PRAISE FOR

Adam and Leonora

"Carol Jameson has a rare talent for delight. In reanimating past artists, poets, and lovers she snares them in a *Midsummer Night's Dream* of pure storytelling intoxication. Even her André Breton is halfway loveable!"

—JONATHAN LETHEM, *New York Times* best-selling author of
Motherless Brooklyn and *The Fortress of Solitude*

"I 'watched' this novel as if I were viewing a Buñuel film, delighted and surprised by the quick geographic and emotional twists, and by a take on romance (mad love!) that characterizes the best of surrealism."

—OWEN HILL, author of the Clay Blackburn novels

"An ambitious blend of fiction and art history, author Carol Jameson explores the powerful and often provocative role that dreams can play in everyday life. Fans of surrealism are sure to enjoy."

—VICTORIA LILIENTHAL, author of the award-winning novel
The T Room

"Jameson has written a wonderful novel, layered with romantic escapades and philosophical musings on Art and Life. She deftly handles different places and historical time periods from Paris on the cusp of war, to New York, Mexico, and Los Angeles. Adam is the archetypal male artist, a modern Don Quixote in search of the Ideal, while André Breton, as Sancho Panza, offers counsel that fluctuates between brilliance and buffoonery. The women—Pauline, Mimi, and Leonora—are visionary artists in their own right. Ada*m and Leonora* is executed in a fluid literary style reminiscent of the great studies of human folly."

—SUMMER BRENNER, author of *The Missing Lover*

Adam

and

Leonora

Adam

and

Leonora

A NOVEL

Carol Jameson

SHE WRITES PRESS

Published 2024
Printed in the United States of America
Print ISBN: 978-1-64742-638-5
E-ISBN: 978-1-64742-639-2
Library of Congress Control Number: 2023919037

For information, address:
She Writes Press
1569 Solano Ave #546
Berkeley, CA 94707

Interior design by Stacey Aaronson

She Writes Press is a division of SparkPoint Studio, LLC.

For my father, Bob Jameson

"When you get into the spirit of how the Earth creates, all kinds of new revelations become possible."

—GORDON ONSLOW FORD (1912–2003)

This is a work of fiction, inspired by the life and art of the surrealist painter Gordon Onslow Ford.

"There are fairy tales to be written for adults,
fairy tales still almost blue."
—ANDRÉ BRETON

Prologue

"It has taken me ten years to hone my palette to only the color of blue. . . ."

Leonora let the declaration float out and up into the air. The students, gathered in Adam's living room, sat on couches and chairs, leaning against golden, avocado, and crimson cushions, surrounding her in a rapt little circle. Some stared at her, puzzled. One let a slow smile spread over her wizened face.

"I think I know what you mean," she ventured.

Leonora gazed at her, questioning yet pleased. "Indeed?"

"Yes, but maybe I should just let you talk and. . . ." The student's voice trailed off. She reached for the glass of water in front of her, softly gulping.

"I don't know that I can explain," Leonora said. "Ten years is a long time. Some of you may understand, others"—Leonora let her gaze rest for a moment on a younger woman who squirmed into the crimson cushion she was leaning on—"may not. Yet. But I think what might best show you what I mean is a tour of Adam's studio. That is, after all, why you are here, is it not?"

They all nodded, eager.

"I only ask that you respect what has been preserved."

Leonora rose, glancing around at the group. Oh, she thought, could she do this? Expose Adam to their collective gaze and questions? Leonora took a deep breath, then felt him, heard him: "You will execute this tour impeccably. No need to analyze so much, Leonora. Show them my work. Let them drink it in. It is there for them. They are why I painted, created for all of those years. . . ."

With a subtle nod, Leonora gently commanded the group: "Please, follow me." Before leaving the room, she glanced up at the magnificent canvas above her, its startling comets golden in the cobalt sky.

The students rose, gathering up their backpacks, papers, and water bottles, before filing out after their host to view the work of Adam Sinclair in his studio as he left it all those years ago.

Leonora

"How do you do?"

Standing at his threshold, Leonora appraised the man before her. He was tall. Yes. And handsome, naturally. A messy burst of thick gray hair atop a square, masculine forehead. Intense blue eyes that pierced her to her core. He wore a painter's smock, splashes of red, orange, blue, and lime covering it in layers. His long legs sported worn jeans. These, too, were splattered with paint.

Nervous, she watched as he eyed her up and down, slowly taking her in. He did not respond with the standard American answer of "Good, thanks," or "Fine, thank you," or "Who the hell are you showing up at my doorstep unannounced?"

Okay, this last, Leonora knew, was not the standard American response, but she half expected him to slam the door in her face. After all, she had never been formally introduced to the famous painter. Who was she to just knock on his door one breezy Monday afternoon?

Yet, she felt as if she knew him. She'd been hiking the ridge above his studio for years, fantasizing about the man who lived and worked in the old barn-like structure below. She'd heard rumors that his wife had died decades ago. He now was alone. A recluse. A man who lived to paint.

But as she stood before him, Leonora felt as if she'd come home. Here was a man, *the* man, that she'd always imagined on her long lonely walks over the years.

Why today? What had finally given her the courage to make her way down the mountain, the trail windy and treacherous? She'd thought of doing exactly what she was doing today so many times. Yet each time she'd considered turning down the mountain instead of continuing along the ridge back to her home, she'd hesitated. She had never taken that fateful turn.

Until today.

And as he stood in front of her, tall and imposing, that air of British properness hitting her square in the chest, Leonora drew in a quiet breath.

He gazed at her for what seemed like an eternity, until finally, miraculously, he responded as she knew he would. "How do you do?" he answered, a slow grin creeping over his creviced face.

Leonora broke into a radiant smile. He was a kindred spirit. A fellow Brit. Of course, when she thought about it later, she realized that she must have known this. It was local lore that he'd come to California from England in the 1950s, that he'd spent time in France and Mexico. Yet the familiar greeting "How do you do?" as an answer to her own "How do you do?" still surprised her. It had been a long time since she'd exchanged such a greeting.

"Do I know you?" he asked.

"I feel like you might," she answered.

"Is that so?"

"Yes, well, perhaps not. . . ." She spied the room behind him, filled with his giant canvases of chaotic color and cosmic energy.

"Then," he stepped aside, wiping a grungy hand on his smock, "perhaps you better come in and introduce yourself. Though I can't entertain for long. I am in the middle of something."

"Oh," she murmured, "I don't want to interrupt your work."

"It's nothing like that," he chuckled, glancing down at his dirty smock. "Appearances can be deceiving."

Leonora nodded. She knew much about appearances. She worked hard to keep hers smooth and unruffled. A researcher by profession, she knew that a calm and clinical demeanor was what her field demanded. Yet she, too, was an artist. She painted and sculpted. Though she knew she had much to learn, to practice with her art. And this meeting with Adam. Would it be the start of a new shift? Would he inspire her in ways that she only dreamed of?

"As I mentioned, I don't have much time this afternoon, though if you'd fancy a spot of tea, I could put a kettle on." Adam motioned for her to come in. "Please, have a seat. It won't take a moment."

Leonora ventured into the great man's living room, taking in the giant canvases and stupendous view of the valley.

What had she gotten herself into? she wondered. Would he think she was some hussy after his fame and fortune?

"Milk? Sugar?" he called out from the kitchen.

"Yes, please, both," she answered, standing awestruck in front of a gargantuan canvas of energetic sprays, lines, circles, and dots leaping off the canvas into her soul.

"That one is still in progress." He handed her a mug of steaming tea. "I needed to get it out of the studio and let it sit for a time. Do you know what I mean?"

Leonora took a sip of the strong beverage, nodding. "Yes," she said. "I think I do."

He eyed her for a moment, speculatively, then motioned her to take a seat.

"Now," he said, "tell me about yourself. Beginning with your name?"

"Leonora," she answered, gazing at him steadily.

"Leonora," he murmured, smiling slowly. "I like it. I knew a Leonora once. You may have heard of her? Leonora Carrington?"

"Yes, of course," she murmured. Images of the famous surrealist's animal heads—goats, horses, owls—atop women's figures leapt into her consciousness.

"So, Leonora, why don't you tell me why you knocked on my door today?"

Swallowing hard, she took a deep breath. "Well," she began, "I hope you don't think me too forward but. . . ."

Leonora stopped, unsure. Adam had looked amused, sipping his tea, studying her. But then his expression changed—almost a look of recognition as if he already knew what she would say. She took a moment to calm herself, to keep her voice from betraying her nerves.

"I have been hiking the ridge above your property for many years now and. . . ."

Pauline

Pauline tore at the blank page, ripping it from the typewriter. Crunching it up into a tight little ball, she hurled it savagely in the direction of the trash basket.

Of course, she missed.

Shit.

She'd been working on the second chapter of her "novel" for over a week and still nothing! Why, oh why, was she even trying to write a novel? She'd been so excited when the first chapter just flowed out, the words streaming from her mind onto the page, her fingers flying over the typewriter's keys in wild abandon.

And it was good!

Or so she thought.

But now?

Nothing.

No matter how much she tried, every time she started to type, the words just wouldn't come out. She told herself, Okay, Pauline, just write anything. Type any drivel that happens to appear. But when she did this, she just couldn't stand it.

Writing.

It was a wicked problem.

It had been so easy last week. And even when she was a child. *The Adventures of Jezebel,* her first play, had streamed out of her hand onto her notebook. She'd been little more than, what?

Twelve? Thirteen? But this first success gave her the confidence to pursue her dream of being a "writer."

What the hell had she been thinking?

Sighing, she gazed out the window, the sky a brilliant blue with creampuff clouds floating by. A burly robin flitted into the sycamore outside her apartment window, his red chest puffed up in avian pride before he belted out a splendid trill. A woman dressed in a lime-green suit strolled down the sidewalk, her little pug in tow. The dog stopped suddenly, yapping at the robin, who flitted away without a care in the world.

Oh, if only she could fly, Pauline thought.

Well, why not?

At least she'd get out of this apartment. She didn't have to work until the evening shift at Ver Brugge's, so why not at least go out for a walk?

LECTURE TONIGHT!

THE ACCLAIMED SURREALIST ARTIST

ADAM HOMER SINCLAIR LECTURES!

SURREALISTS ON FIRE

NEW SCHOOL FOR SOCIAL RESEARCH

8 P.M., 6 E 16TH ST.

ADMISSION: $1.50

The sandwich board on West Fourteenth Street caught her eye. Why, this was right around the corner! Pauline exclaimed to herself, a strange tingling sensation oozing up and over her body.

She stood, transfixed, for a moment, contemplating. She'd never heard of Adam Homer Sinclair, but she adored the surrealists: André Breton, Kay Sage, Apollinaire. These artists and writers intrigued her, what little she knew about them.

But she had to work in two hours. Waitressing? Was this her life?

Hell no. Pauline decided that if she couldn't be a writer herself today, the very least she could do was learn more about writers.

And from an artist.

This, too, intrigued her. Artists were so . . . she struggled for the right word . . . sexy . . . yes, that was it. What could be sexier than taking an image that floated in your imagination and creating a magical reality of it?

So much more fun than writing!

She'd just call in sick to Ver Brugge's. Sure, they'd have her hide, but she felt a pull that she hadn't felt in some time. Was it the surrealists?

Or was it this Adam Sinclair?

Shrugging, Pauline allowed herself a smug little smile as she headed back to her apartment to call in "sick" and find some suitable surrealist apparel for the evening ahead.

He was electrifying.

Pauline sat, entranced, as Adam lectured about his experiences with André Breton in Paris. How the two of them sat in quaint cafés till the wee hours, philosophizing about the blah blah blah. . . .

What was he saying?

Pauline didn't even know. All she knew was that she was totally captivated. It didn't matter what he was talking about. Though she knew, vaguely, that he was telling some charming anecdote about Breton—something about giraffes and champagne?

She perked up for a moment, trying to catch the thread of the story. But then she was too distracted—by his voice, his accent, his manly painter hands. The way they wove expressively over his head and in front of his chest. Exquisite.

I wonder what he paints? she thought . . . with such hands. . . .

"I believe if one can embrace the mysterious energies of nature . . . if one can immerse oneself in its infinite wisdom, then the creative spirit will fly free. . . ."

Pauline pulled herself back to reality. Away from the hands. Into the words.

Did he have the answer to her latest creative block?

Rapt, Pauline leaned forward in her red velvet seat, cupping her delicate chin in her hand, and listened. And listened and listened.

Mimi

A hazy lavender smoke floated seductively, trapped by the ceiling of the Café de Flore, the dilapidated stage lit by a wavy rose-colored light, the tables full of chatter and glasses clinking. Garçons languidly leaned against the bar, cigarettes dangling, waiting for the bartender to fill their trays. A sultry tired tune wound its way through the lavender fog as the lone performer sauntered onto the stage, her tight red dress sparkling, her thick, dark hair draping over one eye.

"Mesdames et messieurs," a hearty baritone boomed out, "bienvenue sur la scene, Mademoiselle Mimi Saucier!"

Adam sipped at his Bordeaux, only half listening to his friend's philosophizing. Not that he wasn't interested. He was. But what danced before him on stage was more interesting.

Much more.

"She is not the one for you, my friend." Breton paused, shaking his head, his bushy mop of hair startling in its ferocity.

Grinning slowly, Adam forced his gaze away from the stage. "How can you be so certain?"

Breton waved one arm emphatically into the air. "Any fool can see that she is only one dimension. A mere distraction. She is not the one to whom you would give your life."

Chuckling, Adam turned his gaze back to the stage. "Who said I wanted to give her my life? I am only looking for a little companionship, n'est-ce pas?"

"Oui, companionship, this I can understand. But my friend, she is dangerous. Can you not see this?"

"Indeed, I do," Adam agreed, his gaze floating back to the stage as the song came to a close, the applause halfhearted, except for a few boisterous fans in the back of the café. "BRAVO, MIMI! C'est magnifique . . . MIMI!"

"Excusez-moi." She stood too close, leaning toward Adam, yet not quite touching him, the cigarette dangling seductively from its holder. "Monsieur, may I trouble you for. . . ?"

Adam glanced sidelong at Breton before flicking the match and holding the flame expertly to her cigarette.

"Merci," she purred.

"You are most welcome," Adam said, motioning to an empty chair at their table.

Breton grunted, pushing back his chair, the legs scraping. "I will find someone else this night for whom my thoughts will elucidate their existence," he said. "I cannot compete with such . . . seduction."

She laughed, the soft notes falling out of her lovely mouth and into the smoky air. "Why, monsieur, I have no designs upon him."

She stroked Adam's forearm, lightly.

Scoffing, Breton shook his head. "Mademoiselle, your designs are as clear as the reality of the blue of the African elephant, the purple of the winter storm, the red of the pestilent scratch!" Grabbing his umbrella, he turned to face Adam, scowling. "Remember you are booked on the passage to New York for the morning crossing."

Adam chuckled, heartily. "Don't worry, André. I won't forget."

He watched in amusement as his friend hustled across the crowded room, joining a familiar group of intellectuals: ". . . I *am in no mood to admit that the mind is interested in occupying itself with such matters, even fleetingly. It may be argued that. . . ."* [1]

Grinning, Adam glanced over at Mimi, her pale skin and dark hair a vision. He hadn't planned any of this, but what fun it was to be out. In the café. With his friend. And this woman. A temptress. A seductress. A sorceress?

All afternoon he'd been holed up in his studio. Working. But the painting was going nowhere. With each stroke of the brush, he stopped. Thinking. Frustrated. Of course, Breton would argue that he was thinking too much. That he needed to simply let the paint flow from the brush, from his arm, from his imagination. Yet, when Adam tried this, why, all he was left with was a muddy mess. A canvas of despair.

And so, he'd given up for the day. Agreed to meet André at the Café de Flore for a drink. And then, here she was.

This woman.

A singer.

A dancer.

A lover?

Adam, turned to her. "Can I buy you a drink, mademoiselle?"

"Champagne." She pouted, blowing a perfect ring of smoke out and over the table.

Adam watched, delighted, as it evaporated into the dusty atmosphere.

"Indeed." Adam waved for the garçon, ordering the drink.

Under the table, he felt a gentle tap on his leg. Glancing down, he saw Mimi's bare foot snaking around his leg, and slinking down his calf.

"Farewell to absurd choices, the dreams of dark abyss, rivalries, the prolonged patience, the flight of the seasons, the artificial order of ideas, the ramp of danger, time for everything!" [2]

Breton waved his hand above his head in dramatic flurry, his crimson scarf blowing madly in the early morning breeze.

Adam had to chuckle. He was going to miss André. His passion. His friendship. His art. But mostly his absurdity.

Not that he couldn't succumb to his own.

Adam sighed to himself, remembering last night with Mimi. Had he acted too rashly? But yet . . . how could he have stopped himself? There she was, in the café, so seductive. So irresistible. And then there they were, in his studio, amid his paintings and his packing. She had feigned interest in his work. "What is this"— she had pointed at his enormous abstract of oranges, cobalts, and violets—"supposed to be, monsieur?"

He had smiled, indulgent. "I don't know. What do you think it is?"

She'd slowly circled the large canvas, her stilettos' tiny clicks distracting him, then she pronounced, "It is an orange in a blueberry muffin!"

Delighted, he laughed, "Exactly! How did you guess?"

Prettily, she'd gazed at him, serious for a moment. "I am an expert on the arts, monsieur. And not just the visual ones. . . ."

And with that they'd fallen into his creaky bed, making mad love till the wee hours.

Now, here with André, and his ship, the *Empress Imogene*, ready to sail off, Adam wondered if he was making the right choice. To leave Paris. And his art. And André . . . and Mimi?

No, she was nothing to him. Not really. A pretty plaything for his last night in the city, and yet, there was something about her. Something that he couldn't get out of his mind. She haunted him.

Was it guilt?

Or was it something more?

"What is it, mon ami? Do you not see that all is before you? That you have earned this chance to sail to New York, to a life free from the strain of our impending doom here in Paris and all of Europe as the matter stands now?"

Adam shook himself from his reverie, "Ah, yes, of course, André. You are right. It is just that I will miss you."

Scoffing, André waved out again at the vast gray sea. "Me? I think not, my friend. It is that vixen who captivated you last night. You are under her enchantment, no?"

"No!" Adam denied a little too vehemently.

"Very well," Breton said, giving Adam a gentle pat on the shoulder. Adam knew immediately that his friend was not fooled. For all his absurdity, Breton was a man of subtlety.

"Off with you!" Breton slapped Adam heartily on the back. "You will find immensity and passion and art and a stampede of chartreuse elephants in that great metropolis that is your destination!"

Laughing, Adam shook his head, "I'm sure I will, André. I'm sure I will."

And with a final handshake, Adam turned and strode up the narrow gangplank to join the rest of the passengers on the *Imogene*.

Exhaling deeply, Mimi blew the smoke ring out the balcony window and watched the vapor rise into the dawn sky. The pinks and grays of the clouds swept it into their embrace. A sweet bird began its morning song to greet the day. The proprietor of the café below raised the enormous metal door in noisy preparation for his first customers, "Hey! Savez-vous le temps, mon ami? Oui. . . ." he called out into the air, the answering volley lost to Mimi's distraction.

Adam was on his ship to New York City by now, she thought. And what of it? Sure, he had been an attractive man. But she had had many attractive men. He was no different.

Or was he?

Mimi rose from the windowsill, kicking a stray stocking that lay forlornly on the hardwood floor. Coffee, that's what she needed. If she had her coffee and then her morning shower, all would be back to normal. She had an audition later that day for a dance revue. It was a seedy establishment, but who could be picky in these times? After that, another night at Café Flore. Where no doubt she would meet other attractive men. Sing to them. Dance with them. Play with them. Make love to them. . . .

Yet, she couldn't shake this feeling of regret. That Adam was gone. Out of her life so quickly.

Would she ever see him again?

Sighing deeply, Mimi gently touched the flatness of her belly.

Maybe she thought. Maybe one day she would. Who knew in this life?

Anything was possible.

But for now, to the café. And coffee. And her life. . . .

Leonora and François

"So, did you finally meet the Great Artiste?" François popped the wine cork with his own artistic flair, before retrieving two glasses and pouring the Château Magnifique sauvignon blanc.

Leonora couldn't help but smile. "Thank you," she murmured, reaching for the glass her husband was offering, a sardonic glint in his eye.

"And?" François chuckled.

She shrugged. How much to tell him? The afternoon with Adam Sinclair was really beyond description. She'd been imagining their meeting for so long. All those long afternoon hikes along the ridge above his grounds. She'd stopped at the turn in the path so many times, only to lose her nerve and continue on her regular route back home to her life. Her work. Her husband.

And now, here was her husband, grinning that grin at her. Was he making fun of her? She couldn't tell. Maybe. Maybe not.

But this was serious. This meeting with Adam. She'd studied his work and his life for years. His paintings called to her. Huge, beautiful constellations of yellows, Prussian blues, crimsons. The energy and daring of them. Why, if only she could meet him. Study with him. Learn from him.

So today, when they'd met, she had to keep her awe in check. She didn't let on how much she admired him, or did she?

Leonora was no gusher. It wasn't like she had a natural propensity to run off at the mouth. She was quiet, measured, thoughtful. And yet, when she'd met Adam, she'd felt unlike she'd ever felt before. He moved her. She shivered as he talked about his work. The tour of his studio. The intricacies of his process.

Why, she was in love.

Careful, she told herself. This was dangerous territory. She couldn't allow herself to succumb to his magic and his power, no matter how much she admired him.

And what had he thought of her? she wondered. Had she told him too much? Too little? He had seemed fascinated by her research around dreams and the artistic process. How if one could record the energy of the dream in a painting, this was the truer "self" that emerged in the image. And her talk of her own art, how she'd had a dream about honing her palette to only blue. How the dream had been filled with aqua waterfalls and Prussian blue pools.

"But why is this, Miss Bloom? Is there something to be gained by such severity of selection?" Adam had asked.

And had she blushed? No, she doesn't blush. But she had become shy. Tongue-tied even. Quite unlike herself.

"Leo?" François interrupted her reverie. "Did you hear me?"

Shaking herself, she gazed over at him. "Yes, yes of course, you asked me what happened, right? At our meeting?"

"Yes, my sweet. What did he look like? What did he say? How did you respond? Come, tell me all, or I will have to take action to pry it out of you!"

A fake dastardly snarl momentarily scarred his handsome face. She laughed softly, knowing now what to do. "Oh, well, you know. He was very . . . how shall I put it?" She took another sip of her wine, savoring the crispness. "He was very . . . British. If that makes sense?"

François grinned, "Ah, yes, the English. Now I understand. Quiet. Proper. No fun at all. Am I right?"

"Perfectly," she answered, rising to make her way to the kitchen. "Would you like salad or asparagus with your filet tonight?"

"Surprise me!"

Leonora opened the refrigerator and peered in, frowning. If only he knew what he was asking.

But the surprise wasn't about the vegetables. No. The surprise was in how much Leonora needed to return to Adam Sinclair's studio. Not next week. Or the day after tomorrow. Or even tomorrow.

Could she slip away tonight?

"You find anything interesting in there?" François asked. She heard the gurgle of liquid as he poured himself another glass of wine. Sidling up behind her, he wrapped his free arm around her slender waist.

"Oh, yes—I think so," she answered before turning and kissing him, the door to the refrigerator slamming shut as he leaned into her.

Leonora let herself be swept away into his embrace, but there was a tug still in the corner of her mind, even as François pressed onward. Adam: Would he agree to her request? Would she be able to persuade him of her sincerity, the validity of her project?

"You okay?" François stopped for a moment, searching her. "You seem a million miles away. Perhaps you do not feel in the mood?"

Shaking herself out of her reverie, Leonora smiled, seductively she hoped. "Oh, I'm sorry, honey. I feel quite fine. Honestly . . . I am all yours . . . always. . . ."

But even as she kissed him, Leonora couldn't help but think about another man, another place, and another scene. . . .

Adam took a step back, and then another—it was no use. No matter what vantage point he took. Close up. Far away. Upside down.

The painting was a disaster. "What the bloody hell am I doing?" he muttered to himself.

It was that Leonora. What did she want? Why did she seek him out? And most importantly, what was he to do with her?

He remembered her questions, so specific, so studied: "How about your paintings of the Inner Earth?"

"Well, it is the creative aspect of the spirit of the Earth. So, you have far more possibilities. You don't have only the things you can see, like trees, birds—you have all kinds of fantastic creation, which you have never seen before. It is like the poetry of Baudelaire. He said, 'I would have liked to have lived in the company of a young Giantess, as a voluptuous cat might sit at the foot of a queen.' When you get into the spirit of how the Earth creates, all kinds of new revelations become possible. You become one with the creative force of the Earth. So, it is a question of love; it is a question of courting, not a question of conquering; it is a question of being worthy." [3]

She had nodded, serious.

Now, Adam stood for a moment, staring at his work in process, the colors screaming at him in their vivid cobalts and offensive oranges. What had happened this afternoon with Leonora? Who did she remind him of? For some reason that he couldn't quite place, she was familiar. She brought him back to a time, to a place, to another woman whom he'd used as a muse, then a lover, then a wife. . . .

Pauline?

No, Leonora was nothing like Pauline. Pauline was full of sass and spontaneity. That first night he'd met her, after his lecture, she'd stood in line, toe tapping impatiently on the cement floor, her frustration at having to wait in the long line written plainly on her eloquent features. She'd handed him the copy of his little book. He laughed quietly to himself now as he remembered how proud he'd been of this small volume, his first on the intricacies of the creative spirit.

"I was beginning to wonder if I was ever going to get through that line," she'd said with a sigh, running her fingers through her thick dark locks. "I just wanted to thank you for the enlightening lecture and to—"

She'd paused, suddenly shy, as he gazed at her intently. Who was this charming thing? Adam knew an enticement when he saw one. But this one, she seemed different somehow.

"Did you want me to sign your copy?" He'd reached out for the volume, which she handed to him, somehow reluctantly.

"Oh . . . yes, please." She'd recovered, quickly.

"And your name?"

"Pauline."

"Pauline. . . ." He'd penned her name, artistically surrounding it with tiny cosmic stars.

"Lovely," Pauline murmured.

Closing the book, he handed it back to her. "I still have a few people to meet, but would you fancy a drink later?"

Adam remembered her sparkling eyes, the quick inhale of breath.

"Oh, well . . . I'm not sure . . . I need to be at work tomorrow and. . . ."

He had shrugged. "I see. Perhaps another time, then?"

She had stood for a moment, contemplating her options, or so it had seemed to him at the time. Later, he came to learn that this was just her way: weighing options, analyzing possibilities, quickly, furtively, before making a decision. Yet on this night, so long ago, he hadn't known this about her. He'd just thought how this one was going to take some work, some finessing, till, she'd surprised him, blurting out: "Oh, what the hell. You only live once, right? When and where?"

"How about the Black Cat Café? Say around ten?"

"Purrfect," she'd said, laughing.

And he couldn't help but join in. Her sudden silliness, contagious.

"Ahhh . . . Pauline," he sighed aloud now. Why had he been drawn to her? he wondered. Of course, she was lovely, attractive, in that way that American girls back then had. The forthrightness. The brazenness. The intellect.

But he had sensed that this girl was different. This girl could be The One.

She could be his lover. His wife. His muse?

Adam shook his head now as he approached his painting again. Was Pauline in this painting?

Was Leonora?

Suddenly feeling exhausted and confused, Adam set his brush back on his palette. He needed to rest, to sleep, to dream.

Yes. Dream. He would dream of this Leonora. The dreams would give him a clue. They always did.

Maybe Pauline would visit tonight in his sleep? Give him some insight about this Leonora?

Adam smiled slowly to himself as he washed out his brushes, covered his paints, and turned out the lights.

Heading out of his studio, he stared up at the night sky. The stars were bright, the moon a sliver. The faint breeze through the pines was soothing.

He would dream tonight. Of the trees. The moon. The stars.

And of his muse . . . Pauline?

Or Leonora?

Sighing, Adam let himself into the house, climbed the stairs, and sank onto his bed.

Pauline and Adam

"The exquisite frown, it is so beautiful, but would you bless a weary traveler with a sunshine smile chartreuse to brighten his most downtrodden mood, mademoiselle?"

"Excuse me?" Pauline glanced up at the bushy-haired visage that was peering down at her. Who was this crazy character?

"It seems to me that every act is its own justification, at least for the person who has been capable of committing it, that it is endowed with a radiant power which the slightest gloss is certain to diminish." [3]

"I don't know what my frown has to do with gloss, but I'm actually waiting for someone." Pauline felt the frown's gloss growing in spite of herself, but hell if she was giving this guy anything. "So, if you don't mind—"

"Ah, but allow me to introduce myself, mademoiselle!" Breton bowed deeply, his hand sweeping dramatically before her. "I am André Breton, a man most sincere in his admiration of gloss and diminishment."

"André Breton? *The* André Breton?" Pauline stammered, mouth agape. Could it really be? What on earth was he doing here at the Black Cat Café?

"Oui, mademoiselle, but s'il vous plaît, call me André—"

"Very well, but . . . "

"May I?" Breton pulled out a chair from her table, motioning a plea for a seat.

"Oh, sure, of course, but like I said, I'm meeting someone, and he should be here any moment. . . ."

Breton grinned, "Ah, a rendezvous. Magnifique! Who might the lucky gent be?"

"Well, I only just met him, but he's the most fascinating person. He's a painter and he just gave this lecture over at the New School and. . . ." Why was she telling Breton all this? Shouldn't she be asking the great man about his own work? But what could she possibly ask him? It wasn't as though she were some expert on the surrealists—though after listening to Adam's lecture, she was beginning to think that their ideas were just what she needed to jump-start her writing. If she could only allow herself the same sort of spontaneity that Adam spoke of in his painting, if she could somehow let go of her insecurities and just write, well, who knows? She might have something to talk to Breton about after all.

"Pauline?"

Adam's voice echoed deliciously behind her.

"Why! Adam! Mon ami!" Breton boomed out, rising and giving Adam a hearty hug.

"André? What brings you to New York?" Adam glanced over at Pauline, his eyes sparkling, shrugging as he disentangled himself from Breton's enthusiasm.

"Oh, you know, this and that. The gloss. The diminishments. The frowns, they are so scintillating. . . ."

André winked at Pauline as he pulled out another chair for Adam.

"Of course," Adam chuckled as he signaled for the waiter to bring them all a drink.

"Three glasses of your best champagne, sir."

"Very good." The waiter bowed. "And something to go with that fine vintage? Perhaps some escargot, oui, mademoiselle?"

Pauline nodded, shyly. What had she gotten herself into here?

"Garçon!" André cried. "Bring it all! The coquilles, the frites, the elephants!"

"Elephants?" Pauline started to giggle. This was going to be an evening that she wouldn't soon forget. With Breton in the mix, mirth trumpeted forth. His language. His images. His hair! Yet there was a part of her that was frustrated. She wanted to talk to Adam. To learn more about his philosophy around cosmic spontaneity. To stare into his sky-blue eyes and lose herself in his chocolate voice.

And with Breton here . . . well, this would be impossible.

"So, Adam, you tell me, where did you find this most beautiful woman to adorn your evening repast?"

Adam smiled slowly. "As a matter of fact, André, I didn't find her. She found me. Can you believe my good fortune?"

André chuckled, wickedly, as the waiter popped the champagne, the golden liquid bursting out into the glasses. "No, mon ami, I cannot. She does seem to be a . . . what do they say here in America? A cut above the type you do usually attend. . . ."

Adam took a sip of his drink. "I couldn't agree with you more, my friend. I couldn't agree more."

Pauline blushed in spite of herself. These two men were absolutely crazy! She took a long sip of champagne, then shrugged and downed the glass.

"More?" Adam asked, his eyes blazing into her.

"Ummm . . . please." Pauline took another sip and felt the alcohol begin to work its magic. She could handle these two. It would take a bit more champagne, but who gives a damn? You have opportunities like this only once in a lifetime, right?

"*Man proposes and disposes. He and he alone can determine whether he is completely master of himself, that is, whether he maintains the body of his desires, daily more formidable, in a state of anarchy. . . .*" [4]

"Anarchy, is it?" Pauline felt Adam's fingers, under the table, run gently over her hand, up her arm. . . . She drew in her breath, quick and ecstatic.

"Do you agree, mademoiselle?" Breton was staring at her, a knowing light in his eyes, a challenge in his smile.

"Oh . . . yes. . . ." She inhaled. "Is there any more champagne? I—"

"Indeed," Adam gallantly hefted the bottle out of its bucket, poured the golden libation into her glass, spilling over its rim, his foot now taking over the under-the-table exploration.

Pauline tried not to swoon; it was an effort. But she wouldn't allow herself to succumb. At least not now—in public—with Breton and his gloss.

She took a large swallow of her champagne, then glanced over at Adam before launching into the fray: "I wonder if anarchy is indeed the answer, André? While I can understand its appeal and sympathize with its constituents, I find that some sort of order is necessary to—"

"Nonsense!" Breton smacked the table. "The giraffes will not stand for it! You mark my words, mademoiselle! And while many will dismiss their acumen in the savannas of Africa, I discern otherwise. . . ."

Pauline burst out laughing; how could one argue with the acumen of the savannas?

Breton stopped his dialogue and, then shrugging, began again. "The red of the elephant will trump all and while those who dismiss the pachyderm for its—"

"The escargot, for you." The waiter set the hot plate down with a flourish. "More champagne?"

"But of course, my good man!" Breton bellowed.

Pauline felt herself fading. She needed to eat. Now. Grabbing one of the appetizers, she popped it inelegantly into her mouth. Delicious. Like the champagne. Like the lecture. Like Breton.

But mostly, like Adam, who had resumed his under-the-table explorations. Much to her gloss-ridden delight.

"I wonder if you wouldn't mind listening to an idea I have for my next lecture?" Back at his studio, Pauline watched Adam as he sifted nervously through the sheaf of papers piled on his desk.

She plopped down on the old creaky bed, uninvited. The champagne gushing through her veins, she grinned. "Sure, of course. Though I'm not sure how much help I'll be."

"Oh," Adam assured her, "don't worry. I just need an audience before the audience, if that makes any sense?"

"It does indeed, and I will be your most attentive student." Pauline grinned, trying to balance on the bed with alert academic anticipation.

"Very well. I do thank you for your kind consideration."

"Is that part of your lecture? I mean, most students don't expect consideration, much less kind consideration."

Adam chuckled softly. "No, no, I—"

"Oh dear, don't be nervous; students will eat you up." Pauline grinned. "I'm just an American girl, and you, you are the British intellectual. But I'll stop teasing. Go on."

For a moment, she worried that she had gone too far, but Adam met her gaze with a smile, took a breath, and began reading:

"I must preface my reading with a note that this description references Matta's *Invasion of the Night*, which will be on display for the audience whilst I offer the following interpretation. Unfortunately, my dear Pauline, I haven't a facsimile of the painting here to accompany my offering for you tonight. However—" Adam cleared his throat and looked up.

"You were saying?" Pauline asked. Arranging herself on the edge of his bed, she loosened the top button of her blouse.

"Errr . . . yes . . . I was simply making the point that you won't have the benefit of viewing the painting as I read, but perhaps this will be a test of my ability to convey the visual without the visual, so to speak."

"So to speak." Pauline smiled slowly.

"Yes . . . er . . . well, I will commence."

"Please, I am all ears."

Adam cleared his throat. "If you would be so kind as to imagine the painting before you here." He motioned to the blank wall behind him.

"Of course, I can do that." Pauline laughed softly. Was it the champagne, or this charmingly shy man? Who would have known the famous Adam Sinclair could be so disarmed? He certainly had not seemed the least bit timid when she'd seen him lecture earlier.

Pauline felt a little thrill as Adam began: "*The horror at the sight of the wet bread and the joy at the sight of a red balloon have married and given birth to a green flower of brilliant conversation. . . .*" [5]

Adam paused.

"Go on," she coaxed. "I am beginning to see it. . . ."

"Yes, very well. Imagine depth dimension to represent time length, breadth to represent the space compartments, and height to represent a measure of sexual power."

Pauline had become more and more entranced with Adam's description of Matta's images. She was beginning to see Matta's *Invasion of the Night*, understand its dimensions. Until, that is, Adam uttered the phrase *sexual power*. She tried to focus as he continued reading, but her intellect was losing the battle to her lust.

". . . in the distance two feelings were formed which finally unite and a flower is born. . . ." [6]

"A flower," Pauline echoed. A sudden vertigo overtook her. The dizziness, though, felt delicious.

"Yes, do you find such a conclusion problematic?"

"Not at all. It's just that. . . ." Pauline hesitated, trying to find the right words, her brain swirling, her body sparking. Her play at being the willing student had given way to a genuine interest in Adam's ideas, but it was late. The copious amounts of champagne and Breton's wild ravings and object poetics were catching up. What had Breton said about women's heels and verse? Something about the foot of imagination yields the rhythms of femininity?

"I am afraid that I've imposed upon your kindness too much with such nonsense," Adam said, interrupting her reverie. He sat beside her on the bed.

"No, not at all," she said. "I just think that I need to have the painting before me in order to understand the depth of your analysis. Plus, it's late . . . and. . . ."

Pauline leaned in to him, letting herself melt. The strange tingly thrill continued to pulse through her. Was it the red balloon? Or maybe it was the green flower? Or was it the gloss of Adam's attention?

He took her face in his hands, kissing her before she could find the depth dimension.

They fell back into the rumpled bedclothes, his sexual power overtaking her in all its delectable conversation. As he began to explore her parts below, a sudden pop sounded in her ears.

"Oh . . . my!" Pauline whispered, "Was that the red balloon? Did you hear it?"

She pulled away from Adam's embrace abruptly. He was too much. His power over her too damning. It was too fast. Why did she think she could manage this? Coming here to Adam's studio so late at night. After all that champagne. After all that talk. And then this "lecture"! The champagne and the red balloon had momentarily clouded her vision. She needed an exit strategy.

"Pardon me?" Adam sat up straight, a bemused twinkle in his eye.

"I think I heard a pop!" she announced. "Or maybe it was the green flower that threw me? I was thinking about it, and if you don't mind, I'd like to hear that part again. . . ."

Pauline's voice trailed off. Tentative. Was this working? She knew she was playing a dangerous game. While he may have wanted the quick interlude, Pauline wanted more—she wanted

his intellect, his respect. Why, she could even be his next inspiration. Why not? But it could all go wrong. He could get angry,
call her a tease, throw her out into the night, and then she would
have missed her chance at knowing a great man. But a truly great
man would be patient. She scanned his face, trying to discern his
emotions, but he gave nothing away. He straightened his clothes
and returned to his lecture.

"The green flower and the red balloon, my dear Pauline, are
only metaphors for the deeper connections one can realize
through the collective unconscious that informs our creative
process. Have you heard of Jung?"

Pauline pulled her skirt down to cover a pale thigh. "Of
course . . . I . . . " Jung? Jung? She knew she'd learned about
him . . . something about archetypes? Dreams? But she was in
no state to feign knowledge of such wispy abstracts now.

"I think I need to go. . . ." she murmured.

"So soon?"

"Yes, well . . . it's late and I have classes tomorrow and work
and. . . ."

"I see." Adam rose. "Do let me call you a cab. It is the very
least I can do after your attention to my er. . . discourse. . . ."

"Yes, well . . . you . . . needed an audience and I was happy to
provide you with one but only up to a point . . . if you catch my
meaning. . . ."

"Indeed, I do." Adam sauntered over to the phone, making
the call. "The cab will be here shortly. Shall I escort you down to
the foyer?"

"Yes, thank you. You are too kind."

"No, you are the kind one." Adam's blue eyes twinkled as he
helped her on with her jacket, opened the door, and followed her
out into the dank, dark mystery of the night.

Mimi and Genevieve

"Mimi, are you listening to me?" Genevieve blew a lazy smoke ring. The perfect circle hung for a moment above the tabletop between them, then drifted back toward Mimi.

Mimi waved her hand in the air, vainly trying to steer the smoke away. Yes, smoking was sexy, but not first thing in the morning. She gazed around their tiny kitchen, the counters cluttered with dirty dishes, the morning papers strewn across the table.

"I am sorry." Mimi shook her head. "I am just tired, that is all . . . What were you saying?"

"I do not think that it is safe for you to remain here in Paris." Genevieve nodded toward the boulangerie across rue Malher that had been shuttered, its Jewish owners "disappeared."

"I am fine, Gen. Why would they come after me?"

"You know they don't need a 'reason.'" Genevieve took a swig of her espresso. "They are looking for anyone that fits their 'profile,' and you, my sweet, with your dark beauty and"—she reached across the table, placing her hand over Mimi's protectively—"and our . . . relationship . . . I fear for you, especially in that dive club you work in."

"You are being preposterous!" Mimi exclaimed. "I am perfectly safe at the club. Gerard will protect me!"

"Gerard!" Genevieve scoffed, throwing her head back, blond curls dancing in the light. "He is a worthless good-for-nothing," Genevieve continued. "Not to mention an atrocious businessman. You would do much better to come to Switzerland with me. We can live in my chalet. Cozy and safe from the world until this horrible doom passes. . . ."

"I cannot leave my job," Mimi declared.

"Why not?"

"I owe Gerard that much. To stay for at least six months. Besides. . . ." Her voice trailed off. What if Adam returned? She knew this was the real reason she could not just "disappear." Of course, he had said nothing of returning. They had made no promises to each other after their one mad passionate night of love. Yet . . . Mimi could not help herself. He had infected her. With his passion. With his art.

With his child?

Again, she felt the slight twinge of nausea rise in her belly. Could it be that she carried his child?

"Are you quite well, ma petit amour?" Mimi felt Genevieve's gentle touch, her fingers stroking her hand. "You do not seem yourself."

"I am fine." Mimi shook off the nausea. The hopes of seeing Adam again. "I am only tired, as I mentioned. And I have a long day and a late night. I need to go to market to pick up some things for luncheon."

"Let me, my sweet." Genevieve snuffed out her cigarette, rising and stretching, catlike in the morning air.

Mimi nodded, her tiredness suddenly overwhelming. "You don't mind?"

"Of course not. I have the whole day before me until I race late this afternoon."

"You will win, my darling." Mimi kissed her lover affectionately on the cheek. "Are you riding Fly with the Wind today?"

"Oui! And I will win with such a steed beneath me!"

Mimi nodded vaguely, slumping onto the sofa as Genevieve rushed about the flat to gather her gear for the race.

"Ciao, ma petite!" Genevieve called out, slamming the door behind her.

Mimi closed her eyes, sighing audibly, a purple cloud of exhaustion floating up toward the ceiling, visions of golden stars and violet roses drifting in front of her. She smiled softly, a sweet tune filling her, as she fell into a deep, deep sleep.

7

François, Adam, and Leonora

"What is my naughty boy frowning about after such a"—François glanced over at his mistress, a silky feline in rumpled moonlight. Marianna smiled wickedly, her dark eyes dancing—"delicious interlude?"

François's frown deepened, "Oh, Marianna, it's nothing, nothing. I am just fatigued."

Marianna pouted, sitting up, her dark curls cascading down her sumptuous back. "I don't believe you. You are thinking of her, aren't you?"

"Who?" François asked.

Marianna laughed ruefully, "You know who! Leonora! You say you are leaving her, but then, when you come to me, you think only of her."

"No, no." François turned his attention to her now. "That's not true. It's just that, well . . . she gets under my skin, you know?"

"Oh, I know!" Marianna rose and stalked over to the window seat, the full moon casting a shadow on her sultry features, her high cheekbones illuminated by the moon's glow.

"No, that's not what I mean. It's this artist . . . she's obsessed with him, and I just don't know what to do about it."

"What artist? How can some artist be a problem? Isn't it a good thing that she has someone, too?"

"No, no, you don't understand. It's not like that. She's obsessed and. . . ."

"I am obsessed, too!" Marianna pranced over to him, pulling the sheets away in playful protest.

"Hey!" François grinned, yanking the sheets away from her, drawing her toward him.

Marianna yelped playfully. "Oh, you!" she cried.

"Yes, me!" François grabbed her, wrapping his arms around her waist and pulling her toward him, kissing her deeply, but still, he couldn't help himself. All he heard about was Leonora and her artist. She was driving him crazy. Why, she even dreamt of him the other night. And when he had asked her what the dream was about, she'd denied it. "But I heard you," he'd insisted after she woke him from a sound sleep. "You were calling his name out. You were very insistent and. . . ."

Leonora had seemed genuinely puzzled. "I don't know why I would call out Adam's name. Unless it has something to do with the questions I wanted to ask him for my research around the process of creativity and its connection to dreams and their—"

"It's not important!" François had cried, impatient with her. Why must she always go on and on about her research? Like this is what he was talking about? No! It was Adam that she had been dreaming of. He had heard her call Adam's name and now she was trying to distract him with this nonsense about her research?

Did she think he was an idiot?

"You were calling out 'Adam, Adam!' You must remember, Leonora!"

He had watched her closely. She shook her head. "I have no memory of this, François. You must be mistaken."

But he was no fool. She was hiding something. And François knew it was more than just a passing interest in a research subject. What the secret was, he didn't know.

But he'd be damned if he wasn't going to find out. Leonora and her dreams. These would be her undoing. . . .

"François!" Marianna pouted now. "Stop thinking of her! Pay attention to me! Now!"

Chuckling, François drew her to him. "Of course, my sweet. How could I not. . . ." And with a dastardly twinkle in his eye, he began a slow methodical inspection of the sensuous hills and valleys of his delectable Marianna.

Adam

It was the dark of night. A full moon illuminated his path through the dense woods. Adam knew these woods, but then he didn't. The path was familiar, but then it wasn't. Yet there was something that compelled him to continue on this trail. Something that he was searching for. A reward at the end of the path, but he had to trust, even though there was a feeling of anxiety and, yes, even fear about the unknown. He came to a fork in the path—one way led down a dark, tunnel-like sphere; the other out into a bright, moonlit meadow.

He chose the tunnel path. He chose the unknown darkness. Why? He could have taken the moon meadow path. This was the known. It was luminous and safe.

Yet . . . he was again compelled to follow the unknown, and as he strode along this path, he felt her. A presence. A spirit.

"Pauline?" he called out, his voice echoing into the dark forest. "Are you there, my love?"

A faint breeze stirred the woods and an owl hooted in the distance before he felt her. Stopping at a massive redwood, Adam gazed up its tall trunk. He could see bright dots of light sparking off the tree's trunk, shooting off brilliant tiny stars into the night.

"Pauline?" he called again. "Are you here?"

"No. . . ." A voice answered. It was familiar, but not his dear wife's. Who was it that had summoned him here to this place?

"Who are you?" he called out.

"Leonora. . . ." the voice echoed into the night.

"Leonora?" he answered, puzzled. "Where are you?"

"I am here, in front of you. Look. . . ."

Adam walked around the tree, glancing up its trunk to see that the tiny sparks had disappeared. "I don't see you, Leonora."

"Yes, you do. Close your eyes. I am here."

"But. . . ."

A cold breeze blew into his room, knocking a stack of papers from his desk onto the bedroom floor. "Leonora?"

Adam sat up, casting about the dark room for her.

But of course she wasn't here. In his bedroom. In the middle of the night.

It was just a dream.

Yet what was it that she had been trying to tell him in the dream?

Those sparks—he shook his head. "What the bloody hell did they mean?" he muttered to himself.

He thought of getting up, heading over to the studio. Painting these bright lights while they were still fresh in his mind. He knew that the sooner he could commit a dream and its energy to his work, the more genuine and meaningful it would be. He had the habit of rising early each morning and heading to his studio at the first dawn's light in order to capture his dreams. The images. The energy. The divine creative spirit.

Meeeooow!

"Ah, Puck, there you are," Adam patted the sleek black feline. "Can you tell me what that dream was all about?"

Meeeoowww . . . purrrrr . . . Puck nestled up against Adam's neck, bumping him hard with his wet nose.

"Okay, okay, sorry to wake you." Adam laughed softly to himself, letting the cat nuzzle his way under the covers. "There, you comfortable now? Guess I'll have to wait till tomorrow to paint that one."

Purrrrrr. . . .

Adam shook his head, pulling the covers up to his chin, the room still chilly from the breeze.

Or was the chill a remnant of the dream?

He closed his eyes. Sighing deeply, he slept again. And Leonora? Did she dream tonight too?

Adam turned over on his side, a feeling of intense slumber upon him. "Adam. . . ." he heard her voice as he drifted off. "I'm here . . . look up . . . please . . . can you help me?"

Adam shifted in his sleep, twitching slightly. *Meeeow!* Puck protested, before they both settled down to finish out the night of dreams and whispers.

Leonora

Leonora felt herself fly, up and up, inside a dark sphere, and then around a massive tall tower. She felt free and joyous. But also divided, fragmented, afraid.

What had she become? Where was she?

She saw thousands of tiny green needles reaching for her, but she was too quick, too smart for capture.

She laughed gaily, her cares and worries gone.

"Pauline?" she heard from below. Pauline? Who was Pauline?

Leonora glanced down, and there he was.

Adam.

She beckoned to him, "Come, join me!" she called.

But he remained below, unhearing.

"Adam!" she called. "Adam, here, up here! I'm here!"

"Hey! Leonora!" François shook her awake. "Wake up, Leonora!"

She fought his command, "Adam . . . Adam. . . ." she heard herself call out.

"Leonora, it's François! Adam's not here, goddamn it! Wake up!"

"François?" Leonora shook herself awake, disoriented, shivering, her gaze finally focusing on her husband's perturbed visage.

"Yes, it's me. You were dreaming. Of Adam."

"Adam . . . ?" Leonora frowned; how did he know this? "I don't think so," she murmured.

"Yes, you were. You called out his name. Twice."

Leonora tried to rouse herself. François mustn't know about this! What had she done? Calling out Adam's name in a dream of all things!

François groaned. "I just want to know what you were dreaming about with Adam!"

"Oh . . . Adam. . . ." Leonora shook her head. She had to distract François. He mustn't know her secret. "I'm sorry, darling," she turned to him, cooing.

"That won't work," François commanded. "Out with it!"

Leonora smiled, slowly, tracing his firm thigh with her fingertips softly. "Are you sure?"

He sighed, suddenly powerless. "Oh, Leo, you vixen, you!"

"Mrrrwww!" Leonora purred, tugging him to her; he spooned into her. She was safe. For now. But she must be more careful, she thought. Though how she was going to control her dream life would be a challenge.

She knew her dream held the key. If she could learn to control it, then she could keep François from prying. She would do some renewed research around this topic in the morning.

But for now, sex was the answer. And with a little gasp, Leonora let herself be swept away, knowing her escape was only a temporary respite from the secret she held so close to her heart.

Leonora had promised herself she would occupy her morning with research, yet, after her daily walk, she found herself knocking at Adam's door again. He greeted her warmly, but with no surprise—as if he expected her. He offered her a cup of tea and they were soon seated in his studio with his paintings crowded on the high concrete wall. Brilliant oranges, olive greens, and golden stars shot forth from the canvases. Leonora felt a chill up her spine as a star hurled itself into her heart.

Gasping softly, she pulled herself away from the image and tried to focus on Adam. What had she missed? He seemed to be mid-lecture. Nodding at his words, pretending she had been following, Leonora took a sip of her tea.

"In the Great Spaces of the Mind, travel is of greater dimensions. Dreams are just a little bit faster than rational thought, but Great Spaces of the Mind can move at enormous speed, although one is not particularly aware of it." Adam paused as Leonora tried to pick up the thread.

"Dreams. . . ." she murmured. Another star flew from the canvas, landing on her bare arm. She glanced down at the warm glow, glimmering golden on her skin, before continuing. "Great Spaces of the Mind," she repeated, "can also be experienced in transpersonal dimensions of lucid dreaming. But they are often difficult to express in words. " [7]

She was still sure of her connection, especially after her dream last night. And the energy of these stars? Did Adam feel them, too? Or were they only for her? How much to divulge to Adam this morning? She remained unclear about which tack to take. What was this fog she seemed enveloped in? And yet, she was also startlingly alive, energized, at the same time. She glanced up at the painting, filled with galaxies and glitter, eyeing a constellation that shimmered in the foreground.

"That is why I paint, Leonora," Adam began. "The images are there, in my mind's eye, and if I capture their energy on the canvas, I experience a sort of widening, a great opening of my consciousness. It is something that I cannot force. It is something that is difficult to articulate in words, language as you say. However, it is on the canvas. This energy. This movement. The dream speaks to me and I translate it onto the canvas."

Leonora nodded. She knew exactly what he meant. It was the same for her. "I understand," she murmured. "Tell, me, if you wouldn't mind, what is it, do you think, that a dream can articulate to you?"

"To me, dreams. . . ." Adam started to speak and then stopped, staring at her. "You know—in that light, your profile. . . ."

"Adam?" Leonora asked.

"Ah . . . yes, what was I saying? You remind me of someone. I'm sorry, but I had a restless night last night. The cat. At it always with the late-night escapades."

Not having a cat, she could only smile vaguely. She had been about to ask, "And who do I remind you of?" but stopped when Adam smiled sadly at her. Leonora flashed back to the photo of the woman she'd seen on her first visit. The dark hair. The pale skin. The brown eyes. They could be twins.

Suddenly, she felt something soft and furry rub against her leg. "Oh!" she exclaimed, momentarily startled. "Who are you?"

She looked down to see a huge black cat rubbing against her leg. She stroked the cat's head, giving Adam time to be distracted from his sadness. He will tell me when he's ready. Leonora continued to pet the cat, who had now jumped on her lap, purring loudly.

"Oh, hello," she murmured.

"Puck, leave her alone," Adam admonished the feline, but only halfheartedly.

"He's fine," Leonora stroked the rich fur as the cat turned in circles several times and then settled into a round ball. "Aren't you, Puck?"

Mrrroooow! Puck took advantage, now standing tall on her lap, rubbing his head against her ribs.

"Oh!" Leonora laughed, delighted.

"He likes you," Adam said. "He's an old man now and doesn't take to many people, but you, he likes."

"I'm flattered." Leonora stroked Puck's sturdy head as the cat circled again and then nestled in for a nap.

"More tea?" Adam asked.

"Yes, please."

As Adam busied himself with the kettle, Leonora stared at another one of his large paintings hanging on the wall opposite. The canvas was enormous. Fifteen by seventeen feet at least. The background layered with rich cobalt and Prussian blues created a lush bed for more of the bright golden stars that leapt off from various egg-shaped circles dancing on it. She felt a surge of energy, a breathlessness, as she took in the painting's mesmerizing world. Waiting for one of the stars to leap to her.

Adam handed her a steaming cup of tea. "That one I call *Universetopia of the Stars*."

"It's wondrous," she murmured.

"Yes, well, I'm not sure of that," Adam frowned. "However, it does speak to your question about what dreams tell me. Can you guess?"

"Oh," Leonora shook her head, "no, I wouldn't presume."

Chuckling, Adam's blue eyes twinkled. "No, of course not. How could you? A painting is uniquely the world of the artist on one level, but on another, it belongs to the viewer. So, tell me, Leonora, what do you see?"

Taking a deep breath, Leonora began, "I see a universe, vast and deep. It is limitless in its scope. It contains all the energy of humanity, but also all of life we cannot know in our narrow perceptions. The stars change and fly. They dart about even though one would believe a painting is static." She paused, glancing down at the still-shimmering spot on her arm. "Yet the dynamism of this painting, why it takes the viewer to a world both inside herself and outside of her reality. It is like a dream. It is a dream. In fact, it is my dream. . . ."

"Your dream?" Adam asked.

"Oh, no, I didn't mean my dream. I meant that. . . ." Leonora couldn't continue. She was grateful for the distraction of the cat on her lap, and she stroked his head again. The cat purred and then turned to nip her hand.

Mrrrooowwwww!

"Puck! Enough!"

"Maybe he's bored?" Leonora suggested, pulling her hand away from the cat, setting her cup down. Suddenly the mood had shifted. Adam seemed upset about her interpretation of his painting and now the cat bite. What to do next? She needed to get out of there before she made an even bigger fool of herself. She looked up at Adam, who smiled at her and the cat.

"Nah, he's just being a nuisance, aren't you, Puck?"

Mrrrrooowwww!

They both laughed as the cat jumped off Leonora's lap and trotted over to the door.

Adam opened the door; Puck dashed out.

"Now where were we?" he asked.

"I—" Leonora glanced at the open door, the bright morning light casting a glittering triangle on the tiled floor. "Maybe we could go on a walk?" she asked.

"Marvelous," Adam agreed. "And after, I can show you my latest work. The painting I began this morning."

"That would be wonderful," Leonora answered, rising and grabbing her jacket. She felt a subtle tingle up and down her spine when she stole a final glance at *Universetopia*.

"You coming?"

"Oh, yes, of course," Leonora answered, following him out into the wooded glowing morning.

Pauline

"Hey, doll! What's a fella gotta do to get a cuppa joe over here?"

"Excuse, me? Miss . . . ? Miss . . . ? I'm afraid my eggs are cold. Can you please get me another order?"

"I've been waiting for over twenty minutes for the check, sweetheart, and I tell ya, I don't wanna take it up with the manager, but you may force my hand if you catch my drift."

Pauline's mind swirled. The demands flying through the air of a busy morning at Ver Brugge's. She didn't usually work the breakfast shift. Not a morning person. Especially after her late night. Needless to say, she hadn't gotten much sleep, what with the lecture and the champagne and . . . Adam. . . . Oh! Last night had been so magical. His lecture. His paintings. His power.

"Miss! I—"

"Okay, okay, hold your horses. I'm coming!" Pauline grabbed the coffee pot and sprinted across the bustling room. What the hell was she doing? Why was she a waitress of all things? She was a writer. A dreamer. A . . . what?

A waitress. At least for now. Pauline sighed, pouring the coffee into the half-empty cup.

"Well, it's about time!" the woman, a reddish sausage of a housewife, harrumphed. "And my side of toast? Where is that?"

"Coming right up, ma'am." Pauline managed a smile that she knew was a grimace.

Racing back across the room, she heard a familiar voice behind her:

"Let us not mince words: the marvelous is always beautiful,
anything marvelous is beautiful, in fact only the marvelous is
beautiful." [8]

Swirling around, she beheld the impish Breton, seated at
one of her tables. How had she missed him?

"Good morning, my marvelous," Breton sang out.

"Uh. . . good morning," she said, her gaze landing not only
on Breton but the handsome man seated at the table with him.
"Adam. . . ."

"Good morning, Pauline," he nodded, his blue eyes twinkling.
"I see you're busy but—"

"We need to whisk you away, my dear," Breton interrupted.

"But I can't." She shook her head. "I'm at work and I can't
leave and—"

"Hey, sweetheart, a little attention over this way," a burly
bear of a man hollered at her from across the room, snapping his
mangy fingers at her.

"You do need to come with us," Adam nudged, rising.

"I'm sure that wherever you're going, it's more. . . ." she began,
blowing a stray curl out of her eyes.

"Marvelous!" Breton winked.

"Marvelous, yes, but as you can see . . . I . . . just can't. . . ."

"Pauline, if you don't take table number two's order right
now, you're fired." A tall, manful presence appeared out of
nowhere behind her. Damn, she thought. Frank. Her maniacal
manager. If she didn't get rid of Breton and Adam pronto, she'd
be out of a job. And loathe as she was to work here, and much as
she wanted to fly away with these two, she knew it was impossible.
At least right now.

"My dear sir"—Breton rose, his hand outstretched—"let me
introduce myself. I am Pauline's uncle and this is her . . . her . . .
brother. . . ."

Adam raised one eyebrow.

"And we are so sorry to interrupt your bustling operation here, but Pauline must come with us immediately. It is a matter of utmost urgency."

"Oh, yeah, and what kind of urgency might that be?" Frank growled.

"Her dear mama is in the hospital. The time left to her may be of a short duration and so Pauline must come with us immediately!"

Glaring at Pauline for a moment, Frank shook his head. "You never told me your mother was in the hospital."

"I had no idea. . . ." Pauline shook her head, trying to hide a smile.

"Yes, this is why we are here, monsieur," Breton continued. "We are, unfortunately, the bearers of this unfortunate news. But time is of the essence and we must convey Miss Pauline to the hospital before it's too late. . . ."

Breton sighed dramatically, his bushy head playing along in mock sympathy.

"It is imperative that she leave immediately," Adam prompted. "Mother dear will not last long, I'm afraid. She is calling for you, dear sister."

Pauline untied her apron. "I'm very sorry, Frank, but as you can see, I have to go. I'm sure Mildred can handle my tables."

"I've got you covered, dearie." Mildred snuck up behind the little group. "Didn't mean to eavesdrop, but then I did, so . . . go, honey. Your mama needs you."

"Thanks, Milly, you're a peach." Pauline gave her a quick kiss on the cheek, shrugging at Frank before heading behind the counter to get her purse and coat.

"Don't think I won't check up on your story," Frank called after her.

"Oh, leave the poor kid alone." Mildred slapped him playfully on the arm. "Her mother's in the hospital for Chrissakes!"

"Hey, lady, some joe!"

"Hold your britches, hold your britches, you big oaf!" Mildred grinned, lumbering skillfully over to table two, coffee pot in one hand, check pad in the other.

Pauline mouthed a silent "Thank you" as she hurriedly followed her two saviors out the door into the crisp, wet morning air.

"Ah!" Breton gave a sweeping wave across the cloud-puffed sky. "It is marvelous! Is it not, my beauty?"

"Yes. . . ." Pauline giggled. What the hell was she doing? Was she crazy? Lying to her boss. Leaving her shift in the middle of the morning rush. Following these two to God knows where.

"Indeed." Adam slung his arm possessively over her slim shoulders.

"Can I ask what that was all about?" Pauline grinned.

"*The fabric of adorable improbabilities must be made a trifle more subtle the older we grow, and we are still at the age of waiting for this kind of spider. . . . Fear, the attraction of the unusual, chance, the taste for things extravagant are all devices which we can always call upon without fear of deception. There are fairy tales to be written for adults, fairy tales still almost blue,*" [9] Breton rhapsodized.

Pauline nodded slowly; confusion reigned on this bright morning. Blue fairy tales? What could he mean?

Throwing her head back, she laughed in delight. "I have no idea what you're talking about, André, but I don't care. Where are we going?"

"To a place where fairy tales and spiders fear not, my dear girl! Taxi!" Breton stepped into the busy street, his arm raised in command.

She glanced over at Adam who, looking down at her, grinned. She felt his soft breath as he whispered in her ear, "I wouldn't ask too many questions if I were you. Just enjoy the unusual. Who knows, you may, in fact, spot the red balloon."

"Oh, now I know I'm in trouble." She laughed softly, remembering the magical night before with him. Red balloons? Hadn't he said something about their power over her unconscious? Or was it a floating cherry in the sky? Or, hell, she had no idea. Yet here she was with Adam and Breton, floating into who knew what.

"Pauline?" Adam gazed down at her, "Are you with us?"

"Oh, yes," she whispered. "Am I ever!"

And snaking her arm through his, she followed him and André into the land of the blue fairy tales, red balloons, and yellow cabs.

Pauline imagined the blue fairy tale. Snow White with her Seven Aqua Dwarfs dancing behind her. Cinderella with her Turquoise Pumpkin ready to whisk her away at the stroke of midnight. Sleeping Beauty with her Scary Blue Lips that only Prince Charming could bring back to life. . . .

"Penny for your thoughts?" She felt Adam's hand gently stroking hers as the cab bumped along the beachfront street.

"Oh. . . ." Pauline tingled at his touch, trying not to let her voice betray her inner whirl. "Nothing . . . I. . . ."

"My dear Pauline," Breton interrupted, turning around to face the two of them from the front seat of the cab. "I do not for an instant believe that 'nothing' hangs in your pretty head. You were thinking marvelous thoughts, were you not?"

"Well. . . ." she laughed softly. "Actually, I was thinking about your idea of the blue fairy tale. . . ."

"Oui?"

"I'm not sure what you meant by that. . . ." What was she doing questioning Breton? Of course she wouldn't understand most, if not all, of what he says. He's surreal! She laughed inwardly.

Breton waved one hand dramatically, gesturing out the window at the sea. "The fairy tale, it is blue. It is purple. It is orange. It is the rainbow. It is color extraordinaire! N'est-ce pas?"

"Uh. . . ." Pauline nodded.

"I think what André means," Adam interceded on her behalf, "is that fairy tales can be any color that we wish them to be. The color is always there. On the page. On the canvas. . . ." He looked over at her, his blue eyes serious. "In our hearts."

"Oui oui! C'est magnifique! That is it, mon ami! The fairy tale, we do always think of it as one color or as one dimension, but in our dreams, in our imagination, why—" Breton's arm swung in a wide sweeping arc inside the cab's interior.

"Hey, watch it, buddy," the cab driver snarled. "I gotta keep my concentration."

"Of course, of course, pardon, monsieur." Breton settled back into his seat, contemplating for a moment, *"The bugbear of death, the music-halls of the beyond, the shipwreck of the loftiest intellect in sleep, the crushing curtain of the future, the towers of Babel, the mirrors of inconsistency, the insurmountable silver-splashed wall of the brain—all of these striking images of human catastrophe are perhaps nothing but images."* [10]

Pauline stared at him open-mouthed. The crushing curtain of the future? The mirrors of inconsistency? The insurmountable silver-splashed brain? Was she supposed to laugh or cry? Understand or question?

Jump out of the cab as soon as it came to a halt and run for her life?

"I myself," Adam began, *"am using divisions on a two-dimensional surface—my canvas—so as to reflect the life pattern that exists in the universe, its tension, oppositions, actions and counteractions, and to explore the cosmic pattern by the way I move the planes back and forth in all directions to form the complete living unit."* [11]

"Precisely, mon ami!" Breton exclaimed, glancing back at Pauline. "Now you do understand, ma petite chérie?"

Pauline nodded slowly. She needed to get some air. And fast. What were these two talking about? She had a vague understanding of Adam's proclamation after last night, but Breton?

Well, the silver-splashed wall of her brain was hurting!

"Six-sixty-six Ocean View, folks." The cab driver ground the taxi to a stop.

"Merci, my good man." Breton climbed out of the cab, stretching his arms to the sky, sighing loudly.

"Here you go." Adam handed the driver the fare, then guided Pauline out of the car into the bright afternoon.

"C'est magnifique!" Breton called out to the sea, waves crashing in thick succession. "The images evolve and revolve. They are here." He waved at the sea and the sky. "And they are here." He pointed to his head, his thick bushy mop bursting in the breeze.

"They are indeed." Adam nodded, hooking his arm through Pauline's.

Pauline breathed deeply, the sea air filling her lungs. Already she felt better.

"Come, come, this way, s'il vous plaît." Breton led them up the garden path to the quaint shingled cottage sitting amid a tangle of white rose bramble.

"You're in for a treat." Adam winked at her.

Pauline smiled slowly. "I am hungry."

Chuckling, Adam tightened his hold on her as Breton knocked vigorously on the old oak door.

The room smelled of violets and vanilla.

Pauline's eyes took a moment to adjust to the candlelit room after the brightness of the beach, yet it was the overpowering cloying smell of romance that struck her senses first. Next, her gaze quickly took in the knickknack-laden shelves, covered in a fine film of one-hundred-year-old dust: tiny figurines of bronzy fishermen and pink ballerinas, an ornate floral teapot with matching tiny cups, ancient books titled *Mysticism Mocks* and *Occult 101*. The heavy floor-length crimson drapes blocked out the dazzle of the afternoon sun, creating a world of smoky intimacy. A pair of golden eyes blinked at her from the ruby-red settee, whiskers twitching slightly at an afternoon nap interrupted.

For a moment, Pauline felt herself swoon as the heavy, musty dankness enveloped her.

"Welcome, my friends, please come in. I am Madame Y."

She directed the little group to sit down at the small round table, her bangles jangling, her wide brown eyes appraising, her voice deep, resonant, low.

"Oui, madame!" Breton hailed her vigorously, bending to kiss both her cheeks, before sitting down. "We are fresh from the sea and the city. We seek your guidance in matters of the mystic."

Nodding slightly, Madame Y waited for the group to be seated before sitting herself, regally, at the spot closest to a spray of violets.

"Please, place your hands on the table," Madame Y commanded softly, "and hold hands with each other. . . ."

Pauline took Adam's painterly mitt and then Breton's warm one, trying to contain both her excitement and her skepticism. Were these guys serious? They'd really dragged her out of work for a séance? Why?

Not that she didn't appreciate the afternoon off, but she wasn't sure why they'd brought her. She had no one she wanted to "communicate" with, even if she believed in such flights of the spirits.

No. Pauline couldn't think of anyone. She would simply go along with it for now. Use the experience as grist for the mill. Why, she could use it as a scene in her novel. Or as research for an article on such matters of the occult.

"Madame," Breton began, clearing his throat dramatically, "I have the desire to communicate with the illustrious crimson spirit of Rimbaud! I know that if I were to speak to him, he could give me much insight into the ways of verse and the lands of the blue fairy tale."

Breton winked at Pauline, who sat wide-eyed at the table across from him.

"Rimbaud. . . ." Madame Y intoned. "Da. . ."

Closing her eyes, Madame Y sang into the air, "Monsieur Rimbaud? Are you there? We wish to speak to you if you are."

"Le soi c'est l'autre, le soi c'est un autre." A faint voice floated overhead, its vibrations filling the room.

"The self is other, the self is another," Adam whispered to Pauline, the scent of violets growing stronger, more cloying in the little room.

"Oui! It is him!" Breton called out excitedly. "Monsieur, it is I! André Breton, your greatest admirer. I wish to ask you, have you seen the pearl glades of the spirit?"

"Oui. . . ."

"Ah, of course! And, I wonder, in these glades, do you often compose your verse, even in the land of the spirits which you now inhabit?"

"Oui."

"Oui, oui!" Breton began to rise from the table in his enthusiasm.

"Please, sir," Madame Y instructed. "Seat yourself. You cannot break the chain. The spirit will flee."

"Oui, oui, of course, of course." Breton fell back into his chair, tiny drops of perspiration gathering at his temple.

"Rimbaud?" Madame Y called out. "We are most apologetic for the disruption. Are you still with us?"

Silence.

Pauline glanced over at Adam, who shrugged, then squeezed her hand. She couldn't help but thrill to his touch even though she was in the middle of this insane séance.

"I fear he is vanished," Madame Y spoke, frowning over at Breton.

"Oh, pardon, madame!" Breton exclaimed. "I just could not believe that it was he! The great poet himself, speaking to us from the pearls of the spirit. I need to get him back. I must ask him about the elephants."

"Elephants?" Madame Y looked down her nose, and then shrugged. "Very well, we will commence. Unless you require a moment of respite?" She eyed Adam and Pauline, who both shook their heads.

Closing her eyes again, Madame Y intoned, "Rimbaud . . . come back to us . . . we ask that you—"

"The elephants!" Breton jumped up. "I must know if they are the answer to the blue fairy tale!"

Pauline couldn't contain herself any longer and burst out laughing. Adam's smile broadened. "Now you really are in trouble," he said.

"I have no doubt," she whispered. "But elephants and fairy tales and—"

"Shhhh!" Madame Y commanded. "Silence. Or we shall never retrieve the communication."

Pauline stifled another giggle as the room filled with vanilla and violets. Violets and vanilla.

And elephants. . . .

"Man is perhaps not the center, the focus of the universe. One may go so far as to believe that there exist above him, on the animal level, beings whose behavior is as alien to him as his own must be to the may-fly or the whale," [12] Breton proclaimed into the murky room.

"Indeed." Madame Y nodded, rising silently. Retrieving a mysterious velvet box from the bookcase behind them, she stood for a moment, still.

Pauline felt an energy pulsating in the darkened room. Her skin tingled as tiny goosebumps rose. What was going on? Should she stay or should she go?

Returning to her place, Madame Y set the tiny box reverently in the center of the table.

They all stared at it. Spellbound.

With a dramatic wave of her slender hand, Madame Y opened the box and revealed a minuscule thimble, golden in hue, with aged indentations of silver and copper.

"A thimble, madame?" Breton asked.

"Yes, monsieur, a thimble."

"Ah. . . ." Breton sat back in his chair, nodding. Pauline felt Adam's hand squeeze hers, communicating what? she wondered. A thimble? What was the significance of this object? She wasn't exactly expecting an elephant, obviously, from such a tiny box, but a thimble?

Madame Y took the thimble from its velvety bed and placed it on the table. Its golden indentations appeared dull, at first, but then as Pauline stared at it, the tiny pinpricks seemed to glow.

Could it be that the thimble was possessed by some higher being, as Breton had suggested?

No, this was ridiculous. It was an inanimate object. It wasn't changing. She was imagining this. Yet as she continued to stare at the object, she watched in fascination as its glowing sparkle began to float, first an inch, then two . . . then higher, till the thimble was hovering in the air above the table.

"Speak, oh Spirit," Madame Y commanded.

Silence.

"We await your instructions, Spirit."

More silence.

Pauline turned toward Adam, trying to catch his eye to gauge his reaction. Was he seeing the same thing that she was? But he stared straight ahead, his focus on the floating object.

"It is I, dear Polly," a faint feminine voice floated into the room.

"Mother?" Pauline's eyes began to tear, her heart pounding. Could it be? Her dear mother who had left her so suddenly, so tragically.

"Yes, sweet girl. It is I."

"Oh. . . ." Pauline gasped, her grip on Adam's hand tightening.

"May I ask a question?" Breton interrupted.

Madame Y arched one patrician brow, "You may. But it is up to the Spirit as to whether or not she wishes to respond."

Breton nodded, "Madame, given your vantage point from the Great Beyond, can you direct us toward the blue fairy tale?"

Silence.

Madame Y frowned. "I fear, Monsieur, that this is not the Spirit's purpose in her visitation."

"Oui, of course, I do beg her pardon." Breton sat back in his chair.

"Perhaps," Adam spoke slowly, "she can illuminate us on the proposition of the Great Spaces of the Mind and the Other Dimension, as it does appear she inhabits this world?"

Pauline's heart continued to race. Why would her mother wish to speak to her? What was Adam talking about, the Great Spaces of the Mind? The Other Dimension? Pauline began to feel lightheaded but, at the same time, hyperalert. As though every cell in her body were on fire.

"I do not know of this Great Spaces of the Mind unless my dear Pauline can explain?" The voice floated into the air, whirls of golden specks sprinkling up and up.

"Uh. . . ." Pauline had no idea what Adam was talking about. How could she? All of this was so beyond her. She tried to summon the courage to speak, but it seemed that her brain could not command her tongue.

"Miss?" Madame Y directed her gaze at her. "Do you wish to ask the Spirit this question? Or perhaps you've another one that presses more upon your soul?"

Pauline sat, silent, her mind racing. What could she possibly ask her mother? There were so many things. Where was she going that night she disappeared? Why had she gotten into the car with a stranger? Who was this stranger?

But all she could do was stifle a sob. "Oh, Mother," she cried. "I miss you so! I love you!"

"And I you, my sweet. I miss you so very much. But know that I love you. I will always love you. From this Other Dimension, as your friend calls it. I am watching over you. Do not fear. Trust these new friends that you have made. They will lead you to places that are vast and unfamiliar, but go. Follow them. Especially the one you call Adam. He is The One, dear girl."

Meeeowwww!

Jumping onto the table, the black cat swiped at the floating thimble, which fell swiftly, a tinny ringing echoing in the room.

"Pushkin!" Madame Y cried, trying to knock the cat off the table with a wide backhand. "Bad, bad pussycat! Off the table immediately!"

The cat glared at her for a moment, his whiskers twitching before leaping off the table. He sauntered back over to the couch. Nonchalantly, he jumped up on its inviting cushions and began licking his left paw.

Madame Y sighed heavily, her brow knit in a fierce frown. "My apologies, dear people. Pushkin can be a bit of a nuisance. I am afraid that our session is over for today. But,"—she gazed across the table at Pauline, her wide brown eyes large and knowing—"I do hope that you have received the information you have come for from the spirits?"

"Ah, yes, madame, indeed, indeed." Breton nodded, rising. "Though I do wonder if we might try one more time to contact another spirit? That of the great Marie Curie and her husband, Pierre. I have a burning desire to ask them how they came about their theory of radioactivity and its relation to the poetics volatile of the blue fairy tale."

Madame Y turned toward him, then smiled slowly. "Perhaps another time, monsieur. And you," she smiled at Pauline, some of her hauteur melting, "did you receive the message you came for from your dear mama . . . I know she speaks to your heart, da?"

Pauline nodded, speechless, then glanced over at Adam.

Grinning, he gave her a sly wink, before speaking for her. "Yes, madame, we thank you. The young lady is quite weary now. I do believe Pauline has all the information she desires. At least for today."

Madame Y nodded, solemnly retrieving the thimble from the table and placing it back in its tiny box, before leading them out of the dim room, the scent of violets and vanilla now only a faint memory as Pauline stepped out into the dazzling afternoon blue.

Mimi and Édouard

Drifting down the rue Dauphine, Mimi could feel every spent cell in her body. She was exhausted. For some reason, she could barely put one foot in front of the other. Her feet seemed to be made of lead bowling balls. If she could just get home, lie down, sink into sleep, then she knew she'd feel better tomorrow. Granted, it'd been a busy night at the café. But wasn't it always? Certainly, the gentleman who had insisted she join his table, even though she was due for another set, had added an extra layer of pique to her night. Why don't they understand *No!* she wondered.

Men. Mimi loved some of them; one in particular sprang to her mind. Yet, she pushed him away. Adam was gone. Out of her life. Busy in his life in America.

He probably didn't even remember her name. . . .

Sighing out loud, Mimi glanced up at the lavender sky, a full moon peeking from behind an elephant cloud. I wonder where Adam is at this moment? she mused. I wonder if he, too, is gazing up at this same sky, seeing the elephant's trunk outlined in the pale moon's glow.

Passing an old building front, vines growing up the walls, she paused, listening.

Tender, romantic notes cascaded out of the open window, into the mist of the midnight air.

Was it Ravel? One of the *Valses Nobles*?

Mimi stood outside the open window, enchanted, her exhaustion beginning to evaporate. Who could be playing the piano so sweetly at this hour?

A musical insomniac?

Mimi laughed softly to herself, edging toward the open door where a golden light cast a rectangle of welcome.

The theme grew in power, the notes floating into the air and dancing around her. Yes, it was one of the waltzes. Venturing softly through the doorway, Mimi tiptoed into the foyer, poked her head slowly around the corner.

He was a small, dark little man, his fingers elegant on the keyboard. Each note caressed.

Could it be the great man himself? she wondered. She'd seen his picture in some advertisement somewhere. An upcoming performance, perhaps? And this man did bear an uncanny resemblance. Yet Mimi found it hard to believe that Maurice Ravel would be playing in such a casual manner, almost as if he were in the open square itself.

She stepped closer, crunching a small leaf that had blown into the entryway.

The music stopped abruptly. The pianist turned toward her, frowning.

"Oh!" Mimi cried softly. "Pardon, monsieur, I am so sorry. I heard your beautiful music from the street and I couldn't help myself. I had to see who was playing. . . ." Mimi's apology drifted into the now-silent space.

The pianist gazed at her for a moment, then shrugged. "It is not a problem, mademoiselle. You only startled me. I thought I was alone. I am afraid that I can get lost, as it were, in the music, and forget that others can hear my playing, which"—he gave a shy smile—"I am afraid, is not very good."

"Oh, but it is! It was!" Mimi cried, stepping forward into the room, her tiredness now vanished as she beheld his sympathetic and humble gaze. "I am no musician"—she shook her head— "well . . . I do sing a little. . . ."

"Ah, a singer!" he exclaimed. "Magnifique. Do you perform?"

She laughed. "I do, but I'm afraid it's just at a seedy café down the boulevard. No one there really pays attention to my singing. Well, almost no one. . . ."

"I find that hard to believe," he said. "Such a charming voice you have. I can only imagine what heights it might reach in song."

"You are too kind." Mimi cast her eyes down, uncharacteristically shy. What was it about this strange little man that had her so rattled suddenly? Was it the power of the music and his talent to bring out its beauty? Or was it his gaze? So gentle, yet so intense. Why, it was as if he were looking into her very soul.

"Allow me to introduce myself." He rose, extending his hand. "I am Édouard Ravel."

"Ravel?" Mimi's heart pounded. "You're not related to Maurice Ravel by any chance?"

"I am indeed. I am his brother."

"His brother? I had no idea he had a brother."

Édouard shrugged. "Very few people do. I am not nearly as talented or famous as Maurice."

"But you are a musician, too? Your playing is divine!" Mimi exclaimed.

"Again, you are too kind, mademoiselle. I am a musician, yes. And the piano is my first love. However, I did not have the immense talent that my brother possesses and so I do not pursue it in any profound way. Though I do love to play his music. Especially his waltzes. They have a certain melancholy that speaks to me."

"You are sad, monsieur?"

Taking a deep breath, Eduard shook his head. "I apologize, mademoiselle. I do not mean to burden you with my woes."

"Oh, it's not a burden," Mimi gushed forward. "I, too, am sad . . . at times and. . . ."

He nodded, gazing at her deeply. Mimi found herself blushing.

What was going on? Why was this man so . . . provocative . . . ?

"I am afraid I have told you more about myself than I usually do upon first meeting. Yet I feel at some disadvantage. I don't even know your name."

"Mimi," she murmured. "My name is Mimi."

"Charming. Would you care to sit?" He motioned to the spot next to him on the piano bench.

Gulping, Mimi nodded before tentatively taking a seat as the music began again.

Genevieve paced the tiny apartment like a caged panther. Damn her, she thought, dragging deeply on her cigarette. Where the hell was she?

Glancing up at the tired cuckoo clock, Genevieve frowned to make out the time in the dark. After two. Sure, Mimi worked late at that goddamn club; why she did, Genevieve would never understand. She certainly had enough money for the both of them.

But then Mimi was stubborn. Claimed she liked it. The singing. The atmosphere.

The men. . . .

Exhaling deeply, Genevieve pictured the worst. Mimi in that slinky red number, singing "Parlez-Moi d'Amour" in that sultry way of hers. And the men. They'd all be eyeing her up and down. Wanting her. And Mimi?

She played right into their slimy paws.

It was disgusting!

Genevieve thought of their time together. The afternoons sipping coffee, then off to the track where Mimi would cheer her on. Then back to the stables for champagne and congratulations, before heading back to the flat for an afternoon of delicious love-making.

Goddamn her! Genevieve swore to herself again. If Mimi didn't walk through that door soon, she was going to have to go out looking for her. And on a night like this, with the moon full and the air so soft, well . . . Mimi could be God knows where.

If only Mimi would listen to her. Quit that job. Get out of Paris while they still could. It wasn't a safe place for the likes of them. But then, Mimi always fudged on this. Claiming she loved women, loved Genevieve, but then saying how she had to please men because of her job.

It was driving her crazy!

"Hello . . . darling. . . ." Mimi flung open the door, floating into the apartment, a dreamy cloud surrounding her.

"Where the hell have you been?" Genevieve demanded. "It's almost three in the morning and I was expecting you hours ago."

"I told you never to wait up for me," Mimi pouted, tossing her black stole on the bed. "I'm starving!"

"Well, there's nothing to eat," Genevieve snarled. Did she think she could just come waltzing in here as if everything were as it had always been?

"Are you certain?" Mimi opened the ice box, peering inside. Genevieve watched her take in the pathetic stalk of celery. A half-eaten coq au vin . . . some moldy brie . . . a bottle of champagne.

"What's this?" Mimi pulled the champagne from its shelf, slamming the ice box shut. "Are we celebrating? Did you win your race today?"

"As if you'd care. . . ." Genevieve pouted. Why did she let Mimi get to her so?

Shrugging, Mimi popped the cork, smiling blissfully. What was going on in that pretty head of hers? Genevieve wondered. There seemed to be something different about her. Something had happened. She had met someone.

Genevieve felt a cold chill down her spine.

"Here." Mimi handed her a glass of the bubbly. "Let's toast to your win."

"How do you know I won?"

Mimi smiled, slowly, "Okay . . . let's toast to your loss, ma chérie. I don't care. I just want to toast."

"Why?" Genevieve couldn't keep the suspicion out of her tone.

"Oh . . . I just love the music."

"What music?"

Mimi's violet eyes grew dreamy and sparkling. "Don't you hear it?"

Shaking her head, Genevieve gulped her drink and grabbed the bottle to pour herself another. "No."

"If you listen, you can hear it. . . ." Mimi cocked her head to the side, and then began swaying slowly to an imaginary tune.

For a moment, Genevieve watched her lover in disbelief. How could Mimi be so oblivious?

A familiar bubble began to rise in the pit of her stomach, and Genevieve felt her self-control evaporate. Gulping the rest of her drink in one swift swallow, Genevieve raised her arm . . . and for an instant, she felt the room spin, the chairs, clock, and Mimi all a misty fog around her. Genevieve felt the light heft of the glass as she glared at Mimi's trancelike dance. "You little whore!" she cried. And with a primal shriek of anguish, she hurled the glass against the wall, shattering it into tiny bits under the clock.

Cuckoo cuckoo cuckoo

"Oh, now look what you've done!" Mimi cried, shock barely registering as she gazed at the shattered bits of glass littering the dank floor.

"I have a feeling it is nothing compared to what you've done!" Genevieve tried to keep the sob from rising into her voice. But she was so sure. It was so obvious. Mimi had met someone and she was smitten.

Mimi sipped her champagne, gazing coolly at her lover. "I've done nothing wrong. I only—"

Genevieve shook her head, then grabbed her own wrap from the back of a worn chair. "I don't want to hear it. Not tonight. I'll see you in the morning."

Striding swiftly across the room, she opened the door, standing at the threshold for a moment. Had she overreacted?

she wondered. Was she simply tired and spent from her long day and the longer wait?

No . . . Mimi was different. She could feel it.

Without a glance back, Genevieve slammed the door behind herself, wiping away her angry tears. Damn her, she thought for the umpteenth time that evening, as she stalked out onto the quiet street, a soft breeze at her back, her feline spirit crushed by unbearable sorrow.

Mimi stood quietly for a moment in the center of the room, staring at the door where Genevieve had just disappeared.

What had she done? Had she really done something wrong? Why was Genevieve so angry? Did she know? But how could she?

Mimi sighed, thinking: Had she fallen in love? Had she fallen out of love?

No, it couldn't be. Not so fast. Not so hard. But yet, when she thought of Édouard, his music, his touch, she couldn't help but smile to herself even as a lurking pang of guilt hit her when she remembered the pain on Genevieve's face.

Swaying slightly, Mimi was suddenly overcome with a euphoric queasiness. Making her way over to the kitchen table, she pulled out one of the little chairs and plopped down. Raising the champagne glass to her lips, she took a sip, sighed, and set it down.

She wasn't thirsty anymore. She wasn't dancing anymore.

The queasiness hit her hard. Mimi felt her belly, a rounded softness. She knew what she needed to do . . . yes, she could seduce him. Or had she already? Smiling slyly, Mimi rose, locked the door, and floated into bed.

Leonora and François

SANTA CRUZ, CALIF., 1992

Leonora stepped over the delicate golden dragonfly etched into the dark tiled floor. Frowning, she bent to examine it, flattened as if so many had stepped upon its intricate golden veins, so delicate but, now, so lifeless.

Yet . . . there was something about it that still held magic and possibility. Gently she pried the wings, body, and head off the floor, holding the weightless golden gift in the palm of her hand. Was that a movement? She looked more closely. Yes! Its tiny antennae were twitching ever so slightly. Trembling with excitement, Leonora carried the fragile being over to the vase of colorful peonies on the table, tenderly placing the dragonfly into the greeny water.

Breathless, she waited and watched as the dragonfly began to come to life. Its antennae now reaching up and out of the water, its wings beginning to fill out and wriggle in the murky liquid, the golden head and eyes now alive and bright.

Suddenly the golden dragonfly erupted out of the water's embrace, flying out into the room in magnificent energy. Leonora gazed at it for a moment in amazement and wonder, before racing to the front door and opening it wide.

The golden dragonfly wasted no time in flying out the door, out into the indigo night, its resurrection a miracle of touch, water, and magic.

François snorted, burbling loudly, mumbling something in his sleep, before rolling over with a contented sigh. Damn, she thought. She wanted to follow the golden dragonfly out into its magical indigo night. But François was a rude awakening into the reality of her life.

Yet, the dream left her with such a feeling of magic and power. She had brought the golden dragonfly back to life. If she hadn't pried it from its flattened grave, it would never have flown alive and enchanted, out into the night.

Leonora rose; quietly she walked over to the open window to gaze out at the setting moon. What did the dream mean? Was it a sign? Obviously, it was telling her something. She had the power to bring life back from lifelessness? Beauty was beneath her feet if only she'd stop and lift it to life? Transformation of a dramatic sort was in her future?

She smiled, remembering her afternoon at Adam's studio. His work, the creative process, energizing her. Now, as she gazed out at the night sky, she remembered the tingle of anticipation upon seeing his work. And she had not been disappointed. . . .

After their hike, she had followed Adam up the gentle slope from the woods, pine needles crunching under their boots. He led her to the large, barn-like structure that was his studio, unlocking the heavy door. Leonora stood at the threshold for a moment, breathless, staring into the cool gray room of his studio.

Great canvases of Prussian blue with emerald comets hung haphazardly on the tall wooden walls. Cosmic sketches of bright orange dots and golden stars were scattered about the gigantic room, tumbling onto the cement floor. In the center of the studio was a long rectangular worktable littered with the usual artist's wares: tubes of paint, brushes, sketch pads . . . and a thimble?

It was prominently displayed in the center of his worktable, posed atop a small, rose-colored wooden box.

Intrigued, Leonora had bent closer to examine the enchanting object.

"A thimble? Do you often prick your thumb when sewing, Adam?"

Chuckling softly, he shook his head. "I suppose that is one interpretation."

"What do you mean?"

"This object has a history, a story that, if you're interested, I could tell you one day. . . ." Adam's voice trailed off, wistful and melancholy.

Leonora nodded, eyeing the thimble on its perch. There was something about it. It seemed to possess an energy. Some sort of field emanated from it. What was the story? Dare she press him? They had only just met, but Leonora felt as though she'd known him all of her life. And this thimble. Was it the key? Could it explain the link between them?

"I understand if the story is one of a personal nature," Leonora began, chills running up and down her spine. What was it about this thimble? Or was it the energy in the studio itself? Or the man before her, suddenly so far away?

Adam sighed softly. "Yes, of course, it is personal, but if you've the time, perhaps I might prevail upon you to listen? It's a story that needs to be told in words perhaps, though. . . ." He motioned at the numerous canvases stacked up behind the staircase, hanging on the walls. "My work has been an attempt to tell its story . . . for many years. . . ."

"Indeed?" Leonora tried to hold her inquisitive nature at bay. Adam wanted to tell her but she felt it was, perhaps, not the right time . . . yet. . . .

"I wonder if we might head back up to the house for a spot of tea?" he asked, suddenly distant, polite.

"Of course," she answered, trying to hide her disappointment.

She saw Adam glance at the thimble, furtively? Longingly? Lovingly?

Leonora was not quite certain. All she knew was that this man had a depth to him; that his art only scratched the surface of his soul.

A story. Yes, Leonora lived for stories. And if she were patient, she knew that one day, maybe soon, she'd learn of Adam's, a pinprick at a time.

François snorted, then grinned in his sleep, turning over with a lumbering heave. "Marianna. . . ." he murmured. "Come hither, my darling. . . ."

They were in a thick wood, green pines towering over them as they danced through the soft pebbled path. François held Marianna's hand tightly; she was laughing, a tinkling delight at his touch. They were so blissful.

Suddenly, a huge grizzly bear appeared between them, a maple-colored, snarling beast. François, at first, was terrified. But then he felt Marianna's hands clutching his, their arms forming a powerful circular embrace around the bear wedged between them. The three of them began to bounce and roll rapidly down the path. The bear was no longer a threat. He was part of their journey. A grizzly ménage, if you will.

François's gaze caught Marianna's on the other side of the bear. She was laughing in wild abandon, ecstatic. François threw back his head and joined her, his manly laughter echoing in the wood. He tightened his grip around the pair, his hands holding fast to Marianna's as they barreled down the path. Suddenly he felt something different. Marianna's touch was changed. More distant, detached. François craned his neck to catch a glimpse of her on the other side of the bear.

It was not Marianna! It was Leonora! Her dark eyes flashing. Her beautiful mouth turned up in a most sinister grin. "Hello, my darling," she sang out, "were you expecting someone else?"

And she laughed and laughed and laughed as the bear trio continued to roll down the path, faster and faster and faster, until suddenly they came to an abrupt halt. François clutched the bear and felt for Leonora.

But she was no longer there.

The grizzly turned toward François and gave a mighty snarling roar, raising his massive paw, claws out. . . .

"Arrrrggghhhh!" François cried out, sitting up in bed, a sick blackness covering his psyche.

"François!" Leonora cried, rushing to his side to comfort him. "Are you quite all right? It was only a nightmare." She touched his hand gently with her own.

François stared down at her hand, cringing inwardly.

"Do you want to tell me about it?" she asked.

"No . . . no, I don't think so. . . ." François got out of bed, trying to control the subtle shaking in his soul. Such a dream.

He must leave Leonora. Now. Before she ate him alive. Marianna was right. If he didn't break his ties with Leonora soon, there would be nothing left of him.

What was Leonora to him anyway? Only an obstacle, an impediment to his true happiness. Besides, she had That Artist, Adam What's-his-name. . . .

Grabbing a cigarette from the nightstand, François lit it, inhaling deeply. He frowned at what he knew to be Leonora's silent disproval, even as she continued to gaze at him with loving concern.

Damn her, he thought. Why must she always choose the precise moment to be "nice" to him? But the dream's power was too strong to ignore, its message too clear.

He needed to leave her. It was time. But how? He still needed Leonora. At least for the time being.

"François?" Leonora said softly. "Come to bed. It's only a dream."

"Yes, you're right." He sighed, stubbing the cigarette out. "It was only a dream. . . ."

But he knew better. And so should Leonora. Couldn't she feel his unhappiness? His distress? Wasn't she the one who claimed that dreams spoke to those who listened?

Well, he was listening now, he thought. He climbed back into bed, pulling the covers over his head.

Pauline and Remedios

Pauline plopped down under the massive jacaranda, its shady violet sanctuary a welcome respite from the intensity of the blazing sun. The hike around the grounds had been a good one. She needed it after her session with Wolfgang in the morning. That man! she thought. He is driven! Not that she didn't revel in the energy of their work. The magazine was coming together in ways that she had never imagined. She was, most of the time, thrilled to be a part of its creation.

Yet, she felt like something was missing. There was a part of her that longed for an abstract idea of pure creation. What was it that Wolfgang had said this morning? *"Works of art are traps set for life—if the trap is well set, life is snared within it forever."*[13]

Sighing softly, Pauline shielded her eyes with her hand, squinting out into the yellow glare. A scrawny brown mutt trotted around the side of the low-slung ranch house, pausing for a moment to sniff before lifting its leg for the ritual marking, then continuing on around the house.

Pauline took a deep breath. It wasn't that she didn't appreciate her life here. Adam's love sustained her. Paalen's project energized her. But there was a longing that she couldn't quite identify. Was it her own writing? Did she need to begin a project that was only hers?

"Hola," a soft voice called from behind.

Turning, Pauline grinned as she watched her new friend climb the gentle slope behind the jacaranda, black curls escaping from their elegant coiffure.

"Remedios!" Pauline, called out. "¿Cómo estás?"

"Bien, bien. ¿Y tú?"

Pauline smiled widely; already she felt better. Why had she been so out of sorts? What had been her problem? Granted, Wolfgang could be demanding and even a bit commandeering, yet she enjoyed their collaboration. Why had she felt so crabby?

"I'm okay." Pauline reverted to English, her Spanish still rudimentary.

Her friend sat down next to her, concerned. "Only okay?"

"Well, now that you're here, I do feel better."

"What is the problem?" Remedios tucked a stray curl behind her ear. "This heat?"

"I thought you'd be used to it, growing up in Spain."

"Ah, well, that was a long time ago. And"—Remedios gave a languid wave at the sweltering landscape in front of them—"it is different here in Mexico. The sun, it is a fire of sparks and magic, but still, it is too hot!"

Both women giggled, delighted by this proclamation. Pauline adored Remedios's talk almost as much as her art. Her paintings were filled with magical worlds of windmill cats, floating eyeballs, and lightning cellos. Why, Remedios almost made her want to be a painter.

Almost.

"Is it a problem with Adam?" Remedios asked.

"Adam? Oh, no, I don't think so. I mean, he is doing well. His work is growing in a new direction. I think this place, the nature, the solitude, the air . . . it feeds him."

"And you?" Remedios touched her friend's hand gently. "Is this place good for your writing?"

Sighing, Pauline shook her head. "I'm not sure. I mean . . . you know I'm working with Wolfgang on the journal?"

"Yes, *DYN*? It is interesting, no?"

"Yes, yes, it's interesting. He's interesting. I feel privileged to be working with him on this project. Breton's *Manifesto* has been the bible of surrealism for long enough. Wolfgang has another vision that needs to be heard. And . . . I. . . ."

Pauline's voice faltered. A tiny violet flower floated down from the bough of the massive tree, landing softly on the ground in front of her. She picked it up, gingerly, holding it in her palm.

"Beautiful. . . ." Remedios murmured.

Pauline nodded, twirling the flower round gently. "I wonder if I'm like this flower. . . ."

Remedios smiled tenderly. "Yes?"

". . . one minute I am anchored to my home, safe, above danger. And then the next, I am set free, floating down, down, down to the ground, to be picked up by a stranger or trampled on by. . . ."

Pauline felt a sudden familiar surge in her chest. She would not cry. Not in front of Remedios.

"My dear friend." Remedios took her hand, carefully lifting the flower from her palm and then softly blowing it into the breeze.

"You will fly. See?"

The two women gazed at the lavender speck floating out and up on a sudden welcome breeze.

"Do you really think so?" Pauline asked.

"I know so," Remedios grinned. "Now! Come with me! What you need is a tequila!"

Laughing, Pauline rose, allowing Remedios to snake her arm through hers, the two friends following the path of the magical jacaranda's blossom, its scent lingering in the hazy azure air.

"Merde! That is what it is!" Breton stormed into Adam's studio, letting the screen door bang shut.

"Good afternoon, André." Adam stepped back from his easel,

squinting, the wild golds of the stars jumping off the canvas and into his consciousness.

"You must put a stop to her!" Breton cried, pacing across the cement floor. "It is little bits of fecal matter"—he tossed a slim volume onto Adam's worktable—"here . . . and here . . . and why, look at this!" Flipping through the magazine, Breton pointed at various offenses on the page.

"Fecal matter?" Adam stepped back toward the easel, eyeing a corner, then reached for a brush, dipping it into luminous golden amber, and applying it to the canvas.

"You do know what I mean!" Breton huffed. "Listen to this: *The Manifesto turned around the method of automatism, defined as 'pure psychic automatism, thought's dictation without conscious, aesthetic, or moral control.' The whole effort was to provoke the inner murmur, and Breton stands like a signalman at night, signaling the passage of a great lighted train, the passive life of the intelligence.*" [14]

"Ummm. . . ." Adam continued to apply paint to the canvas, a bright cosmic star beginning to take shape.

"Do you not understand, mon ami? Pauline! She is a woman! What can she know of the *Manifesto*'s provocations?"

"It sounds like she knows quite a bit. . . ." Adam stepped back again, then pointed to one corner. "It needs something there. What do you think, André?"

Breton took a deep breath. "A blue giraffe. That is what it needs, Adam. A blue giraffe will satisfy that space."

"Indeed?" Adam chuckled, cocking his head slightly. "Perhaps."

"*The idea, the woman, disturbs it, disposes it to less severity. Their role is to isolate one second of its disappearance and remove it to the sky in that glorious acceleration that it can be, that it is,*" [15] Breton proclaimed.

"Do you think Pauline would agree about the blue giraffe?" Adam asked, grinning.

"Arrgggh!" Breton threw up his hands, wild above his head. "I do not talk about the blue giraffe! Pauline and Wolfgang, they must be stopped. This crazy journal that they have begun. It is a travesty. I am the *Manifesto*!"

"Yes, well, it seems that Pauline would agree with you there."

"On the surface, oui, but underneath, can you not see? She is the subversive element. She and Wolfgang, they will ruin my life's work if you do not stop them."

"I'm afraid that I have no control over them, especially Pauline. You can't control your wife, can you?"

Breton sputtered. "No ... I. ..."

Adam stepped back toward the easel, considering. "Pauline writes as she wants to write, just as I paint as I want to paint, and you rant as you want to rant!"

For a moment, Breton stared at his friend, shock oozing out of his blazing eyes. Then a slow grin turned into a delighted chuckle. "Ah, mon ami, you are so funny! Of course, I do see your point. But it is such a pity that you are not still the one to speak for the Movement. Of course, I mean no offense. Your wife, she is a most intelligent woman, but she knows not what she writes of. She does not have the experience that you do. I only wish that you had stayed in New York, continued your lectures. Your word spread the *Manifesto* with such style and verve."

Wiping the brush on the side of his pants, Adam reached for the Prussian blue and squeezed a healthy blob of it onto his palette. "You know that I couldn't stay in New York any longer, André. The pressure was too much for me. And while I appreciate your praise around my articulation of the *Manifesto*, I had to stop. I had to leave the city. I needed to come to a place that was away from the crush of humanity. I needed nature and solitude and sky and trees and light and water and . . . I'm not sure about the giraffe, André, perhaps an elephant?"

Laughing, Breton shook his head. "Oui, an elephant. A zebra. A grizzly bear. It is you who will allow the spirit of intuition to guide you. Listen to her."

"Like you do to Pauline?"

"Ah, okay, I take your point. I will listen to Pauline. I will give her a chance. But women, they are a problem. I adore them, but. . . ."

"Hola!"

Adam grinned, nodding toward the door. "I think we have company, André. Hola, Remedios. ¿Cómo estás?"

"Bien." Remedios's dark eyes danced behind the screen. "May we come in?"

"We?" Breton frowned for a moment, eyeing the journal still open on the worktable. Shrugging, he reached for it, stuffing it in his jacket pocket.

"Hi, darling." Pauline opened the screen door without waiting for an answer. "We come bearing gifts."

"If that is the tequila," Breton held the door open for the two women, "then please, do enter."

Chuckling softly, Adam lay down his brush, reaching for the glass that Remedios held out to him.

Mrrrrooooowwww!

"Oh, Pablo! I didn't know you were following us!" Pauline exclaimed, bending to scoop up the large white cat. "Are we interrupting?" she asked, stroking the purring beast.

"No, not at all." Adam wrapped his arm around her. "André and I were just chatting about your work with Wolfgang."

"You were?" Pauline caught her breath. Did she dare ask them what they thought?

"It is a work of genius!" Breton exclaimed, helping himself to a drink.

"You think so?" Pauline blushed.

"Magnifique!" Breton winked at Remedios, who shook her head, warning him with her dark eyes.

"I am so hungry," Remedios said, glancing over at Pauline.

"Oh!" Pauline tried to keep the disappointment out of her voice. She wanted to hear what André thought of her article. Yet there was a part of her that feared him. Though he seemed more than enthusiastic at the moment.

"Sweetheart." Adam headed over to the sink to begin rinsing off his brushes. "Do you think we could find some accompaniment to this charming cocktail you've brought us?"

"Of course." Pauline glanced over at Breton, then at Remedios and finally at Adam's unfinished painting. What was that in the corner, under the shooting golden fire?

A blue giraffe?

Shaking her head, Pauline turned toward the group. "Come, everyone, let's see what we can rustle up."

Snaking her arm through Breton's, Remedios guided him out into the golden haze. "Do you enjoy our Mexico, señor?"

"Ah, I do, I do," André answered. "May I tell you of a dream I had or maybe it was not quite a dream, but . . . *One night, before falling asleep, I became aware of a most bizarre sentence, clearly articulated to the point where it was impossible to change a word of it, but separate from the sound of any voice. . . .*" [16]

"Pablo! Let go of that right now!" Pauline hissed at the cat.

The large white feline stared at her placidly, the steak dangling from his mouth, his tail twitching slightly, before turning and sauntering away.

Remdios's hearty laugh rang out. "Oh that gato! He is a one, isn't he?"

"You could say that," Pauline sighed, exasperated. The cat was the least of her worries. She'd get the steak back from him in a minute. He wasn't moving too fast.

It was Breton that she had real concerns about. Had he really meant what he said about her writing? Did he really think it was "magnifique"? She found this hard to believe. Breton wasn't one to roll over and give up the surrealist mantle to anyone else.

Settling down at the bright red kitchen table, Remedios took a gulp of her drink. "Breton, he was very flattering, sí?"

"Yes, yes. . . ." Pauline hesitated. How much did she divulge to her new friend about her worries? Remedios seemed like a sympathetic ear, but she didn't know her very well. Yet, Pauline was a firm believer in intuition. And in her soul, she felt that she could trust Remedios. That Remedios would tell her the truth.

The fluttering notes of one of Ravel's waltzes drifted through the open door and into the cozy kitchen, a recording of Claudio Arrau, one of Adam's favorites. Pauline paused for a moment, transported to another time and place . . . Adam's studio, late at night. Or was it the afternoon? The light was dim, but the paintings sparked, their cosmic lines and planetary shootings jumping off the canvas. Ravel had been in the background. Adam was in the foreground, painting? No . . . he had put down his brush. He was turned toward her. His brilliant blue eyes fixated on her as only an artist can fixate.

Pauline recalled how her heart fluttered, her skin tingled. He was so magnetic. And for some reason, he liked her.

"Pauline?" Remedios's gentle voice brought her back to the sunny kitchen. "Where did you go?"

Smiling shyly, Pauline gazed over at her friend, "Oh . . . I. . . ." Should she tell Remedios about her courtship with Adam? How fast she fell? How a mysterious medium at a beachfront séance brought about their marriage?

"I was just thinking of Adam. . . ." Pauline shook her head, sighing softly.

"Yes?" Remedios asked.

"Oh . . . nothing . . . I. . . ."

"It did not seem like 'nothing' to me," Remedios began.

"Yes, well . . . I don't want to bore you . . . I. . . ."

"I am not easily bored."

Giggling, Pauline grinned. "No, I would imagine not."

"And things are fine with Adam?"

"Yes, yes, everything is fine. Actually, it's my work that I feel is not. . . ." Pauline paused.

What was it about her work that seemed not quite right? Did

it have something to do with Adam? Or with Wolfgang? Or Breton?

"Your writing is wonderful," Remedios beamed. "Your ideas are complex, and your language communicates them so clearly. You have a great talent."

"Do you think so?" Pauline caught her breath. Why would Remedios say such a thing if she didn't believe it?

"Yes, indeed I do."

"Then why do I feel like my creative inspiration is. . . ? I don't know how to say this. . . ." Pauline blushed shyly in spite of herself. Here she was, a wordsmith, or so she called herself, and she couldn't find the words to express her lack of spark? Is that what it was?

" . . . it seems like I don't have the spark, the passion, that I had back in New York, about my writing. . . ."

"Sí, sí, sí . . . I do understand this completely." Remedios nodded, pouring herself another drink from the bottle of tequila in the middle of the table. "Would you like?" She held the bottle out to Pauline.

"Sure, why not?" Pauline held her glass out as Remedios poured.

"Now!" Remedios took a hearty swig of tequila. "The inspiration. It comes from many places."

"Where does it come from for you? Your paintings are so heavenly. They portray a world that is mesmerizing and unique."

"Gracias." Remedios gazed out the window for a moment, the evening light golden now on the violet jacaranda tree on the horizon. "I think, for me, my inspiration often comes from my dreams."

"Ah . . . yes, Adam says the same thing," Pauline nodded. "I don't think my dreams are very inspiring though. They often follow a mundane narrative around a day working at the restaurant or a paper not completed for a course."

Remedios laughed. "Yes, of course. I, too, have mundane dreams. But these are not the ones that I speak of. You know the painting of the gato and cello?"

"Yes, of course. It's one of my favorites."

"That came from a dream."

"Wow! That must have been some dream!"

"It was. I was walking down a quaint alleyway here in Mexico or perhaps in my homeland of Spain. It was night and the stars were out. Ahead of me, leading the way, or somehow I was following, a pack of cats pranced. I was delighted to be following their lead down this winding cobblestone street. All of a sudden, the cat in the lead, a large white beast—"

"Like Pablo?"

Remedios laughed, "Why, yes, exactly like Pablo. In fact, it was Pablo. He was so white that he glowed in the dark night. All the other cats—there were orange ones and striped ones and brown ones—they all followed him. I followed at the rear. All of a sudden, Pablo burst into a sparkle of greens, silvers, golds, and aquas. Like shooting stars he became, bursting up and into the night air. And I thought to myself, Pablo has entered the Other Dimension."

"The Other Dimension?" Pauline asked, her heart quickening. What was it about this term that seemed so familiar? Was it something that Adam had said? Or Wolfgang?

"Yes, 'the Other Dimension.' And I immediately woke and hurried out to my studio and began to paint. The cat in the painting, as you know, is not white, but a burnt sienna, and the cello? I am not sure where that came from, but the sparks are from the cat. From his energy. He is reaching for the Other Dimension. . . ."

"As only a cat or a cello can do, right?" Pauline smiled and nodded.

"Sí, sí . . . as only a cat or a cello can do," Remedios agreed. "But you see my point? The dream, it was just the spark, just the tidbit that I needed to spring to action. I had to paint that dream, and I had to paint it immediately before its energy dissipated."

"Yes, Adam speaks of this, too. How a dream is something that he has to paint immediately. Otherwise, he will lose its energy.

But. . . ." Pauline hesitated for a moment. What could she say here? That she thought that dreams might be just fine for painting but not for writing? That writing down one's dreams was the height of cliché?

Remedios gazed at her, then smiled brightly. "I only share this dream to demonstrate one method of inspiration. I am sure that your writing may come from other sources. It is not the same as painting, I know. But perhaps you may pay more attention to your dreams and see what they may show you."

Pauline nodded. "Yes, that's a good idea. I will do that, but for now, I have to find that stupid cat. He has our dinner! Pablo! Pablo, where the hell are you?"

Stepping out onto the veranda, Pauline shaded her eyes to search the horizon for the large white cat.

He was nowhere in sight. Glancing down at her feet, then gazing up a few feet to the tabletop, she spied the scattered remains of their dinner, bits of chewed on meat, bordered with tiny teeth marks.

"Oh, Pablo. . . ." she murmured, walking over to pick up the pieces of gnawed meat. "Now what am I going to make for dinner?"

"Perhaps I can help?" a rich baritone rang at her side.

"Oh!" Pauline gave a little start. "Wolfgang, I didn't hear you come up. . . ." Her voice trailed off as she beheld the solid, handsome man standing before her. She tried to keep her flutterings in check, but when he looked at her like that. . . .

"I don't mean to startle." Wolfgang grinned. "But it seemed as if you could use some assistance?"

Smiling slowly, Pauline nodded. "Well, yes, as you can see, the cat ate most of our dinner."

"Then allow me." Wolfgang took her gently by the elbow and began to lead her away from the house back toward his studio.

"Oh. . . ." Pauline glanced back at the screen door where she could see the shadow of Remedios standing.

"I think I have just what you need back at my studio." Wolf-gang guided her across the dusty courtyard.

Letting herself be led, Pauline told herself that Wolfgang was only trying to help. But there was another part of her that couldn't help but be thrilled. Working with Wolfgang had been challenging. The collaboration a tricky proposition. For many reasons.

The least of which was this energy she was feeling now.

Aha! Energy! Perhaps inspiration would come to her at last!

Mrrrooowwww!

"Pablo!" Pauline cried at the sound and sight of the white beast. "You're a bad boy!"

Wolfgang chuckled as he led her up the steps to his studio, "He certainly is. And"—with a wink, he opened the door—"he's not the only one!"

Catching her breath, Pauline stepped into his studio, sketch-books scattered on the slanted draftsman's table, a large canvas of a painting in progress, opaque skulls floating in a sea of azure and emerald, sat on an easel in the center of the cool room. And the white cat already inside, leading the way to inspiration and mischief. As only a white cat can. . . .

Mimi

HOLLYWOOD, CALIF., 1942

"Mama! Loooook!" The child held up a smudgy paper, the bright lemon, lime, and red scratchings careening off the sides of the page.

"That is très bonne, ma petite sweetums," Mimi murmured, trying to keep the tired boredom out of her voice. The child was engaged. Busy. Creative. Artistic? Did she take after her father?

Mimi sighed, turning back to the stove to stir the canned tomato sauce for pasta. All children drew pictures, made art, right? It was not a thing that was unusual. But yet, part of her hoped that Adam lived on in this child. His child.

Ah . . . why did she even bother? Adam was so long ago. Not a part of her life at all. Who knew what had even happened to him? He'd gone off to New York, leaving her in Paris. She had been nothing to him. Or . . . ?

"Hallooo?" Édouard let the screen door slam loudly.

"Papa! Papa! Look what I made!"

The child jumped from her chair at the kitchen table, tumbling into the living room where Édouard scooped her up.

"My! What have we here?" He kissed the top of her curly head, glancing over at Mimi and winking.

"It is a picture! I made it just for you!"

"For me?" Édouard took the drawing, held it out to examine it.

"Why! It is wonderful, my petite one! I like especially this part here."

He pointed to the red blob at the corner of the paper.

"That is the dog!" the child exclaimed excitedly.

"A dog? A red dog?"

She nodded, serious. "Yes, Papa. A red dog. Do you like it?"

"I love it!" Setting her down, Édouard strolled over to where Mimi stood, still stirring the sauce. "And how was your day?"

Mimi shrugged, taking off her apron. "I have to go. The Hotsy Totsy phoned and wants me to fill in for one of the girls who called in sick."

Édouard frowned. "Oh . . . that is too bad. I was looking forward to spending the evening with my two favorite girls."

"Papa! Look at me!"

The child spun around on the worn living room rug, her dark curls flying in wild abandon.

"That is a very beautiful dance!" Édouard exclaimed, clapping his hands.

"I made a salad. It's in the ice box," Mimi said, grabbing her purse from the hook behind the door. "Don't wait up for me. I will be late."

The child stopped spinning, staring at Mimi. "Mama! No! Don't go!" A wail began, low and soft but gaining quickly in tempo and volume.

Mimi stooped to hug the child. "Mama will be back, sweetums. She just has to go to work and sing a song and—"

The child's tears slowed. "Mama sing a song?"

"Yes, Mama sings songs. And then she will come home. You be a good girl for Papa, now."

The child nodded as Édouard stood behind her, his hand gently resting on her slim shoulders. "Come, my petite pet, let's have some spaghetti and then you can show me more of your drawings!"

Brightening, the child hopped into the kitchen, leaving Mimi and Édouard alone for a moment. "She is very excited about her art," Mimi murmured, her hand on the door.

Édouard nodded, "Yes, I can see that . . . she is very special."

"Yes, she is," Mimi assented, letting herself out the door into the early dusk light.

Breathing in the soft L.A. air, Mimi strode down the tree-lined sidewalk to catch the bus. She felt so free to be out of the house and its stifling atmosphere. The child. Camilla. She loved her. Adored her. But . . . Mimi knew that the child wasn't enough. She needed to be more than just a mother and wife.

Yet, what was this elusive "something"? A singer? No, this wasn't it. She could perform, yet the nightclub scene wore her out. The late nights. The constant battles of fighting off "admirers" and negotiating schedules with her boss and fellow singers.

Mimi wanted more. An actress? Like Lana Turner? Mimi smiled to herself as she boarded the bus. Who wouldn't want to be Lana Turner? Yet, she knew that this, too, was only a fantasy. That to be an actress in Hollywood was a dream that probably would never materialize.

If only things had been different.

Staring out the window at the pale industrial landscape, Mimi sighed out loud. A frumpy middle-aged woman glared at her from under her gaudy lavender hat. Mimi gave her a big grin and a little wave. The woman looked away.

Mimi chuckled to herself. People were so funny. Why had that woman taken such offense at her sighing? What did it matter to her?

The bus's brakes screeched to her stop, and Mimi hopped out, the darkness now taking over the sky, the clouds gray and indigo.

The Hotsy Totsy's neon sign blinked brightly at the end of the block. Its orange-and-red letters proclaimed a night of wild abandon with THE CITY'S JAZZIEST GIRLS.

"Hey, baby, what's the time?" A lone shark eyed her as she weaved through the cramped arrangement of tables and chairs.

"The time?" Mimi smiled, charming. "Do I look like a clock?" she asked.

"No, baby, I just thought—"

But Mimi didn't wait to hear his answer as she headed back behind the stage to change for her first number.

Adam sipped at his drink, waiting for André to get back from his "meeting" with a couple of poets he'd spotted when they came in. "Will you excuse me, mon ami? I won't be long. The blue giraffe will keep you company in the immensity of my absence."

Glancing around the dark little room, Adam shivered. What was it about this place that seemed so familiar? He'd never been here before that he could recall. Yet there was an energy in the venue that he couldn't pinpoint. Had he been here in a dream? Or maybe in another life?

He was here in L.A. to meet with a gallery owner interested in his work; Pauline had stayed in Mexico, saying she had work to finish with Wolfgang. A deadline looming. "I would love to come to L.A. with you, darling," she'd said. "But I simply can't at the moment. You understand, don't you?"

And Adam thought that he did. Or did he?

"Farewell to absurd choices, the dreams of dark abyss, rivalries, the prolonged patience, the flight of the seasons, the artificial order of ideas, the ramp of danger, time for everything!" [17] Breton appeared in front of him, announcing his proclamation with a flourishing grin. "Poets! They are the promulgators of the surreal in a world that values only its own reality. How was the blue giraffe?"

Adam chuckled softly, "Oh, she's fine. Just fine . . . though. . . ."

Breton seated himself opposite his friend, eyed him seriously. "Yes?"

"It's just that this place . . . I'm not sure how to describe it, but I feel as though I've been here before. . . ."

"Aha! Naturally! This is called the déjà vu! You know it?"

"Yes, of course, but it's not quite that . . . I. . . ." Adam took a long slow sip of his drink, contemplating. What was it about this place? It was as if someone he knew, someone from his past were watching over him. Adam sighed softly.

"I think you need to concentrate on this energy you speak of, mon ami! The time is now. You are here! You must listen to that which speaks to you. It is important. It is a danger, perhaps, but this danger cannot be ignored!"

"You think there's something dangerous here?" Adam gazed pointedly at Breton. "Why do you say that?"

Breton shrugged, "Oh, it is nothing. Just a whim. Soon the show will start, and this will be a fine distraction, no?"

Shaking his head, Adam smiled softly, "Yes, you're right. About the show that is. The danger? I'm not so sure."

"Good evening, ladies and gentlemen!" The MC had bounced onto the small stage, a cane and black cape to accent his appearance. "Tonight, we have a special treat for you. A singer of unparalleled beauty and talent. She comes to us from none other than gay Paris. Please welcome Mademoiselle Mimi Ravel!"

Adam turned toward the stage and stared in astonishment. Could it be? After all these years?

"Bonne soirée, messieurs-dames," Mimi sang out, sultry, alluring. "I have for you tonight a special number. One I think you will all enjoy. . . ."

Seating herself on a tall stool in the center of the stage, Mimi looked out at the audience, surveying the house before beginning. The usual crowd of drunken leeches leered at her, tongues hanging out, beers in hand. A couple of women, dressed in black sequins, blinked behind glasses of champagne, cigarettes in hand, blowing bored smoke rings into the hazy air. A table of two men, one with an enormous bushy head of hair, gesticulating wildly, while the other. . . .

Blanching, she felt her heart flutter. It couldn't be. Not here. Not now . . . and yet . . . there he was. . . .

Adam. . . .

Steadying herself, Mimi smiled brightly at the crowd, and then began:

Parlez-moi d'amour
Redites-moi des choses tendres. . . .
Speak to me of love
Tell me sweet things again. . . .

"*It is not the fear of madness which will oblige us to leave the flag of imagination furled.*" [18]

Breton sank back in his chair, letting Adam take in his profundity.

"I beg your pardon?" Adam continued to stare at the stage where Mimi had stood singing, just moments before.

"The woman and the elephant. You have not imagined her, mon ami."

"Indeed. . . ."

"Good evening," she cooed.

Breton brightened. "Ah! Mademoiselle! What a divine delight you are upon the stage. Bravo!"

"Merci." Mimi gazed down at Adam, who remained transfixed. "May I join you?"

"Oh, please, yes, do." Adam stood and pulled out a chair for her. Mimi sat, lit a cigarette, and signaled the waiter. "A glass of champagne, please. And for the gentlemen?"

"Bring a bottle of your best!" Breton jumped up, waving green bills at the server.

"Very good," the waiter said, nodding.

"It is good to see you, Adam," Mimi purred, trying to keep the tingle she was feeling at bay. How had this happened? To find him here. At her place of work. After all these years? Why, who could have predicted it? She took another long drag of her cigarette, blew a smoke ring out into the dark room.

"Yes . . . yes . . . and you, too. . . ." Adam began.

"We were entranced by your performance, ma chérie," Breton exclaimed. "My friend here, especially, could not remove his eye from your form."

Mimi nodded. "That is so kind." She turned toward Adam. "How is your painting?"

He gulped the last of his drink. "Well . . . very well. . . ."

"That is wonderful. And what brings you to L. A.?"

"Adam has a friend, a patron if you will, interested in showing his work at the Gallery Gilded on Wilshire Boulevard. Do you know it?" Breton moved up and down in his chair, nearly knocking over the waiter who delivered the champagne.

Mimi watched as the waiter popped the cork and poured out the bubbling beverage. It was all so strange. Surreal, as these two would say. She smiled to herself. She hadn't meant to follow Adam's career for the past years, but he had been in the papers. And there was the matter of the child. Should she tell him?

Mimi took a delicate sip of her champagne. That remained to be seen. Things were complicated.

"I must go," she rose. "I have another set."

"May I see you after you're finished?" Adam asked.

"I would like that," Mimi said, tracing his arm lightly with her fingers. "Meet me backstage?"

Adam nodded as he watched her weave among the tables and chairs, pausing to chat with a customer here or there.

Mimi felt his eyes upon her and smiled. This was going to be a delicious night.

"This idea, this woman, disturb it, they tend to make it less severe. What they do is isolate the mind for a second from its solvent and spirit it to heaven, as the beautiful precipitate it can be, that it is. When all else fails, it then calls upon chance, a divinity even more obscure than the others to whom it ascribes all its aberrations." [19] Breton gazed at Adam seriously. "Do you not agree, mon ami?"

Adam continued to stare at Mimi as she climbed the stairs and sat again on the bar stool. Her voice rang out sexy and sultry.

Breton sat back in his chair and grinned and grinned and grinned.

Leonora

"More wine?" François held up the bottle of Pinot Grigio. Grinned at Leonora.

"Oh, thank you, but no. No more for me now." She placed her hand over the top of the wineglass. "I have much work to do this afternoon."

"Work, work, work." François shrugged, pouring himself a hardy second glass. "I view it as a necessary evil, but on an afternoon such as this. . . ." He waved his hand dramatically up at the blue, blue sky and pink-blossoming cherry tree. "I cannot but succumb to the call of spring."

He took a long sip of wine and gazed at Leonora, who frowned slightly across the table from him. The birds chirped sweetly in the bougainvillea surrounding the outside patio at the Crêpe Place.

"Yes, well. . . ." Leonora pushed a stray bite of her veggie crêpe around on her plate. "It is tempting, but I really do have to work on a dream that—"

"Oh, your dreams!" François scoffed. "Don't you tire of this obsession with your life that is not really your life?"

Leonora felt her cheeks flame. What gave him the right to judge her? Why must he always taunt her? He knew how important her work was. And now that the pressure of her publisher's deadline for the dream work was looming, she couldn't afford to dawdle away an afternoon, no matter how enchanting. Leonora felt a rising anger that she checked. François's dismissal of her work was vexing. Adam would understand. He would support and encourage her in contrast to François's constant jabs to undermine.

Sighing, Leonora pushed her plate away. "You know that I don't view my dreams as separate from "this life." They are inextricably intertwined with my waking life." She paused for a moment, eyeing François lounging in the sun opposite her. His grin broad, his swagger sure. What was it about him that kept her tied to him?

Chemistry.

She couldn't deny it. Yet, they were so often at odds. He simply didn't understand her. While Adam. . . .

"Good afternoon," a deep familiar voice interrupted her thoughts.

"Why, Adam!" she murmured. "I was just—"

François glared at her, then turned toward the tall interloper. "Yes?"

"Allow me to introduce myself. I'm Adam Sinclair."

"Ah . . . of course." François rose, shook hands. "I should have known."

"May I join for a moment?" Adam asked, gazing down at Leonora.

"Oh, yes . . . of course."

"I thought you had to get back to work?" François muttered.

"I do . . . I mean . . . I will . . . but since Adam is here, and it's such a lovely afternoon and. . . ."

"I don't mean to intrude," Adam said. "I was just waiting for someone and saw you—"

"Oh, by all means, sit, please!" François commanded, reseating himself and reaching for the wine. "Mademoiselle!" he called out. "Another glass, s'il vous plaît!"

The hippie girl waitress, her lavender apron flowing, gave him a spacey smile before disappearing into the kitchen.

"I am sure she will return shortly." François settled back in his chair. "In the meantime, Adam, tell me, what do you think about dreams and reality?"

"I beg your pardon?"

"I mean, Leonora here would have us believe that there is no difference. That what happens in our dreams is just as real as what happens to us now, in reality, this day!" François gave them a sweeping gesture upward and out, pointing to the trees, the sky, the hippie girl, who'd returned with the wineglass.

"Just set it down, my dear. For the gentleman. And bring us another bottle of this fine wine, would you?"

"Sure. . . ." The hippie girl, spacey and slow, sauntered back across the patio.

"François, I said—" Leonora began.

"But surely, my dear, now that we have our illustrious company, you can stay? Don't you want to hear what he has to say about my question?"

Leonora scowled, glancing over at Adam, who gave her a stupendous smile. "I would have to agree with my dear friend here, and also your question reminds me of another friend, you know him, I'm sure, as a Frenchman? André Breton?"

"But of course, please, continue." François was filling the empty wineglass, setting it in front of Adam, who nodded in thanks.

"Breton, as you know, was one of the first to put forth the idea that dreams and reality were not as separate as some believed. He said, and I quote, *'I have always been amazed at the way an ordinary observer lends so much more credence and attaches so much more importance to waking events than to those occurring in dreams.'* [20]

"But I disagree!" François grinned, enjoying the joust. "How can one attach any importance to dreams? Why, they are nothing but the incomprehensible mishmash of our days and perhaps our emotions. . . ." François paused, glancing over at Leonora, who had poured herself a hefty glass of wine.

"I believe," Adam continued, "that Breton was merely making the observation that our dreams contain just as valuable information and experience, perhaps even more, than our waking lives. Our daily lives are so often filled with the banal, do you not agree? While our dreams . . . these can provide us with insight and magic and beauty."

"Beauty?" François leaned forward, his eyes glinting in the afternoon light.

"Why, yes. What we dream can transform our consciousness in such a way that we may view the sublime. And then, if we are blessed, we can translate such beauty into our daily lives. Whether that be in our writing, or our art, or music. Why, there are myriad examples of many great artists who were inspired by their dreams."

"Okay. . . ." François conceded. "But what about those who are not so 'blessed' as you say? What about the poor plebeians who are not artists?"

"I believe all human beings are artists," Adam proclaimed gravely. "It is more the pity that we don't allow ourselves to delve into our unconscious impulses that are presented in our dreams and work to manifest these impulses into art, whatever the medium." Adam took a sip of his wine, his gaze holding François's in steady uncompromising authority.

"I am not an artist," François proclaimed. "And I have no inclination to become one."

"That's not entirely true," Leonora said. "Your photography? What about that?"

François shrugged. "It is nothing. Just a dabbling. It cannot be compared, I am sure, to the art that Mr. Sinclair speaks of."

"On the contrary," Adam continued. "Any endeavor that captures a creative moment is art. It is a making. I cannot claim that all of my paintings are great art. But I paint. I will always paint. It is what I do. I cannot imagine life without it. Nor can I imagine life without dreams, my friend."

"Excuse me?" A slim woman stood at their table, her chocolate eyes round, her long dark hair, streaked with crimson, shimmering in the light.

"Ah, Annabelle!" Adam rose. "I did not see you come in. I hope that I have not kept you waiting?"

"No," Annabelle murmured, pushing a stray strand behind a pale ear.

"Allow me to introduce you. François, Leonora, this is Annabelle. She's here to help me with the organization of my studio."

"Pleased to meet you." François rose, bowing slightly, taking her hand. "Enchanté."

Leonora glanced over at Adam, puzzled. Who was this Annabelle? And what was she really doing meeting Adam at the Crêpe Place? Leonora didn't believe for a moment that she was some sort of assistant. Adam would never allow anyone to come in and "organize" his studio. He was so private. So particular. But then, if not, who was she? She was very pretty.

Leonora shivered a little despite the afternoon's warmth.

"Thank you for the wine." Adam pushed his chair under the table. "And our little talk. I hope that it was illuminating?"

"Very. . . ." François nodded. "Nice to meet you, Annabelle."

"You too, monsieur," she answered, turning to follow Adam to a table at the other side of the restaurant.

"Well, well, well. . . ." François grinned at Leonora. "It seems your artiste has himself a little paramour, oui?"

Leonora frowned. "I need to leave now. I honestly have no idea who this Annabelle is."

"A little jealous are we, my love?"

"Not at all. I just have to get to work."

"Very well. As you wish. I'll get the check."

"Thank you."

Leonora grabbed her purse and weaved among the tables to leave. Adam and Annabelle were seated near the wall, the bougainvillea shadowing them in intimate cover. She felt a twinge of something. Was it jealousy? But she had no romantic inclinations toward Adam. . . .

Or had she?

Leonora hurried out of the restaurant onto Pacific Avenue, climbed into her car, and instead of heading back up to her studio, turned right and drove to the beach.

The sea would calm her. Give her clarity. This she knew.

Parking on the bluff, Leonora climbed out of the car and made her way down the sandy path to the beach. She kicked off her sandals, digging her toes into the warm afternoon sand as she strode out toward the shore. The gulls squawked overhead. The sea breeze hit her deliciously in the face.

She felt better already. Reaching the water, the icy waves shocked at first. She took a deep breath . . . exhaled.

Gazing up at the sky, Leonora marveled at its blue blueness. And then the blue ocean. And then her blue toenail polish, shimmering in the shallow water.

Blue. It was her color. It had been her color her whole life. She remembered when she was a child, how her mother had asked her what her favorite color was and she had said blue. And so they had painted the walls of her bedroom blue. Each wall like the sky.

Leonora reached the end of the beach and stood for a moment, letting the wind caress her. The sea now a blue gray. The sky now a golden blue. And she knew that blue was more than blue. It was purple and golden and pink and green. It was aqua. And Prussian and turquoise and periwinkle.

Her palette. So many colors, yet . . . all she desired was blue . . . And this made sense. Didn't it? But she had to think that the blue was more as she watched the sun hide behind a golden cloud, turning the sky into a blue diamond. She remembered the golden dragonfly. Flying away into the midnight blue night of her dream. It was power and resurrection and transformation, and now. . . .

She sighed, sitting down on the beach for a moment, savoring the light. Why was she so agitated? François was just being François. Playing devil's advocate with her and Adam about work and dreams. She knew this. Why did she let him upset her so? Why indeed?

Sometimes, Leonora wondered why she stayed with François. They had met so young. He had been dashing in that way that only Frenchmen can be. Chic and sophisticated, full of attitude and swagger. The chemistry had been beyond her control that first night she had met him at the gallery on the rue Daphne. The paintings were awful. Big atrocious portraits with eyes that followed you as you moved through the room. And François. He had lit upon her. Had come over, offering a glass of champagne, murmuring how some art was best left in the studio.

And she had laughed because this was exactly what she had been thinking.

And then there was Adam. Leonora could not stop thinking of him. His art. His passion. His dreams.

His Annabelle?

Who was this Annabelle?

Was she really some "assistant" to help with his large works?

"Hello, ma chérie," a familiar baritone floated through the sea breeze.

"François!" Leonora rose, dusting the sand from her slacks. "What are you doing here? How did you know?"

He grinned. That crooked one that made her swoon every time. "I had a small feeling that you would be here. That you weren't really rushing back to work after our luncheon. You seemed upset, luv. I was concerned."

François gazed over at her as they began to stroll back down the beach together. "Adam and Annabelle," he said, "do you want to talk about them?"

"No . . . no. . . ." Leonora shook her head. Why would she talk about Adam to François? What was he up to? she wondered.

"Are you sure?" He bent down to pick up a swollen seaweed pod, tossing it back into the ocean.

"Yes. I just needed to walk. Be here. . . ." she murmured, squinting into the sun, the sky now a purple blue, the clouds a pink orange. The sun disappeared behind the horizon.

"It is too late for you to work now, oui?" he asked. "Shall we go home?"

She nodded, letting him take her hand, the blue of the afternoon lingering in her consciousness as an inquisitive squawking gull circled overhead.

Pauline

"*It is not the fear of madness which will oblige us to leave the flag of imagination furled. The case against the realistic attitude demands to be examined, following the case against the materialistic attitude. The latter, more poetic in fact than the former, admittedly implies on the part of man a kind of monstrous pride which, admittedly, is monstrous, but not a new and more complete decay. It should above all be viewed as a welcome reaction against certain ridiculous tendencies of spiritualism. . . .*" [21]

Breton tapped his knuckles on the table, exhaling noisily as Remedios gazed serenely over his head out the window.

"If it weren't for spiritualism," Pauline interrupted, "I never would have married Adam."

"Sí, sí. . . ." Remedios murmured, gazing directly now at Breton. "That is very true."

Breton shook his tumbled locks. "Oui, okay, yes. I take your point. However, that is not what I am suggesting. I only mean that those quacks that espouse the philosophies of the Other World are ludicrous as purple elephants atop giraffe legs!"

"Oh, now you reference Dalí?" Remedios's dark eyes glimmered as she raised the bottle of tequila to pour another shot for Pauline.

"Dalí?" Breton stood, glaring at the two women. "But of course.

His perspective supersedes all drivel surrounding spiritualism."

"Yet, don't you think that his dreams were a way to access this Other World?" Pauline asked, winking at Remedios.

Breton gazed at the two women; Pauline first and then Remedios. For a moment, all was still except for a lone black fly buzzing lazily around the windowsill. "I proclaim to both of you, goddesses of the spirit world, that dreams are lotuses floating in the sky. I write those dreams on my lotus as I dream. I am my own destiny. The dreams manifest as they do in my poetry, my art, and my consciousness. The material reality is poppycock. That is all I have for you today!"

A sparkling tinkle of laughter erupted from Remedios, who stood and stretched. "A walk, my friend?" She nodded to Pauline.

"Oh, yes, that sounds divine." Pauline grinned. "Will you join us, André?"

"No, no, not at this juncture. I have much work to do."

"As you wish." Remedios tossed back the rest of her tequila, holding the bottle aloft toward Pauline. "I bring the bottle with us, sí?"

"Sure, why not." Pauline held the screen door open for her friend, leaving Breton at the kitchen table scribbling furiously on a pad of paper, the sound of the pen scratching reminding her that she, too, had work to do.

Yet as she followed Remedios out into the late-afternoon light, the heat hit her, wilting any motivation she might have had to work on her—what? Was it a novel? Or a play? Or simply the scribblings of a want-to-be writer? And her work with Wolfgang? It was important, wasn't it? They were writing a *New Manifesto*. One that would show the world how the conscious mind and the life of the dream were in fact not so far apart as most believed.

Remedios fanned herself. "*Muy caliente. . . .*" she murmured, heading toward the jacaranda tree's vast shade.

"Yes, it is," Pauline agreed.

Was it the heat that kept her from writing? Or something

else? Adam? Pauline stopped her thoughts, afraid to venture down that road just yet.

Remedios plopped down under the tree. "It is too hot for walking now. Let us rest for a moment, and you tell me what you think now."

Sitting down next to her friend, Pauline sighed. "I am thinking that . . . oh . . . I don't know, Remedios!"

Her friend brushed a stray violet from Pauline's shoulder. "What is it, my friend?"

"Oh, I don't like to burden you with my problems," Pauline sighed. "You must think I'm an awful baby."

"Not at all. I know the difficulties of life."

Pauline gazed at her friend, feeling the warmth from her soft brown eyes, "Yes, I believe you do. And frankly, I don't think that I have any real difficulties. I just have this feeling. . . ."

"Yes?"

Pauline breathed deeply, the warm air filling her lungs, the sweet scent of the flowering tree giving her courage. "I am probably just imagining this, but Adam seems different since he came back from Los Angeles."

"Different?" Remedios took a long swig from the bottle of tequila. Handed it to Pauline, who followed suit. "How different?"

"It is hard to explain. I mean, Adam is always involved in his work. Obsessed actually. But that is what artists do, right?"

"Sí, that is quite true. But there is something else?"

"I think so. I am not sure though . . . He just seems more distant. Like his mind is elsewhere. And not . . . not just on his painting or his writing, but on. . . ."

Pauline shook her head. What was she thinking? Let alone divulging to Remedios? That she thinks Adam is having an affair? But how could that be? He loved her. He married her. Why, tomorrow was their anniversary. Would he remember?

"You think Adam is with someone else?" Remedios asked gently.

Pauline wiped a tear away. "How did you know what I was thinking?"

Remedios shrugged. "It is hard for you, I know, if it is true. But it is an old story. My first husband, he was so full of himself. He thought all of the ladies were his kingdom. And I did discover that yes, there were a few affairs."

"How did you find out?"

Remedios shrugged. "Oh, the usual way. A carelessness on his part. A smudge of lipstick on his collar. A matchbook in his pants pocket."

"That sounds just horrible!" Pauline exclaimed, shivering despite the afternoon heat.

"It was. At the time, I did not handle it well. I was, how do you say? Hysterical? Confronting him. Screaming at him. Throwing things at him. . . ."

"Throwing things?" Pauline leaned closer, her voice shaking.

"Yes, whatever was at hand. I remember one night he came home. It was late. I had been waiting. I knew that he had been unfaithful. When he walked in the door, I was ready. A large platter. Of his mother's. I hurled it at him as he walked into the room. . . ."

"Did you hurt him?"

"Oh, no, I just wanted to scare him. I didn't hit him. If I had wanted to, I could have done this thing. But he was not worth it. So, we divorced."

Pauline was silent, soaking in the story. Would she behave in such a way if she discovered Adam were having an affair? What would she do? Confront him? Should she? What proof did she have?

"I don't know what to do, Remedios. I have no proof like you did. It is just a feeling. He seems different. I don't know how to explain it."

Remedios nodded. "I suggest to you to wait. Watch. See how he behaves. If he remembers your anniversary tomorrow, is it a genuine celebration or does he proclaim too much? Do you know what I say?"

Pauline nodded. "I think so. I guess that's the best course of action for now. Though there's more to the story, too. . . ."

"Yes?"

"Well. . . ." Pauline hesitated. How much should she tell her friend? Her feelings for Wolfgang were so new. So exciting. Forbidden. Who was she to accuse Adam? Perhaps she was even projecting her own guilt onto her husband. Freud would say as much.

Remedios nodded, encouraging. "I think I know what you are thinking again."

Pauline laughed softly. "Are you telepathic?"

Grinning, Remedios shook her head, "No, no. It is just that I have seen you with him."

"Him?"

"Señor Paalen. He is very handsome, sí?"

"Yes . . . yes, he is. Very attractive. And he pays attention to me. Praises my writing and my ideas."

"But does not Adam do the same?"

"No, no . . . not lately . . . That is why I wonder if he is having an affair. . . ." There it was. The word, hanging in the air, under the sweet lavender blooms of the jacaranda.

"It is too hot." Remedios rose. "I do not think that you need to worry of Adam now. Yes, it may be true. What you suspect. It could be. But on the contrary, it could not be. It could be a fantasy. Not a pleasant fantasy, but one nonetheless. I suggest to you now . . . oh, it is so hot!" she exclaimed. "Let us swim in the lake. It is there for us!"

Remedios waved her hand dramatically toward the horizon where the shimmering blue silver of the lake awaited them. Turning toward her friend, she grinned, then sprinted off in a surprising run.

How can she move so fast in this heat? Pauline marveled, rising and trotting after her.

Remedios had thrown her blouse off, and now her skirt.

Dashing toward the shore of the lake, she splashed into its cooling embrace.

"Ah! Pauline! It is fantástico!" she called out, swimming toward the center of the lake.

Pauline had stripped down to her underthings now, too, splashed into the cooling water. The tiny waves lapping at her slim legs before she plunged underwater, closing her eyes, feeling the euphoria that swimming always brought her.

Yes, Remedios was right. It was too hot to contemplate infidelity. She dove under the surface of the water, holding her breath and feeling the refreshing coolness of the lake. Stroking strongly out into the center, she followed Remedios's lead.

"Hello? Pauline? Is that you?"

A canoe appeared in front of her, its oars resting now on its occupant's lap.

"Oh! Wolfgang!" Pauline gasped. What was he doing out here? And where had Remedios gone?

"Are you okay?" he asked, his blue eyes sparkling.

"Sure, sure, I'm fine. We just got too hot and decided to take a swim and. . . ." Pauline glanced down at her nearly naked self. Could he see her? Part of her was embarrassed, but another part, a bigger part, tingled with anticipation.

"Maybe I'll join you." He grinned, stripping his shirt off.

"Hola, señor!" Remedios appeared on the other side of the canoe. "Will you swim, too?"

"I will indeed," Wolfgang chuckled, throwing off his pants and diving overboard into the blue murky coolness of the water.

The creature is wet and slippery. Pauline struggles to control it. To get it to stay under the man's blue shirt. But she can't. What is it? A kind of sea creature? Or another sort of water animal? It wraps itself around the outside of the man's shirt, brown and wriggly. Like a watery donut come undone. Pauline is frantic. She must get it to stay under

*the man's shirt. This creature . . . what is it . . . ? She sees its little
snout. And its whiskers. Its lanky shape. Ah, that's it! A river otter.
Dark brown and even cute? Yet it will not be contained. It wants to
escape. And Pauline knows that if she lets it go, it will run out of the
empty warehouse, out through the glass doors, into the city, where
danger awaits. And who is the man? Why is he just standing there,
watching her trying to stuff the river otter back under his shirt? Why
doesn't he help her?*

*Pauline is frantic. She can't contain the river otter. No matter how
many times she stuffs it under the man's shirt, it pops back out, its
slippery form eluding her grip. She glances behind the man at the
doorway. It is lighter out there. Not as dark as the empty warehouse,
yet she knows that she can't allow the river otter to escape. If she
does. . . .*

"Good morning, luv," a man's familiar baritone rouses her
from the dream. Pauline struggles to bring herself back to consciousness, but the dream is strong. The urgency of saving the
river otter tugs at her.

"Pauline?" She can half-hear the concern in his voice, yet
still the dream holds her in its grasp. The river otter. She must
keep it from running away. She must tuck it back into the man's
blue shirt. The man. Is it Adam? Wolfgang?

"Wolfgang . . . ?" she murmurs, her eyes fluttering open.

"I am afraid he's not here, Pauline."

She hears the clank of a tray being set down, the tinkling of
silverware, then the smell of strong tea.

"Adam?"

"Yes, it's just me. I thought I'd surprise you for our anniversary, but it seems you were expecting someone else. . . ."

She sits up slowly, rubbing her eyes. "I was? But . . . I. . . ."
Should she tell Adam about her dream? What did it mean? Yet
even as she sat up, groggy, she knew she should keep the dream
to herself.

"Yes, you called for Wolfgang."

"I did?"

"Yes, you did." Adam poured out the tea, handing her a cup.

"Thank you," she murmured, grateful for the caffeinated distraction.

"Do you know why?" he asked.

"Oh. . . ." Pauline held a sweet mouthful of the hot beverage for a moment before shrugging. "I'm sure I don't know. I was having a dream and. . . ."

"A dream?" he sat down on the bed next to her. "It must have been an interesting one."

She glanced away from him, suddenly hungry, the smell of toast and eggs wafting in the air. "My! This looks wonderful, darling!" she exclaimed, reaching for a piece of bacon.

"Please, help yourself. I did want to surprise you, and it appears that I have. Care to tell me about this dream of yours?"

"Oh, it was nothing." She bit into a piece of toast, crunching noisily, hoping to distract him from his line of questioning. "Just a silly dream. About a river otter of all things!" Why was she telling him anything? Damn! she thought.

"A river otter?" He grinned. "Now that does sound enticing."

"Oh, it wasn't!" Pauline took another sip of her tea. "I can't believe you did all of this! Making me breakfast in bed. And the beautiful rose. My favorite!" She bent over, smelling its sweet fragrance. "You are such a dear!" Giving his cheek a buttery kiss, she sank back into her pillows.

Adam rose, paced over to the window, and gazed out. "I just wonder what the river otter has to do with Wolfgang," he asked, his back to her.

Pauline chewed, trying to think. But she hadn't had enough caffeine yet. And here he was asking all these questions about a silly dream. Yet was the dream that silly? Was the man in the dream Wolfgang? And if it had been, well. . . .

"I have no idea," she answered, taking another sip of tea, her brain finally beginning to join the conscious world. "I suppose that was the river otter's name!" She laughed, nervously, hoping he'd take up the joke.

Adam turned around, smiling now. "Its name was Wolfgang?"

"Yes, I guess so. I really don't remember, darling. Is it important? It was just a dream."

"That depends. You know what I think about dreams. How they tell us what we already know."

"Oh, so I know now that Wolfgang is a river otter, okay?" she grinned. He can't seriously be jealous. How could he be? And besides, she was the one with questions. About him. His trip to Los Angeles. His change in demeanor. Was this breakfast a . . . what had Remedios said? A genuine celebration? Or did it proclaim too much?

Adam sat back down on the side of the bed, pouring himself a cup of tea. "I wonder what you think that means."

"That Wolfgang is a river otter?"

"Yes." Adam sipped his tea, his blue eyes blazing into her.

"Oh, darling, it's nothing. Just a silly dream. Now, if I were a painter, like you, maybe I could render the little creature on canvas in all its brown, slippery glory. . . ."

Adam sighed. "I know what you are doing."

"You do?" Pauline felt her heart pound. How could he know her that well? He couldn't know her dreams. She must tread softly here. If he suspected anything about Wolfgang, well . . . she must not allow his suspicions to ruin her day!

"You are trying to distract me with your beautiful whimsical humor, and for today, I will allow it. But I won't forget this dream you've told me. I suspect there is much more to it."

"Ah! Bonjour! Good morning, mon ami!" Breton's booming greeting interrupted, echoing from outside their closed door. Pauline sighed inwardly. Thank goodness for André. Just in time!

"André, please come in." Adam rose, letting him in.

Breton swept into the room, taking in the breakfast tray and the single red rose upon it. "Ah, a thousand apologies! I am so sorry to intrude. But I have someone here who begs to have an audience with you."

"Is that so?" Adam glanced over at Pauline, who had quickly grabbed her robe, sashing it around herself.

"Oui. A most charming young woman. From you will never guess where."

"Where?" Pauline asked.

"Why! Paris! Can you believe such luck! A fellow Parisian come all this way. And she seeks you, Adam."

"Does she now?" Adam stroked his chin, his beard scratchy from a day's growth. "Well, very good. I would love to meet her. She must be an old friend from when I visited briefly. But that was so many years ago and. . . ."

"Enchantée," a strong female voice rang in the room as the tall, elegant woman strode in, extending her hand for Adam to shake.

Pauline took in her chic blond haircut, her wide emerald eyes, her smart white pants topped with a shimmering golden blouse. Who the hell was this? And how did she know Adam?

Taking her hand in his, Adam returned her greeting. "Do I know you? Have we met?"

"Not exactly." The woman smiled. "My name is Genevieve. And we have a mutual friend."

"Is that so. . . ." Adam shifted uncomfortably in the center of the room.

"And who's that?" Pauline called out, her spine tingling, a curious anxiety spreading.

"Her name, mademoiselle, is Mimi."

"Mimi?" Pauline whispered.

"Oui. And I have some information that I think you both will be interested in."

"Ah! Divine!" Breton exclaimed, clapping his hands. "Shall we all convene in the main house for a more spacious breakfast?"

"Oui, that sounds lovely," Genevieve said, glancing at Pauline and then Adam before turning and striding back out the door. A scent of bergamot and cinnamon lingered in the room, swirling round in Pauline's consciousness, before floating out into the ether . . .

Mimi

Mimi exhaled her cloud of purple resignation. Gazing out the living room window, the leafy trees lining the quiet street, she shook her head. Such a scene! Yet, Genevieve had been magnificent. Mimi would grant her that. Though now the whole drama didn't seem real. It was like a dream. Or a nightmare. What had Adam called this space between dream and reality?

Surreality?

Yes, that's what it had been. Surreal. And now, here she was at home with her family, seemingly safe from Genevieve's threats, yet . . . if she did find Adam and tell him about the child, her precious Camilla, then would Édouard leave her? Would Adam come and take Camilla away from her? Oh, this she could never bear! Yet, didn't Genevieve have a point that Adam had a right to know about his own child?

Genevieve had been so angry. Why did she care? What did she hope to gain from such a revelation? Was it a sinister spite that had been simmering for years? Or retribution for a perceived wrong? Perhaps the reason didn't matter. What did matter was her fury.

Mimi exhaled again. This time the purple cloud circled around her, swirling and spinning, making her dizzy. She watched in fascination as the cloud rose, purple, then lavender, then fuchsia, and then . . . red. A fiery passionate red enveloping the room, her consciousness.

"Who do you think you are?" Genevieve had cried. "Playing God. Keeping the child from its father. You have no right."

"Genevieve, darling. . . ."

"Don't call me that," she'd hissed. "I am no longer your 'darling.'" Genevieve had glanced around the tidy living room, taking in the child's toys strewn about the braided rug, the worn baby grand piano, the soothing print by Monet.

Mimi had nodded. "Of course, I just don't understand why you're here. How did you find me?"

"It wasn't difficult. I know the kinds of places you frequent."

"But how did you know we were in California? In Hollywood?" Mimi's heart had pounded. She had to get Genevieve out of the house before Édouard and Camilla came back from the park.

"Does it matter?" Genevieve had sneered. "I found you. And now that I have, you need to be honest with your . . . is he your husband? Does he know that the child is not his?"

"Yes, Édouard and I are married. And, of course, he knows the child isn't his."

"Does he know who the child belongs to? The famous artist?"

"Well, I'm not sure how famous he is. . . ."

Genevieve had cackled, lighting a cigarette and pacing across the room. "Oh, he's famous all right. I read all about him in the *Times*. He is part of a group called the Surrealists. I'm sure you've heard of them."

"Yes, of course, he's told me—"

"I bet he has! When did you see him last?"

"I. . . ." Mimi had turned away from Genevieve's stare. What did she want? If she wasn't here to rekindle their relationship, and it seemed obvious that this wasn't her intention, then what could she possibly want from her? Had she really come all this way, gone to the trouble of seeking her out, finding her place of work, her home, to do what? To tell her that she must be honest with Adam? Tell him about his child?

Why did she care?

"I know you saw him when he was in town this week." Genevieve had blown a smoke ring into the air. Mimi watched in fascination as it mingled with the crimson cloud floating near the ceiling. "What are you staring at? Are you listening to me?"

"Yes, of course," Mimi had said, trying to focus. "How do you know I saw Adam?"

"I have my ways." She had dismissed the question with a wave of her hand.

"What do you want, Genevieve?" Mimi had asked. She'd had enough of this. Édouard and Camilla were due back soon.

"I don't want a thing." Genevieve had stubbed her cigarette out. "Or maybe I do. . . ."

"What could I possibly have that you could want?"

"Oh, you don't have anything, but Adam . . . now, he might have something for me."

"What do you mean?"

"He's made quite a name for himself, hasn't he? Sold some of his paintings. Given some lectures. Written some books."

"Is it money you're after?" Mimi had cried, astonished. Why would Genevieve go after Adam for his money? And did he even have that much? Certainly, he had more than she did, but still. It didn't make sense.

"No, I don't want his money. Or yours. If you had any."

"Then what do you want?" Mimi had cried, exasperated, tears beginning to form.

"I want you to tell Adam that you have his child. That you've kept her a secret for all these years. He has a right to know, don't you think?"

Mimi had nodded, a tear falling down her pale cheek. Of course Genevieve was right. Adam did have a right to know. But if he knew about Camilla, would he want her precious child? Would he take her away from her? And why, oh why, was Genevieve here threatening her like this? It didn't make any sense.

"You are right, of course. Adam should know. But I can't tell him. Don't you see? If I tell him, he might take her from me. And Édouard would leave me. Without the child . . . our marriage, it would. . . ." Mimi had choked softly. Her misery shaking her to her core.

Genevieve had sighed, stubbing out the cigarette. "Ah, poor Mimi. You are in a pickle, are you not, my petite songbird? I will never forgive you for leaving me the way you did. So cavalier. So confident. Just out the door without a glance back. I loved you. . . ."

Mimi had glanced up, sensing the emotion in Genevieve's tone. "Yes, I know you did . . . but. . . ." Mimi had exhaled softly, her voice shaking, "I never saw myself with a woman. Living a life like that. It wasn't for me. I. . . ."

Genevieve had turned upon her, her emerald eyes darkening with a fury: hot, black, treacherous. "Then why did you say you loved me? Why did you do the things you did to me? You bewitched me, Mimi. I gave my soul to you and you took it and threw it off the balcony into the Seine. I watched it sink down into the inky waters, and I thought it had died. But now, when I see you today, here in your life, with your quaint little home and your devoted husband and your precious child, well . . . it makes me sick."

Mimi had stared at her. How could she still feel like this? It had been years. She had no idea that Genevieve felt this strongly. Well . . . no, actually, she did know. But she had been younger then. And full of adventure. Genevieve had been so thrilling. Yet it was true, she had never pictured her life with a woman. And so, when Camilla had come along, and Édouard had agreed to marry her, be the father of her child, it seemed like such a perfect solution.

Little did she know that Genevieve would come back to haunt

her. The fury that she had kept inside all these years would impel her to seek her out today and make these threats of going to Adam.

Why, it was retribution pure and simple, wasn't it? She had to be stopped. But how?

What the hell was she going to do?

The screen door slammed, rousing Mimi from her thoughts. Camilla skipped into the room, spinning around and around. Édouard lingered at the threshold, his dark brow smitten. Suddenly, Genevieve appeared. Floating into the kitchen on a cloud of forest green. Where had she come from? Mimi wondered. Has she been lurking in the house this whole time? Or had she floated in from some other dimension?

Mimi watched in horror as Genevieve extended her hand to Édouard. "Hello, I'm Genevieve."

"Are you a friend of Mimi's?" Édouard asked, puzzled.

"You might say that."

"Hello! My name is Camilla!" The child interrupted, bouncing up and down in wild abandon.

"My, that is a pretty name!" Genevieve exclaimed, patting the child on the top of her head.

Bored, the child spun in tiny circles. "Mama!" she cried, dancing around Mimi, giggling with joy. "Papa said you would sing to me! Will you, Mama?"

"Of course, my pet." Mimi scooped the child up into her lap.

"*Frère Jacques, frère Jacques. Dormez-vous? Dormez-vous. . . ?*"

"Would you care for something to drink, mademoiselle?" Mimi saw Édouard incline his head toward Genevieve, always the polite host.

"Yes, I'd be delighted. Merci, monsieur."

Mimi cringed at Genevieve's sweet smile for Édouard. Patting her daughter's soft hair, Mimi kept the purple cloud inside herself now. She had to. For Camilla's sake.

Camilla swayed on her lap, mimicking her mother, her little girl's voice floating into the air. "*Dormez-vous? Dormez-vous?*"

Édouard

Who was this woman?

Édouard leaned against the worn kitchen counter in baffled awe. Genevieve sat at the little yellow table in the middle of the room, cigarette dangling from one hand, a glass of Chablis in the other. Her words spewed forth, venomous in their fury. What was she saying? Something about Mimi? When she lived in Paris many years ago? Something about a horse race? That Genevieve had won this race, but Mimi had not given a goddamn?

Genevieve stopped talking for a moment to catch her breath, wiping a golden wisp of hair from her eyes.

"I am so sorry, mademoiselle, that you are upset. Perhaps we could take a walk around the neighborhood? It is charming."

Édouard watched her take in the suggestion, her long limbs crossing and uncrossing beneath the table like a feline caged.

"Yes, yes." Genevieve nodded. "This is a good idea. Let us walk."

She rose, snuffing the cigarette out and downing the last of the wine in her glass. Édouard finished his own glass, then surveyed the half-full bottle next to him on the counter. "We shall take it with us, no? You would like to continue with another drink?"

Genevieve laughed, tossing her head back, her emerald eyes sparkling. "I like you!" she exclaimed, following him out the back door into the afternoon light.

"*Frère Jacques, Frère Jacques. . . .*" The faint notes of Mimi's lullaby floated out with them as Édouard walked down the steps. He felt a tinge of melancholy. What was this Genevieve after? Why had she come here, to their home? What was her connection to Mimi? For she was connected to his wife. And it was more than a day at the races. He could feel this. But this did not surprise him. Mimi was a woman who attracted. He had always known this. Yet he also knew that she adored Camilla.

Why did he think of the child at this moment?

"Penny for your thoughts, as they say?" Genevieve startled him from his questions.

"Oh, I was just thinking of ma petite fille. How delighted she was today at the park. Playing with the other children. Singing her little songs. Just like her dear mama."

Genevieve eyed him for a moment, then sighed. "Yes, well, I have something to tell you about her dear mama."

"Do you?"

"Yes, I do. And I'm afraid you may not like what I have to say."

Édouard nodded, serious. Was there anything that she could tell him that he didn't already know about his wife? Perhaps. Did he want to know what Genevieve had to tell him?

Perhaps.

But there was a bigger part of him that did not want to know. He wanted to walk with this woman, enjoy her brash loveliness. She was captivating.

Édouard smiled to himself as he strolled down the sidewalk, the leafy shadows dancing in magical patterns under his steps. Her scent of bergamot and cinnamon enchanting him.

Genevieve paused under a giant sycamore and gazed up, an enormous black crow cawing from its top.

"Okay, monsieur, this is the spot. Are you ready to hear what I have to say?"

"If you wish, mademoiselle."

Édouard seated himself on the grass in the shade, leaning against the tree. Uncorking the wine bottle, he poured them each a glass.

Genevieve took out another cigarette. "Do you have a light, monsieur?"

He lit her cigarette. She took a long drag, then gazed at him for a moment, before beginning.

Adam

She was intoxicating. Adam envisioned Mimi lying on one of his enormous canvases, nude, paint covering her pale skin, cascading down her hips, breasts, belly. Languid sexy circles of stars and comets; blooms of Prussian blue, Hooker's green, permanent rose dripped from her in sensual streaks, creating a painting like none that he had ever imagined.

He nodded as she sat across from him in the dimly lit café; she'd just finished a set.

Mimi was talking. Fast and strong. Then a pause, her voice light, fluttering, halting?

What was she saying?

"And so, Adam darling, I'm so happy that you could meet me tonight. There's something I need to tell you. . . ."

Adam fingered the stem of his wineglass, still picturing her on his imaginary canvas. The Hooker's green blending into the Prussian blue in a cascade of color. An ocean of starburst.

"Adam?" Mimi was frowning. Adam wondered why she was so intense tonight. Usually, she was all lightness and sensuality.

"I'm sorry . . . what were you saying?" he asked.

Mimi glanced around the crowded room. "I could use a refill." She held her empty glass aloft. "Maurice! Merci! Another round please!"

The waiter sauntered over, so French in the middle of L.A. "Oui, mademoiselle. And for the gentleman?"

Smiling slightly, Adam nodded. "I will join the lady."

"Very good." Maurice whisked away their empty glasses, the scent of tired service wafting across the thick air.

Mimi tapped her fingers on the tabletop; turning to Adam, she gave him a delicious but weary smile. "I think the set went rather well tonight. What did you think?"

"Your singing always charms me, Mimi. You know that."

"Yes," she cooed, "but it's nice to hear you say it."

"You bewitch me. I am under your spell." Adam grinned as he watched the waiter set down their drinks. Why, oh why, had he let her beguile him so? Of course, it was flattering. But Pauline. His wife. What was he thinking, meeting Mimi like this? It was a risk. He knew her power over him. It had been such a long time and now, well, it was like no time had passed at all. She still beguiled him with her song and her charm.

Mimi scooped up her cocktail, taking a long sip, sighing.

"I know!" she giggled, but Adam sensed a forcedness to it. What was going on? She seemed on edge tonight. It wasn't like her to be nervous. Yet, he could feel that something was different about her.

"You were going to tell me something?" he asked, sipping his Merlot.

"Yes, well. . . ." Mimi tossed a dark curl out of her eyes, then stared into her drink for a moment before continuing.

He saw the permanent rose bloom over her cheeks, a sensuous veil. "It seems as though you've something significant to tell me?" he asked gently.

She laughed softly. "Yes, well . . . you know me, words aren't my strong suit."

"Maybe you should sing for me?" he joked.

Sighing, she gave a little shrug, "I wish I could but. . . ."

"Adam! Mimi! Hello, mes amis! How is all going tonight? Such a radiant night we are in!"

Breton burst into the café, hailing them from across the dusky room. Damn, Adam thought. What the bloody hell was André doing here tonight? How had he known they'd be here? Had Mimi said something to him? Glancing across the table at her, though, he could see that she was just as surprised as he was. Though was there a hint of relief, too, spreading across her fine features? Was the permanent rose fading?

"André!" Mimi rose, embracing Breton, kissing him on both cheeks. "How splendid to see you!"

"Enchanté, mademoiselle." Breton returned her kisses with a flourish, pulling out a chair and plopping down.

"André." Adam nodded. Normally he'd be delighted to see Breton, but tonight there was something going on. Mimi wanted to tell him . . . what? A secret? Yes, he could sense it. And now, with Breton here, he doubted that she would. If he could somehow get Breton to leave, then Mimi would tell him her secret. Yet, now. . . .

"It seems to me that every act is its own justification, at least for the person who has been capable of committing it, that it is endowed with a radiant power which the slightest gloss is certain to diminish. Because of this gloss, it even in a sense ceases to happen. . . ." [22] Breton waved his hand in front of them. All drama and vigor. Adam thought of an imaginary fly buzzing silently over the table. The hand disrupting its flight pattern. "Pardonnez-moi. Have I interrupted your tête-à-tête?"

"As a matter of fact," Adam nodded across the table at the now silent Mimi, "you have come at a bit of an inconvenient time, André."

"I see. . . ." Breton, nevertheless, continued to sit at the little table with the two of them. "I simply desired your opinion on the manifestation of 'the gloss,' mon ami."

Adam chuckled; he couldn't help it. What the bloody hell was

André talking about now? A gloss with a radiant power? Yet, hadn't he heard this before? Adam stared at his friend, raised one eyebrow, then shrugged.

"I could use some gloss about now," Mimi ventured, exhaling softly into the dusky air.

"Ah! Mademoiselle, you are gloss itself!" Breton proclaimed. "But no, you are not gloss." Breton shook his messy mop. "No I rescind that assessment. You are the Radiant Power. You sparkle and shine. You emanate light and music and sensuality!"

Adam grinned, of course. André had said the same thing to Pauline. Hadn't he? It had been a long time ago and the memory was vague. Yet . . . was André making some sort of veiled suggestion here? Or was he only being his crazy self? Tonight, though, as always, there did seem to be a perverse logic to his proclamation.

"Radiant Power?" Mimi murmured, then smiled. Adam was enchanted by the sparkle shining in her dark eyes. "Oui, monsieur, I wish it were so, especially tonight. I could use such a power."

"Why is that?" Adam asked.

She shook her head, sighing again—

"MIMI! MIMI! Where are you? Your next set is due in five!"

"Oh, damn!" she muttered. "That's Jean-Claude. I have another set. Will you gentlemen excuse me?"

"But of course, mademoiselle, share your Radiant Power with the world. They will be the most fortunate of folk! They will beam a light of orange giraffes who crane their necks for a glimpse of your Power."

"Orange giraffes?" Mimi giggled. "I hope not, monsieur!"

"Unfortunately, Mimi," Adam said, "I must leave. I have an engagement early tomorrow and so—"

"No, please, stay," she begged. "I do need to talk to you."

Adam glanced over at Breton, who shrugged.

"Very well, I will stay," Adam conceded. "But I must leave soon, before midnight if possible."

"Oh, that will be possible," Mimi said. "I promise. Now, you boys sit back, drink your wine, and enjoy the show."

"Ah, that we will, mademoiselle," Breton nodded, hailing the waiter.

Adam settled back into his chair, watching her sway away toward the stage. Should he wait for her? It was dangerous. Part of him knew that he should leave immediately. But another part pulled him toward her, the ocean of creativity, the Radiant Power.

He knew she was bad for him. Very bad. But he couldn't help himself. Mimi beguiled him. He was powerless to stop her.

Breton

This Adam! He is a fool! He comes to this town. He meets this trollop—granted, a very enchanting trollop, but a trollop nevertheless—and there is no talking to him. He will not listen. He knows that what he does is not an honorable thing. But he is dazzled by her, beguiled by her. She has bewitched him. And for what? A few nights of delight between the sheets?

Ah! Bosh! It is poppycock! He must disentangle himself. He must come to his senses. He will never win this game. His charming wife. She will discover his misdeeds. She will never forgive him. And who could blame her? She is an angel. That Pauline. She is heaven on earth. She was the first of the gloss! Why Adam takes her for granted so. I am completely baffled by such a one as he. The dreams. They will haunt him. They will not let him sleep. He will find no peace. There will be gargantuan dinosaurs and fiendish elephants that will trample him in his dreams.

And this Mimi? She, too, has the gloss, the Radiant Power. It is true. But with her it is not the same as with Pauline. With Mimi, the gloss portends doom. That is the reason why she must be avoided. Or else. . . .

Ah . . . why do I even give Adam a second thought? It is his life. If he wants to have his fun, then let him.

But don't come crying to me, dear sir, when your world comes tumbling down in the name of women. In the name of muses. In the name of the Radiant Power!

Leonora

"Pardon, me . . . sorry to disturb you." Leonora poked her head
into the cool, cavernous studio. "I was looking for Adam."

"He's gone downtown. Can I help you with something?"
Annabelle smiled warmly at her, a luminosity emanating from
her. She was busy with buckets of greens and crimsons, an
enormous canvas spread out on the concrete floor in front of her.

Leonora shivered slightly, the chill of the studio seeping
from the cement floors, the thin walls. Gazing around the place,
she couldn't help but be entranced by the huge canvases hanging
on the tall walls. Prussian blue backgrounds with shooting golden
stars flying into the sea. Lemon circles and curlicues, spiraling
into infinite designs of cosmic certitude. Crimsons, tangerines,
and purples forming enormous continents of color.

Adam. He was here. Even when he was not. His work was him.
Leonora could feel him. His strength. His magic. His passion.

Did this Annabelle feel him, too?

Leonora wondered, again, what this woman was to Adam, as
she watched her wipe her delicate pale palms on her apron.

"I don't think I need help with anything." Leonora tried to
keep the primness out of her tone, but it was hard. This girl—for
she was that, she couldn't have been more than twenty-five,
maybe thirty—and her solicitude, brought out a strange defen-

siveness in her. Leonora knew that she was prone to this attitude, and usually she tried to keep it in check, but today she didn't care. She wanted to find out more about this Annabelle. And maybe Adam's absence was a sign that opportunity was at hand.

Sweetly nodding, Annabelle wiped a large brush on a paint-splattered cloth. "Okay, well, that's fine. Do you want to help?"

"Help?"

"I'm just laying on the colors for Adam's next work and, damn, I'm getting a bit winded, if you know what I mean?" Her laughter tinkled softly, echoing up and into the air.

Leonora smiled despite herself. The girl was enchanting. How could she have such a power over her? And so quickly? Why, a moment ago, Leonora had been ready to go on the attack. Barrage the girl with questions about her background, how she knew Adam, what her connection was to him.

But now?

Annabelle held out a bucket of paint filled with golden swirls and pumpkins. "What do you think? Is the color right?"

Stepping forward, Leonora shook her head, "No, not quite . . . though I'm not even sure what your task is. But there's something about the mixture that could use a dab more of"—Leonora surveyed the various buckets lining the floor—"that red."

Leonora pointed to a bucket of dark cadmium red paint at the top of the canvas.

Brightening, Annabelle clapped. "You're absolutely right! Why didn't I think of that? How did you know?"

Leonora shrugged, watching as Annabelle hefted the bucket of red off the floor and then splashed a waterfall of crimson onto the canvas, the paint spilling into bright stars of passionate appeal.

"Wow!" Annabelle exclaimed, pushing a dark curl out of her eyes. "Would you look at that?"

"Yes," Leonora grinned, unable to contain her delight. What was it about painting, about letting it have its way, that was so satisfying?

"Hello, ladies." A rich baritone interrupted their play.

"Hey, Adam!" Annabelle called out. "Look what your friend Leonora just did!"

Leonora felt herself blush inside. Damn. What would he think? Would he like it? Why was Annabelle saying that she'd done the deed? After all, it was Annabelle who had thrown the paint with such abandon.

Leonora watched as Adam slowly walked around the huge canvas, stroking his chin, nodding slightly. Stopping at a bucket of purples, he stared at the spreading red for a moment, before hefting the purples up and tossing a juicy jolt onto the crimsons.

"Wow!" Annabelle exclaimed. "That's super awesome!"

"Indeed." Adam grinned, turning to Leonora. "What do you think?"

Leonora stared into his eyes for a moment, calculating. "I think it's a start, but. . . ."

"Yes?"

She strolled around the canvas, surveying the various buckets that Annabelle had filled. Golds. Greens. Whites. Blues. . . .

Stopping at the bucket of Prussian blue, Leonora glanced over at Adam, who nodded at her imperceptibly.

Bending to lift the bucket, Leonora paused, a swift fleeting image filling her consciousness. A blue sky filled with orange birds, their wings beating, their cries filling her with joy. She heaved the bucket up, taking a deep breath, closing her eyes for a moment, feeling his eyes on her, hearing the delicate jangle of Annabelle's bracelet.

Then eyes open, she lifted the bucket up and over the canvas, tossing the brilliant blue onto its surface. The blue fell and spread and moved into the reds, creating a stunning purple here, leaving a spot of white or rose there.

Grinning, she stared at the canvas in wonder. It was alive. The paint moved and flowed of its own volition. The colors dynamic. The shapes fluid. Who knew what would appear next?

"I like it," Adam nodded.

"Me too! I think it's divine!" Annabelle exclaimed.

"It's a start," Leonora murmured, setting the bucket down, backing away from the canvas, and exhaling a deep, deep breath.

"Hey, isn't that Adam's 'friend,' Annabelle?" François stared with unabashed abandon out the windshield of his 1976 BMW coupe, the car's motor purring like a sacked-out kitten as they sat at the light. Leaning forward on the steering wheel, his eyes followed Annabelle. Hungry.

Leonora bristled. Why must he always stare so? He had this infuriating habit that he claimed he was unaware of whenever she confronted him about it. "Don't stare!" she'd hiss as his eyes homed in on some pretty filly while they sat sipping gimlets at the Teacup Bar. He'd raise an eyebrow, grin his crooked grin, "Was I staring? Sorry, luv." And then go back to his drink and their conversation as if it were no big deal.

But it was a big deal. Wasn't it? Leonora felt it was. But then, sometimes, she wondered if she were overreacting. That men stare. It was just in their DNA. So, let them.

Yet today, she just wasn't in the mood. She was tired and cranky. She just wanted to get to Bookshop Santa Cruz to pick up a copy of *Dreams Unleashed: Unlocking the Power of Animal Imagery* before dinner. And now, here was Annabelle. Presenting herself as the object of his stare.

Damn.

Annabelle was ambling down Pacific Avenue, her arms laden with various bulky packages, brightly colored bags with images of Frida Kahlo and frolicking farm fowl. Her walk was slow. Swaying . . . spacey . . . pretty. . . .

Of course, François was going to stare. Frankly, Leonora stared, too. And again, the questions came into her mind. Who was this girl? What was her connection to Adam? And where was she going?

"She looks like she could use a lift." François stepped on the accelerator as the light changed.

"She's going in the opposite direction," Leonora pointed out.

"That is true, but maybe she wouldn't mind a little detour to the bookshop and then we could stop off at the Teacup for a drink. She's new in town, isn't she? We could give her a wee tour of the local hotspots."

Leonora sighed inwardly. On the one hand, she did want to just get her book and head back up the hill to dive into its dreams' treasure trove. On the other hand, she liked Annabelle, especially after their day of painting. She was sweet and enthusiastic and maybe even talented. Yet, there was François. He was way too interested.

Leonora knew to be wary of this. Yet. . . .

"Okay, we can stop and see if she wants a ride. But we have to let her know that we're going to stop at the bookshop first."

François grinned. "Lovely!" He pulled over to the curb, rolled down the window, and whistled. "Hey, darling!" he called out.

Leonora rolled her eyes. It was just too much, and she had to laugh to herself. François was François. Maybe it was the French in him. Maybe it was being a man. Maybe it was just him. But there was nothing she could do about it and she may as well enjoy the ride.

Annabelle paused, shifting Frida Kahlo over to the other shoulder. "Oh, hello." She smiled sweetly.

"You need a ride?" François asked.

"Sure, that'd be great," she answered. "If you don't mind."

"The thing is," Leonora leaned over toward the open window, trying to be heard over the engine's purr and François's bulk, "we're on our way downtown to the Bookshop Santa Cruz first, and then we'll head back up the hill. . . ."

"Not before we stop at the Teacup for a drink!" François winked.

"The bookshop? I adore bookshops! And what's the Teacup?"

"Hop on in, ma belle, and we'll show you the delights of this lil' hamlet that you've never dreamed of!" François leapt from the car, gallantly taking the bags from Annabelle, who climbed into the backseat.

"This is so cool," she gushed. "I was just thinking how I was never gonna make it back up the hill with all those packages!"

"The advantage of a small town, ma belle." François had stuffed her bags into the trunk, and then hopped back into the driver's seat. He threw the car into gear, gunning down Pacific Avenue. "You never know who will swoop down and scoop you up for an adventure or two!"

Leonora stared out the windshield as they pulled into the parking lot behind the bookshop. He was beyond impossible. But another part of her tingled in anticipation. She couldn't help but be swept up, too. The energy in the little car was infectious.

But to business now. She must get this book. It was vital to her work. As Leonora climbed out of the car, she stretched toward the afternoon sun. An elephant cloud floated by in the afternoon haze. Elephants, she thought. Didn't she just have a dream about elephants? Yes, yes, of course! In the dream, she was on a dusty road by herself, walking toward a little cove. When she rounded the corner and beheld the beach, it was dotted with families picnicking and frolicking in the waves. The water was a deep azure, and the waves were gentle, almost nonexistent. In a sheltered corner of the cove—she didn't see them at first, but on second glance—she saw a ring of baby elephants, six or seven of them, partially submerged in the water, their faces and trunks under the sea as if communicating. All she could see was the back of their heads, bobbing slightly, an elephant caucus. She so wanted to join them! And so she did. Submerging herself in the water, too, taking a place in their circle. She was nervous about joining them, but excited, too, to be a part of the elephant caucus. Just as she was beginning to relax, she felt a horrendous scratch on her leg, and the pain and shock of it caused her to cry out. What was it? One of the baby elephants had claws? But no, it was a huge, black furry claw; an enormous underwater black cat had reached up and scratched her.

What did the dream mean? Leonora had a few ideas, but she was certain that *Dreams Unleashed* would give her vital insight into the dream's meaning and—

"Hey, Leonora!" François called out. "You coming, sweetheart?"

Leonora shook herself out of the dream. She was in it again, and here she was standing in the parking lot behind Bookshop Santa Cruz in a daze.

"Yes, of course, sorry . . . I was just dreaming . . . I mean thinking . . . I. . . ."

Annabelle grinned and strode back for her, linking her arm through hers. "That's okay, Leonora, I do that all the time!" Her laugh was soothing and conspiratorial.

Leonora smiled and allowed herself to be led out of the parking lot and round to the front of the store, feeling the girl's gentle heat as the afternoon sun warmed the back of her neck.

"Ohhhh, kitty! So adorable!" Annabelle bent her pretty head toward the large white feline. He gazed at her, serenely, his golden orbs glittering in the afternoon light. "A cat in a bookstore! How cool is that?"

Leonora nodded, smiling as Annabelle cooed over the cat. "His name is Melville."

"Of course, it is!" Annabelle exclaimed. "Nice to meet you, Herman!"

François chuckled as he sauntered into the stacks, heading for the magazines and weekly papers. Leonora headed toward the clerk seated at the counter, poring over a copy of Anne Rice's latest. "Excuse me?"

The clerk stifled a yawn, gazing at her in unbridled boredom, or was it simply that infuriating Santa Cruz mellow pothead persona?

"I ordered a copy of *Dreams Unleashed*?" Leonora began, tucking a dark curl behind her ear.

The clerk gave her a lopsided grin, his stringy hair hanging in his gray-green eyes. "Sure, man. Just a minute. Let me check the computer, okay?"

Leonora nodded as the clerk slowly rose from the stool, stepping over to the computer at the pace of a snail crawling through molasses. What is it about Santa Cruz that makes everyone so goddamn slow? she wondered. Was it too much sun? Too little to do? Too many drugs?

"Here we go." The clerk nodded slowly. "I see that you ordered it three weeks ago?"

"Yes, that's right. And someone named Autumn called me and said it was in."

"Autumn? Oh, yeah . . . that chick. Sure, she's on vacation now, but I can see if she left a note somewhere about your book. It sounds like a cool read, man. Dreams and all. I have these dreams that rock, man? You know? Like I'm at the beach and I'm walking along by the shore, and all of a sudden, a piece of the sand, like it's a flying saucer, you know, man? It appears out of the sand and it's like all cool colors, like silver and gold and it just lifts out of the sand and it flies up and over me, like wow, man, have you ever had a dream like that?"

Leonora shook her head. "No, I can't say I have. Did you find a note from Autumn?"

"Give me a minute, man, I'm gonna try one more place."

Leonora sighed, stepping away from the counter. Part of her was peeved that the book wasn't just sitting behind the counter, waiting for her. But another part of her was intrigued by the clerk's dream. She usually didn't engage with strangers about dreams, but maybe she should. There was an untapped wealth of material, perhaps, in interviewing the man on the street.

"Hey, Leonora! Have you read *The Secret History*?" Annabelle held up the massive tome, grinning. Melville sat atop the stack of Donna Tartt novels, grooming his wide white face in meticulous cat fashion.

"No, I haven't," Leonora answered. "I don't read many contemporary novels."

"Really?" Annabelle began flipping through the pages. "That's a shame. This looks fantastic. Listen to this: 'Beauty is terror. Whatever we call beautiful, we quiver before it.'"

Annabelle gave a low whistle. "Wow! What do you think about that, Leonora?"

"I am all aquiver!" François sidled up next to Annabelle, grinning.

Annabelle giggled, stepping away from him. Leonora glared at her husband. What the hell was he doing? Must he always flirt with the pretty girls in front of her? They had had horrible fights about this. He always claiming that it was nothing. Just good fun. And she always telling him that it hurt her feelings, even though she might not show it at the time. Should she show her feelings now? In the bookshop? In front of Annabelle? No, she would not. But later, when she and François were alone, she'd let him have it. Or no. Leonora knew him. The answers she would get. The endless loop that they'd repeat. Why fight it? Yet, there was a part of her that needed to. She would think about it.

"Hey, man, I found your book. . . ." The clerk was back, waving a hefty volume at her. "You wanna pay for it now or are you still looking around?"

"I'll pay for it now." Leonora turned away from François's cocky stare, pulling out her wallet to pay for the book.

"Can you get this for me, too, Leo?" François tossed a copy of *Rolling Stone* on the counter. "And maybe Annabelle wants something, too. If you're buying?"

Leonora sighed. "Sure, if she wants the Donna Tartt, I can get it for her."

"You hear that, Annabelle?" François called over to her. "Donna Tartt is yours. My lovely wife is buying today."

"Really? Cool! But honestly, I couldn't. It's expensive, and well. . . ." Annabelle's voice trailed off.

"It's no problem," Leonora said. "My treat."

"Okay, well. . . ." Annabelle placed the book on the counter, smiling shyly.

François grinned broadly. "I'm ready for a gimlet, how about you girls?"

"What's a gimlet?" Annabelle asked.

"Stick with me, sweetheart, and I'll show you all the drinks of the rainbow." François winked at Leonora, who stood for a moment, bag of books in hand, glaring at him.

"Rainbows?" Annabelle asked. "That sounds so beautiful."

"Yes, but it's not the same kind of beauty that Tartt is writing about," Leonora said as she strode out of the bookshop, the orangey sun lighting brick-lined Pacific Avenue. Shading her eyes, she reached for her sunglasses and placed them firmly on her pert nose. Annabelle was chattering about beauty to François, a pair of pigeons swooped down from an eave, and Leonora smiled to herself. It was a beautiful afternoon. And the Teacup Bar. Always divine.

She looked both ways before crossing Pacific Avenue, heading toward the Teacup's noir stairway and a much-anticipated gimlet.

As soon as she entered the Teacup's murky enclave, Leonora spied Madame X starting to mix the gimlets. She knew. And what more did anyone need in a bartender than someone who knew what you were drinking without even asking?

Yet, Madame X was more than your ordinary bartender. She was a Santa Cruz institution, running the bar upstairs while her husband ran the Chinese restaurant below. And while Leonora knew that "inscrutable" was no longer a politically correct descriptor, it was the one that so aptly fit Madame X. Always impeccably dressed in her crimson Chinese cheongsam, Madame X exuded an aura of old-world China.

"Good afternoon, Madame X." Leonora took a seat at the bar. Madame X nodded, her deep chocolate eyes taking in Leonora.

"Good afternoon, Miss Leonora. Gimlet." Madame X placed the lime-green drink on the counter before her, her graceful palm presenting it with an exquisite flourish. "Please, enjoy."

"Yes, thank you. Wonderful." Leonora took a sip, wondering where François and Annabelle were. She thought they were right behind her, but evidently not. She took out her book, holding its delicious heft, gazing at the cover of purple elephants and orange giraffes surrounded by a moonlit glow of palm trees.

This book was going to be most enlightening, she thought, flipping to a random page, her eyes alighting on a quote by Carl Jung: *"The unconscious does not harbor in itself any explosive materials unless an overweening or cowardly conscious attitude has secretly laid up stores of explosives there. All the more reason, then, for watching our step."*[23]

Leonora shivered. Was her unconscious sending her a warning? Did she dismiss her dreams as inconsequential or mine them as only fodder for her art? She didn't believe this to be true. She analyzed her dreams, made connections to her life and her attitudes. Yet . . . were her dreams, especially those that featured animals or people that she knew, full of hidden power that she needed to dig deeper to understand? Explosives. Yes, she felt dynamite inside of herself but rarely allowed it to burst open her conscious life. Why? What was she afraid of? Was it François, for instance? The way they had met? How it had seemed so fated. Out of her control. And now, here today, she still felt this uncanny impulse to just let him do what he would. That she had no control over him. When all she wanted was control. Was her desire for this unequivocal control an earthquake waiting to happen?

Was it François that she needed to be more suspicious of?

Had she been too sure of his love? Of her power over him? Was he the reason she needed to watch her step?

"Hey, Leonora!" Annabelle's cheerful voice rang out, breaking her reverie. "Look what we found!"

Annabelle opened her cupped palms to reveal a tiny golden sculpture. "Isn't it marvelous!" she exclaimed as she placed it on the bar counter.

Leonora stared at the golden lump for a moment before discerning its shape. Why, it was a tiny golden goat! How astounding! "Where did you find it?" she asked.

"Out on Pacific Avenue, just outside the bookshop," Annabelle said.

"Yeah, I would've just walked on by it, but Annabelle here, she has a good eye." François sat down next to Leonora as Madame X slid a gimlet in front of him.

"It was easy to miss!" Annabelle sat down on the other side of Leonora. "I just happened to see a sparkle in the sidewalk and had to investigate. Imagine my surprise when I saw that it was a tiny goat!"

"Yes, imagine," Leonora murmured.

"Gimlet for you, too, miss?" Madame X stood before Annabelle, completely ignoring the tiny golden goat, or was she? Leonora thought she caught her taking it in before asking Annabelle about her drink preference.

"Sure, I hear that they are divine!" Annabelle grinned, gazing proudly at the tiny goat now standing upright on the counter. "What do you think it means?" Annabelle asked. "I mean, how often do you find a golden goat sculpture in your path?"

"Indeed," Leonora moved to touch it. "May I?"

"Oh, yeah, sure, it's not mine!" Annabelle said. "I wonder whose it is?"

"That's a damn good question, ma belle." François took a sip of his drink. "C'est magnifique, Madame X, as always!" he proclaimed.

Madame X nodded inscrutably, now openly staring at the

goat. "If I may say, madame, sir, miss, the goat is an important symbol from ancient Chinese myth. It is the spirit of Yang Ching, the god of Fan-Yin. He is the transcendent goat with white face, horns, and a long beard and—"

"But this goat is gold!" Annabelle exclaimed. "And maybe he has a beard, but I can't really tell. . . ."

Madame X paused, gazing at the girl for a moment before continuing. "He is a Mongolian god. In Chinese, the goat is yang and so represents the sun and the man. He also is symbol of peace and good."

"Cool!" Annabelle nodded, gazing in wonder at the goat. "That could be one meaning. I wonder what else it means?"

"Why don't you ask the goat?" Adam's voice wafted through the ether of the bar, floating into their sphere.

"Ask the goat!?" Annabelle exclaimed. "Wow! What a great idea! Oh, Mr. Goat—'cause I think he's a mister 'cause of what she—what's your name?"

"Madame X."

"Yes, what Madame X said. Mr. Goat, can you tell us what is the meaning of my finding you today on Pacific Ave?"

Leonora felt Adam behind her, his energy and strength and trust in this process. But she couldn't help smiling to herself. Ask the goat. Indeed!

They all bent over the counter, attentive. The goat stood motionless on the counter.

"Baaaaaaa!" François bellowed.

Annabelle clapped her hands. Adam frowned. Leonora sighed. And Madame X?

"Please for everyone, another gimlet?" she asked.

"Let's ask the goat!" François joked, as Adam stepped away to greet a tall shapely woman who had just entered the bar.

His hand on her back, possessive, he guided her over to the group, "Have you all met Marianna?"

Leonora gazed at the woman. There was something familiar

about her. Had she met her before? Had she been in a dream? But as she turned to greet Marianna, she heard a deep inhalation from François. Glancing over her shoulder, she caught him. He was too late to cover it up. She could tell he knew Marianna. And knew her well.

Leonora decided to take matters into her own hands. "It is a pleasure to meet you, Marianna. We were just discussing the meaning of goats. Do you have any ideas?"

Marianna smiled charmingly, then shrugged her shapely shoulders. "I don't know," she murmured. "Why don't you ask the goat?"

Pauline

Stunned, Pauline stared at the rumpled bed, the unfinished breakfast, the cold tea. Some anniversary! she thought. What the hell had just happened? One moment, she and Adam were in perfect anniversary bliss—well, okay, if she were being honest with herself, it wasn't perfect. There was that little matter of Wolfgang-as-a-river-otter dream that Adam had been grilling her about, but still, there had been breakfast in bed, and morning sunlight warming their cozy bedroom, and the anticipation of their special day—and then, this woman! Who the hell was she? What right did she have to come barging into their lives?

And who the hell was Mimi?

Pauline sighed, shaking her head in disbelief. What should she do? Should she join the group for brunch and revelations? Or should she go for a walk around the lake?

Or should she just climb back into bed and try to forget the entire episode?

It was tempting, yet Pauline knew that denial never worked. It just prolonged the situation that she was trying to avoid.

Like Wolfgang. She knew that there was something there, but she told herself that there wasn't. After all, she was a married woman with a devoted husband.

Or was he?

Mrrrrrooooowww! The large white cat rubbed up against her bare legs, demanding attention.

"Oh, Pablo!" she murmured. "What should I do?"

Mrrrowwww meoooww meeeooow purrrrrr! the cat answered.

"You don't say? Okay, then a walk it is. I think you're absolutely right. Some fresh air will clear my head and help me to see things more clearly."

Meeeoowww, the cat agreed, standing at the threshold, waiting for her.

"Okay, okay, just a minute. Let me get dressed." Pauline laughed in spite of her upset. It only took a large white cat to impart his wisdom. And for her to listen to him.

Throwing on a pair of black slacks and a clean blouse, Pauline looked in the mirror, running her fingers through her dark locks. "Not too bad," she said to her reflection. "Especially considering what you've just been through."

MEEEEEEOWWWWW! Pablo cried, dancing at the door.

"Okay, I'm coming," she laughed, grabbing a bright orange sun hat from the rack and following the cat out into the morning light.

Resting under the umbrella shade of the massive jacaranda, Pauline took a long deep breath. The walk around the lake had helped. She was tired now: this spent feeling always helped her feel better. Two mighty black crows swooped down into the grass in front of her, cawing ferociously over some tidbit.

Pauline watched their battle, for that was what it was. One crow cawing at the other. The foe cawing back even louder, flapping its wings before taking off. The winner stood for a moment, its beady black eyes glinting in the morning light, before pecking at a prize leaf with much ferocious vigor.

Sighing, Pauline sank back against the tree's embracing trunk. Closed her eyes. Breathed in the sweet heat that was beginning to build.

"Hola!" Remedios called, trudging up the little hill.

Pauline opened her eyes, grinning. Thank goodness for Remedios. Maybe she could shed some light on the situation, especially if she'd been at the main house when the Mysterious Woman had appeared.

"Hola. ¿Cómo estás?" Pauline scooched over, making room for her friend, who sat down with a thankful plop.

"Bien, bien, y tu?"

Pauline sighed again, "I don't know if you saw her. . . ."

"Oh, yes, I did see her!" Remedios nodded.

"You did?"

"Sí, sí. She is quite a beautiful woman."

"Yes, I suppose. . . ." Pauline felt a familiar flicker of energy in her solar plexus. "Did you talk to her? Did Adam say anything? I. . . ."

Pauline paused, feeling the tears begin to well at the corners of her eyes. No! She would not cry! Not now. Not in front of her friend.

"Are you okay, mi amiga?" Remedios asked.

"I'm fine . . . I just was wondering. . . ." Pauline's voice cracked as she fought the tears.

"Oh, you are upset," Remedios murmured, placing a hand on hers. "I understand."

"You do?"

"Yes, of course. Today is your anniversary, is it not?"

"Yes."

"That is a day for the couple to celebrate. Just the two of them. And now, there is this beautiful woman. She has intruded upon your celebration. It is a travesty!" Remedios declared.

Pauline laughed. "Oh, Remedios! You are just the best! Thank you!"

Remedios nodded.

"I just don't know what to do. Who is this woman? She barged into our bedroom. Well, care of Breton, of course."

"Of course."

"And announced that she was a friend of some woman named Mimi that Adam knew. Oh, Remedios. You should have seen him. He turned so pale. Like a ghost from the past had arrived on our doorstep."

"Perhaps this is exactly what has happened," Remedios nodded.

"What do you mean?"

"Only that this woman, she is from his past, and, yes, it does seem that Adam has . . . what is the saying?" Remedios paused, searching. "Unfinished business?"

"Unfinished business," Pauline agreed ruefully. "Exactly."

"So, it is hard for you, I know. But it is business that Adam must finish. Or at least get started to finish!"

Pauline laughed. "Oh, Remedios. Yes, you're right. Of course, I knew that Adam had a life before he met me. I just never thought it would find its way down to us here in Mexico."

"Yes, well, the unfinished business has a way of traveling to places that we had never dreamed of."

Pauline nodded, gazing out at the shimmering lake as the sun's heat intensified. "How about a swim?" she asked.

Remedios nodded. "Yes. That is a good plan. But first there is something that I need to tell you."

"There is?" Pauline felt her heart beat faster, the strange energy rising again from her core.

"Yes, my friend. But on second thought, it can wait. Like you said, a swim."

Pauline shook her head. "No, now I'm not sure I would enjoy the swim without knowing what you need to tell me."

"Trust me." Remedios rose, stretching languidly toward the lower boughs of the tree. "You will feel better for the swim."

"You're right. We always swim. So, okay, let's, and then we'll talk, though. . . ." Pauline paused, a little irked. Why couldn't Remedios just tell her what was going on? She really didn't want to swim right now.

Laughing, Remedios promised, "I can see you are thinking, my friend. But do not worry. We will talk. But not until after our swim. Now let's go! Vamos!"

Remedios took off down the hill. Pauline watched her friend, her long dark mane of hair blowing in the breeze.

What the hell, she thought. Remedios was right about one thing.

A swim always helped.

Pauline started down the hill toward the lake, a black crow cawing overhead, the breeze caressing her psyche as she tried to push away the nagging feeling that what Remedios had to tell her was anything but an anniversary present.

Floating in the cool green water, Pauline exhaled deeply. Ahhhh . . . it felt so good to be in the water's buoyant embrace. She gazed up at the pale blue sky, hazy in the late morning light, a sprinkling of puffy sheep clouds dancing overhead. The water felt cool, crisp; she felt weightless, free.

If only she could just float out here in the middle of the lake all day, she thought ruefully, everything would be okay. Yet she knew that eventually she'd have to swim back to shore and face reality. Whatever that might be.

What did Remedios have to tell her? Why couldn't she have told her earlier? Was it really that . . . profound? Devastating? Life-changing?

Pauline knew that it must be something about that Mystery Woman and Mimi, whoever she was.

Mimi. That was a frilly name, wasn't it? Why would her Adam ever have anything to do with someone named Mimi? He must have been very young. Or very drunk. Or very vulnerable.

Or this Mimi must have been very alluring. Sexy. French? Yes, the woman this morning was definitely French, Pauline thought. And French women, well, they were trouble. Or at least she'd always heard this. Being the American girl that she was, Pauline could only guess at the wiles a French woman might possess!

"Bonjour!" Pauline heard a sultry voice hail her from behind. Startled, she straightened to a treading water position to behold just the woman she'd been thinking of. Well, not Mimi, but Mimi's emissary or whoever she was.

"Oh, hello," Pauline managed, wiping a lakey drip from her eyes.

"I hope, mademoiselle, that I am not disturbing? But it is such a beautiful day, and when I saw that you were swimming, I thought to myself, a dip in the lake would be just the thing to wash the dirt from my travels. I do adore a swim!"

"Yes, it's the best." Pauline nodded, still taken aback. Was this the best place to be conducting introductions and uncovering secrets?

"I'm Pauline and. . . ."

"Yes, I know who you are." The woman swam easily toward her, her stroke strong and graceful. An athlete. "I'm Genevieve."

"Genevieve? That's a pretty name."

"Yes, it is." Genevieve tossed back her head and laughed up into the sheepy sky. "But so is *Pauline*."

"Oh, thanks. . . ." Pauline continued to tread water, wondering how long they could converse afloat in the middle of the lake. Genevieve seemed to be in no hurry to either continue her swim or the conversation. Pauline took a deep breath. "So . . . you're a friend of my husband's?"

"No, not exactly. Like I mentioned before, I am a friend of Mimi's. A very good friend in fact."

"I see. . . ." Pauline, despite the rising sun, was beginning to get both tired and cold. "And who is this Mimi? Is she a friend of my husband's?"

"You might say that, oui, she was a friend of his; though the evidence would point to much more than just friends."

"What do you mean?" Pauline's heart raced. "What evidence?"

"Have you spoken to your husband since my arrival?"

"No."

"I think that I could tell you more, but I will refrain. You need to speak to Adam. He will tell you what I told him."

"But couldn't you just give me a hint?"

Genevieve laughed, then turned around abruptly, kicking the water into sparkling waves of mirth.

Pauline watched her swim away, barely a splash breaking the surface of the glassy green lake. Should she follow her? Pauline took a deep breath and started to swim to shore, the rhythm of each stroke echoing the thoughts in her brain.

Damn, Adam! she thought. Damn this Genevieve!! But most of all, damn Mimi!

In wonder, Pauline gazes down into the murky sap-green water of the little pond. Rising from its depths, a snowy white round shape, fuzzy edged and wavy, slowly floats up and up toward the surface. Pauline isn't sure what it is until she sees that it is her large white cat, Pablo, rising up from the murky bottom. His form becomes clearer to her the nearer he rises to the surface. She can make out his head and then his ears, his large paws are tucked under him, donut style, instead of reaching up and swimming like a cat would. He is simply floating up and up. Then she sees him turn from snowy white to a dark forest green, his back become a shell, his legs jut out and begin to move, swimming. He is a turtle! And, now as a turtle, he swims up and up toward the surface, where atop him rides a child, her long dark hair flowing like a mermaid in the water's green glow. The child is laughing, a magical joy emanating round her watery being as she breaks through the surface of the water and. . . .

"Pauline? Pauline . . . darling, are you okay?"

"Hola?! Pauline! Wake up!"

She resisted opening her eyes, fighting the desire to stay in the dream. To talk to the child. Who is she? She is so happy. So full of life and joy. Pauline doesn't want to wake up but. . .

"Pauline, wake up!" a strong voice commanded.

Defeated, she opened her eyes to behold the little group gathered around her. Breton. Remedios. Wolfgang . . . And Adam. . . .

"Oh, I must have fallen asleep after my swim. . . ." she murmured, sitting up and wiping the sand from her eyes.

"Sí, sí, I saw that you were here, resting, my friend, and when I couldn't wake you. . . ." Remedios stared down at her, concern written in her warm chocolate eyes.

"I was having the strangest dream. . . ." Pauline took a deep breath, shaking her head. "It was about Pablo and then he turned into a turtle and then there was a child and. . . ."

She saw Adam look away, just for a moment, but it was too late. A child? Is this what the dream was telling her? What could Adam have to do with a child?

Breton boomed out, proclaiming, *"It is in discovery alone that one recognizes the marvelous headlong rush of desire. It alone has the power to enlarge the universe!"* [24]

"I'm not sure that it was about desire," Pauline shook her head. But then glancing over at Adam, she couldn't help but think that, yes, the dream was all about desire. What can happen when desire is fulfilled?

"Ah! Here you all are!" Genevieve strode up to the little group, running her fingers through her short golden locks. "What is happening?"

"That's exactly what I'd like to know," Pauline said, rising wobbly. Wolfgang reached over to steady her. She felt his heat pulsing through his touch. Yet she must focus, she told herself, pulling gently away from him.

"Yes, there is something that I need to tell you, darling." Adam linked his arm through hers, taking possession.

"Can that wait?" Genevieve grinned. "I'm starving! What's for lunch?"

Breton took the bait. *"If a bunch of grapes contains no two alike, why do you need me to describe this grape among others, among all others, to make a grape worth eating?"* [25]

Genevieve threw back her golden head to laugh uproariously. "C'est magnifique, monsieur! Grapes sound a divine start to any luncheon!"

Breton beamed, looping his arm through hers to lead her back toward the main house. *"Our brains are dulled by this incurable mania for reducing the unknown to the known, to the classifiable. The desire for analysis wins out over feeling. It results in lengthy statements whose persuasive force derives from their very strangeness, and only impress the. . . ."* [26]

Pauline felt Adam's strong arm wrapping around her, leading her away from the others. Part of her wanted to follow Remedios and Wolfgang, who trailed a few yards behind Breton and Genevieve. If only she could just join the group, partake of the luncheon and Breton's crazy stories.

"Darling, how are you feeling? Do you need anything?" Adam asked, leading her back up to their wing of the hacienda.

"The only thing I need," Pauline said, "is an answer to my question: Who is this Mimi and what is she to you?"

Adam nodded as he opened the door and gently propelled her back to the unmade bed. "Yes, darling, I will answer all of your questions, but first, it is our anniversary, is it not? And I do believe we need to celebrate. . . ."

He bent down toward her. His kiss was delicious. Pauline swooned, but not before an image of the joyous child riding atop the giant tortoise sailed before her . . . The child's laughter ringing in her ears, her eyes dancing in the light, her arms outstretched toward her. "Mimi!" she cried, before disappearing into

Pauline's consciousness as Adam's strong embrace enveloped her completely. She was powerless. For now.

Pauline knew she was no match for his ardor. Yet, later, she told herself, she would get answers. For now, though, she would succumb. After all, it was her anniversary.

She kissed him back, passionately. They sank into bed, the early afternoon light filtering through the curtains as a gentle breeze blew through their cozy little room . . . Pauline shivered, but in a good way, as she closed her eyes and murmured, "Yes, yes . . . yes. . . ."

"There was this other woman . . . before I met you. She meant nothing to me . . . please believe me, darling . . . it was just one night . . . one foolish night . . . I had no idea that there was a child . . . believe me, if I had known, I would have told you . . . yes, of course, I understand why you are upset . . . I am angry, too. I cannot fathom why Mimi never told me about my child . . . yes . . . of course . . . I don't mean to upset you . . . she meant nothing to me . . . yes, I realize I have already said that, but Pauline, you are the love of my life . . . yes, I know the child will complicate things, but I must see her . . . I don't know what I will do once I meet her . . . Mimi? I haven't seen her in years . . . and. . . .

"Pauline? My friend? Are you okay?" Remedios asked gently.

Pauline stared blankly at her friend, Adam's words running through her mind. She couldn't stop them. Another woman? From his past? Of course, she knew that he had had other women. How could he have not? He was seductive, mysterious, attractive. Hadn't she, too, been seduced by him from the moment she met him? Yet, this other woman, this Mimi, had had his child. Granted, Adam had not known about the child, but still . . . where did this leave her? And now he was off to Los Angeles to meet his child. And maybe even reconnect with this Mimi. How could he not? They shared a child together.

And for herself? Did she even want children? What if he brought the child back here? Would she be able to fulfill the role of stepmother? What if the child didn't like her? Resented her?

"Pauline? Can I get you anything?" Remedios stood at her easel, paintbrush in hand, the unfinished canvas before her. Pauline stared at her friend, barely registering her questions. Then her eyes floated over to the canvas. A woman, hair wild and free, bursting out of a wall, her eyes on fire, her hands reaching for some sort of magical chalice on a small round table. White and golden wisps spun out of the chalice, up into the air. The woman in the painting glowed in tangerines, lavenders, and cobalts. Tiny furls of golden-spun plant life created a frame around the woman.

Pauline wanted to jump into the painting. Be this woman. Drink from the magic chalice and be transported from her life.

Oh! Whatever was she going to do?

"I will get you something to help. . . ." Remedios left the room quietly, leaving Pauline in the cool comfort of the studio.

Usually, Pauline felt safe here. In Remedios's world, all could be painted away. She could watch Remedios work, feel her energy and passion. "No, I don't mind," Remedios had always said when Pauline asked if she could just sit and soak in her friend's creative flow.

But today, Pauline's agitation was acute. She couldn't shake Adam's confession. And she couldn't believe that he was gone. Back to this Mimi and their child. It was all too much for her.

"Here, drink this," Remedios said, handing Pauline a tall glass filled with cool cucumber liquid.

"I'm not really thirsty," Pauline said, but accepted the glass, taking a tiny sip.

"That is better, is it not?" Remedios asked.

Pauline nodded, swallowing the cooling liquid and then taking another sip. "Yes, thank you. You are too kind." She felt a slight tingling behind her eyes, a subtle feeling of relaxation.

Remedios nodded. "I know that Adam has told you something that has upset you."

"Yes, how do you know?"

"It is painted on your beautiful face."

Pauline nodded. Somehow everyone seemed to know Adam's secret before she did. How could this be? That Genevieve! She had started it all. Yet, she couldn't excuse Adam. It was like a double betrayal that he had told these others before her, his wife. But it didn't matter now. The secret was out and she was left here without him.

"Oh, Remedios. There is another woman! And she has a child! His child! What am I going to do?" Pauline set the glass down, and wiped the tears from her eyes. No, she told herself, I will not cry right now. I will not break down in front of Remedios.

Remedios nodded, then glided across her studio to a tall cupboard on the opposite wall. Opening the enormous doors, she began to collect various items: a large black bowl, a jar filled with glowing liquid, ornate utensils of silver and gold.

Her arms filled, she floated back over to her worktable and arranged the items in careful sequence. She placed the large bowl in the center of the table, and then plucked a few golden flowers from a vase behind it. She laid the flowers in a wreath around the bowl, and then uncapped the jar of glowing liquid and poured it in. Pauline watched in fascination as wisps of glittering stars floated up and out, toward the sky. Remedios next took one of the utensils, a beautiful golden spoon, and began to stir the contents.

Mesmerized, Pauline continued to stare as Remedios worked her alchemical magic.

"Come," Remedios motioned for Pauline to approach her. "You are in a state of pain and confusion. Do not be afraid. This will soothe you. Come. . . ."

Pauline rose from her stool, venturing timidly toward the

magical bowl where golden stars continued to shoot out into the cool darkness of the studio.

"What is it?" she asked, softly.

"It is a healing potion. Please, now, close your eyes," Remedios commanded softly.

Taking a deep breath, Pauline stood near the table, allowing Remedios to take her hand and place it over the air above the bowl. Closing her eyes, Pauline felt a tiny tingling in her hand and then she was floating! Up and up and up. She was a comet. She was a star. She was a bird.

She felt the cool air surrounding her. She breathed in the scent of the stars and the cosmos.

Pauline grinned. She had never felt so free. She had never felt so limitless. Anything was possible. And she was her own mistress.

At last.

Mimi

Mimi was no stranger to secrets. Why, there had been that devilishly handsome winemaker from Bordeaux who'd demanded she not tell his wife and children about their trysts. As if she would! And then there was Henri. Oh, Henri. What a romantic! The time she met him at his apartment, followed the rose petals up to the boudoir, and then . . . why, the memory would make her blush. That is, if she were prone to blushing.

And of course, the biggest secret, one that she still had only divulged to but a few, was Genevieve. Genevieve and her horses. Genevieve and her tirades. Genevieve and her advances. Mimi was powerless to resist, even though she had been wary at first. She'd never been with a woman before. But Genevieve had been convincing. Very. And Mimi had been swept away into her embrace. They had been happy, hadn't they? She thought so. But there was always a part of her that didn't quite fall. And Genevieve sensed this; yet they both were having such a fine time!

And then came Adam.

With his piercing blue eyes that read into her very soul. His words were few but intoxicating. The music of his language touched her more than the meanings of the words. He spoke of art and creation and dreams. She had never met anyone like him.

And so, for that one night, she'd succumbed. And it had been delicious. She had thought that he would come back for her, but he never did.

Mimi sighed her purple cloud of resignation.

He was back, all right, and it wasn't for her. He was back for Camilla. The way he had stormed into the bungalow yesterday, all fire and hell. Demanding to see "his" child. As though she hadn't been taking care of her all these years. Granted, he hadn't known about her, but still . . . Mimi stared out the window at the sparkling light drifting through the leaves of the sycamore tree.

What was she supposed to do now? She couldn't let Adam take her child away. To Mexico of all places! Yet, his fury had scared her.

"I cannot fathom why you would keep such a secret all these years!" he had bellowed at her, stepping into their tidy living room. Fortunately, Camilla was at the park with Édouard, but Genevieve, she was right behind Adam, wearing a big satisfied smirk.

"Adam?" Mimi had murmured, "Whatever are you talking about?"

"You know bloody well what I'm talking about! The child. My child! How could you keep her from me? My own flesh and bloody blood!"

Mimi closed her eyes for a moment, letting the afternoon light play upon her. If only she could stop his voice in her head. If only she could go back and change the past. If only, if only, if only. . . .

Softly, she began to sing, the sorrow in her heart taking flight in the words and melody.

Je suis seule ce soir avec mes rêves
Je suis seule ce soir sans ton amour. . . [27]
I'm alone tonight with my dreams
I'm alone tonight without your love. . . .

Swaying softly, she rose and turned round and round, her arms encircling Adam. They were back in Paris. He held her so tenderly, but yet . . . so strong. She felt his breath on her neck, tingling in anticipation. "Oh. . . ." she murmured, "Adam. . . ."

"Mama!" The child's voice burst into her consciousness, and then into reality. Mimi opened her eyes to behold her dear daughter.

"Camilla, my baby!" Bending down, Mimi scooped her daughter up, nuzzling into her soft curls. "Did you have a fine time at the park with Papa and Mr. Sinclair?"

"Yes, Mama! We went on the swings. And we made a sand-castle!"

"She has a great artistic talent," Adam murmured, eyeing Mimi pointedly before glancing over at Édouard, who smiled shyly.

"Yes, we have encouraged her to draw, to paint. And the music. She enjoys the piano, too."

"Very good." Adam seated himself at the kitchen table, leaning back in the sturdy chair.

"You are thirsty?" Édouard asked.

"Yes, but do not go to any trouble on my account," Adam answered. Mimi felt his stare, boring into her soul, as she set the child down.

"I'm going to make a song now! Listen to me!" Camilla called out as she rushed into the living room, the sounds of banging coming from the keyboard.

"Camilla, softly, softly!" Mimi called after her, frowning. "I am sorry. She needs lessons. . . ."

"She sounds perfect to me," Adam said as he took the glass of wine Édouard had poured for him.

"Mimi?" Édouard handed her a glass. Mimi took the drink, thankful for its distraction and hoping for its potency.

"So . . . here we are," Adam pronounced, reaching for a cig-arette.

"Yes," Mimi answered, still standing in the middle of the kitchen.

"Papa! Come! Watch me!" Camilla cried.

"I am being summoned." Édouard smiled, leaving the room with a look and a shrug.

Mimi took a long sip of wine, then exhaled, purple turning to crimson, her breath lingering in the room.

"I will take the child with me," Adam said.

"No, you can't," Mimi began, panic beginning to grip her.

"There is no other choice. We discussed this yesterday, Mimi."

"But the child needs her mother."

"And her father," Adam said, finishing his wine. "I leave tomorrow. Have the child ready by nine a.m."

Mimi stood, striding over to the counter, pouring herself another glass of wine. "You will not take her. I will not allow it!"

"And how do you propose to stop me?" Adam glared down at her, his being fierce, resolved.

"We can come to an arrangement, can we not?" Mimi cried softly, tears beginning to puddle in her eyes.

Adam sighed, shaking his head. "An arrangement? What kind? I cannot remain here. You cannot come with me back to the hacienda. And Pauline. She is my wife. She will take good care of Camilla. I promise you," Adam said.

Mimi sensed him softening. He knew she was distressed. Her tears were real, but why not let them flow and flow? Why was she trying to control herself? Damn him, she thought.

She began to sob, the tears falling in enormous splats. "I will not allow you to take her. She is mine. You cannot take her."

Adam stood, shaking his head, "Oh, Mimi, I am sorry. Truly. But you cannot keep her from me. I will raise her. Teach her. Love her. And so will Pauline."

Mimi wiped the tears away. Pauline! Who was this Pauline? She would not allow Adam to take Camilla away to be raised by another woman. Not today. Not tomorrow. Not ever. She had to find a way to stop him.

"Very well, I see that I cannot win this battle. I will have her ready for you tomorrow."

"Excellent." Adam finished his wine, rising to follow the cacophony of notes in the other room.

Mimi watched his back, tall and straight and strong. I will not let you take Camilla, she thought. You will not take her away. I will find a way to keep her.

"Mama! Come listen!" Camilla hopped in front of her, sparkle in her step and light in her locks.

"Of course, sweet baby, Mama will be right there."

The child hugged her tight, then turned and ran back into the other room. Mimi wiped the last tear from her cheek, swallowed hard, and followed her daughter into her future.

Édouard

"Mamaaaa! I want Mama!" The child cried piteously as Édouard pulled the brown sedan over to the side of Coast Highway.

They were only at Oxnard. Still more than an hour away from his family's ranch in the mountains of Santa Barbara. They would be safe there. His family, an uncle, an aunt, would take care of them. Would hide them from this interloper on his family. This Adam Sinclair who claimed to be Camilla's father.

What proof did he have? Édouard asked himself as he turned to try to soothe his daughter. For, yes, she was his daughter in every way that mattered. Hadn't he been the one to rise at four in the morning to take care of her when she had a fever? Hadn't he been the one to take her to her first day of school, a frightened and shy little girl? He had urged her to go into the schoolyard. To make friends. To share her art and her smiles.

And this Adam? He had been off in Mexico with his wife and his art and his bohemian ways. What did he know of fatherhood? Of caring for his dear sweet Camilla?

Nothing.

"Papa!" the child whined. "I'm hungry. I want Mama! I—"

"Hush, mon petit bonbon," Édouard said gently. "Here, take this. A snack for you." He handed the child a graham cracker and watched in tenderness as she took it, the munching taking the place of the whining.

What was he going to do without Mimi? But Mimi had been no help. She had been ready to surrender the child. Her guilt eating at her. Adam's power over her too strong to resist. He shook his head as he shifted the car back into gear, pulling into traffic, remembering Mimi's defeated attitude of the night before.

"We have no choice, Édouard. She is Adam's child, too. I

have kept her from him for too many years. It's not fair to him. Or to Camilla. She needs her father, too."

"But what of me? *I* am her father!" Édouard had demanded, abandoning his usual gentle tone. "We are a family. We have been all these years. The child knows no other. What will this do to her? To rip her from her family? To let this stranger take her to this faraway place to a woman who may or may not want her? Don't you care about our family, Mimi? Don't you care about your daughter and her happiness? Who is this Adam to take her away from us like this?

"He is her father," Mimi had sighed, resigned.

"But what about his wife? This Pauline? How do you know that she will care for our daughter? That she even wants her?"

Mimi shrugged. "I do not know. I only know that Adam demands to take Camilla. And what can we do?"

"We cannot allow it!" Édouard had proclaimed.

"What do you propose?" Mimi had asked, suddenly alert even after several glasses of wine, the horrible argument with Adam.

"I have a plan," Édouard said.

"A plan? What?"

"It is a risk. But I see no other alternative. I will take the child. To my family's home."

"Take her?" Mimi asked, stunned. "You mean kidnap her?"

"No, no. It is not a kidnapping. She is my child. She is your child. You will come, too. Later."

"What do you mean?" Mimi cried. "What about Adam? Won't he follow you?"

"No, no. He cannot be allowed. You must keep him here. In Los Angeles."

"But how?"

Édouard had paused, stymied for a moment.

"What are you two talking about in here?" Genevieve had entered the room, stealthy as a cat. "Are you plotting a secret getaway?" she had grinned maliciously.

Mimi had glared at her. "No, of course not. But even if we were, why would we confide in you? It is because of you that we will lose our daughter. Our family."

"Families!" Genevieve had sneered. "Who needs families? You threw that away, Mimi, when you left me all those years ago."

"What do you mean?" Mimi had asked. "Would you have raised Camilla as your own like Édouard has done?"

Genevieve had shrugged, taken a long drag off her cigarette, "No, probably not. But you did not give me a chance, Mimi. You left me for this"—she had glanced over at Édouard, her look scathing—"man, and now, you have to pay for your betrayal."

"Betrayal?" Mimi had asked.

"Pardon," Édouard could take no more. He did not need to see or hear about his wife's past lover. It was too much on top of Adam's threat to take Camilla. "I am tired. I will retire now, Mimi. Remember what we spoke of."

"Yes, but we did not finish—" Mimi began.

"Do not worry. I will take care of it," he replied.

"Take care of what?" Genevieve asked.

"None of your business," Édouard replied. And turning from the two women, he left the tidy kitchen and headed upstairs to begin packing.

Édouard glanced into the rearview mirror. Camilla sat quietly now, chewing her crackers, her dark curls blowing in the breeze as the hills and coast whizzed by them. Relieved, he turned his attention back to the road as the car picked up speed, hurling them toward the hopeful sanctuary of his family's compound in Santa Barbara.

Mimi

Mimi stared out the kitchen window, morose, defeated, alone. A cup of coffee sat before her, cold and sad. She watched a sweet squirrel family of three in the sunshiny dirt: two cleaning each other, their little paws busy with grooming their partner's sleek little heads. The third lying flat in the dirt, soaking up the morning sun. A family of three? Herself, Édouard, and Camilla? She frowned, sighing her purple cloud. Or it could be Adam, Pauline, and Camilla. Another family of three.

No, this cannot be, she thought, taking a sip of the cold coffee, a tear falling into the murky liquid.

She wondered where Édouard and Camilla were at this moment. Hoped they had arrived safely. She still couldn't believe that she let them go, but what choice did she have? Adam would have taken her daughter. And she could not allow it. So when Édouard came up with this plan, she could think of no alternative.

At least this way, Camilla was still here in California. And Adam was on his way back to Mexico, without her. Mimi watched as the baby squirrel dug a little hole into the dirt, disappearing into the safety of this tunnel.

Oh! Would her family ever be safe again? Would she see them again? Emotion overtaking her, Mimi cried softly, "I miss them so!"

"I bet you do!" Genevieve had slunk into the kitchen, her perfume filling the air, her tone jarring Mimi back to reality.

"Why are you still here?" Mimi asked, collecting herself.

"Don't worry, I'm on my way out. I just wondered what happened with Adam. And Camilla? And where is your husband?"

"Not that it's any of your business, but Adam has gone back to Mexico. And Édouard and Camilla, they are just out for the day."

Genevieve stared into her, the green of her eyes sparkling

with malice. "Oh, I just bet they're spending a day at the park. What did Adam say about that? I thought he was taking his daughter back with him this morning?"

"He changed his mind," Mimi lied. "He realized that he couldn't just tear the child away from the only family she's ever known." Mimi flashed for a moment on Adam's fury that morning when he discovered the child was gone. "What do you mean she is not here? Where have you taken her? I will not tolerate this, Mimi. I will contact the police! I will report this as a kidnapping!"

And she had stood firm, shaking her head, "Go ahead. Call the police!" she had cried. "I don't care! You will not take my child away from me. She belongs here, with me and her father in the only family she knows!" And Adam had given her one last scathing glare before turning and storming out of the bungalow. Had he contacted the police? So far, no sign of the law. And yes, Mimi was frightened by his threat. But she would gladly give up her freedom, go to jail, if this is what it took to keep her daughter in the country.

"Mimi?" Genevieve stood close to her now; Mimi could feel the power of her heat, the pull of her strength. "I was asking you a question."

"Were you?" As Mimi rose from her seat, a familiar swoony feeling crept over her. Yet she shook it from herself. She would not allow herself to be intimidated . . . or seduced.

"Yes, I was asking what happened to Adam and Camilla and Édouard. And all I got from you was what I know to be a lie!"

"Well." Mimi smiled sadly. "I don't care if you think what I told you is a lie. I don't owe you anything, especially the truth about my family after what you have tried to do to us. I do not understand your malice, Genevieve. We used to be in love. Or so I thought."

"Love!" Genevieve scoffed. "You call what we had love? Lust perhaps or. . . ." Genevieve inched closer to Mimi, her perfume's scent strong and dizzying.

"I must go now." Mimi tried to move past her, but Genevieve put out a strong arm to hold her back.

Mimi was too weak to resist, her energy sapped from the last few hours. Feeling herself begin to fall, Mimi struggled to remain conscious as the black veil descended upon her. She saw the blackness, she felt its power, even as she heard her child calling, "Mama! Mama!" before sinking into Genevieve's arms.

20

Leonora

Leonora rested against the crooked trunk of the giant redwood, sketchbook on her lap, pencil poised. The goats grazed noisily in their pen, snorting happily in competition over the fresh stash of grasses just left for them from the goat girl.

She smiled as she began to draw. Their outlines first, goat #1 and #2 (mom and dad?) were bigger, taller, their girth rounder than the other two smaller goats, #3 and #4, teenagers now bucking each other to try to get to the freshest bits of grass.

Leonora loved the goats. She came here whenever she needed that animal energy. There was something so therapeutic about them. And this was a good opportunity to sketch quickly, she thought. Their focus will be all on the feeding for a few minutes at least, so they won't be gamboling about like they usually do come late afternoon.

Drawing, she worked methodically yet quickly. After drawing their big shapes, she glanced up at them for more detail, penciling in their eyes—strange square, almost-alien slits, then their big ears, their funny tails, and their sturdy hooves. For each goat, she worked the lines of the pencil, sketching minute hairs and whiskers, the sun beating down on her as the shade moved from where it had first sheltered her.

The heat of the afternoon seeped through her clothes, her

skin, filling her with a lazy relaxation even as she drew. Soon she felt her eyelids' weight, the drawings of the goats blurring. Leonora leaned against the trunk of the redwood and closed her eyes for a moment.

A sea of brightly packed cars flooded her consciousness. The traffic jam was monumental: the cars all at a complete stop, honking their horns, drivers leaning out of windows, fists pumping the air in anger and frustration. Leonora, from her vantage point high above one side of the traffic jam, gazed at the rooftops of yellow, orange, and red cars packed into the large tightness of the square. Before her vision rose black chords, octaves of Rachmaninoff, C sharp minor, B minor, and then A major. The chords floated over the throng of packed cars, their power in vision rather than sound.

On the other side of the sea of cars, she could see another set of chords, floating into the sky, the majesty of their black stems growing larger and more vivid as they floated toward her. She knew, absolutely, that these chords belonged to Adam's vision. His rose, too, above the packed cars. But where was Adam? She couldn't see him. But she knew he was there. His Rachmaninoff chords answered hers. Would the Russian composer rescue the drivers from their stationary hell? Or did the chords travel to her from Adam as a kind of communication, a conduit, between her consciousness and his? Leonora saw another set of chords rise up and float into the blue sky. . . .

"Leonora? Hello? Are you okay?"

A tender voice entered her consciousness, stopping the progression of the floating chords. Leonora resisted the voice's entreaty, but it was insistent in its gentle questioning.

"It's Annabelle. Leonora? Hello?"

Leonora opened her eyes, the last of the black chords fading from her vision. The young woman stood over her, concern and tenderness written on her sweet face. "Are you okay?" she repeated.

Blinking, Leonora sat up, disoriented. What had happened? She'd been out here, sketching the goats, and then what? She'd fallen asleep? But how could she let herself do such a thing? Granted, she was tired lately, but was she so exhausted that she could just fall asleep like this? In the middle of the day? In the middle of the woods? All by herself?

Baaaaaaaa! Baaaaaaa! a goat called, cranky and loud.

Giggling softly, Annabelle sat down next to Leonora. "I'm sorry to wake you up, but I was a little worried about you. You were singing a melody . . . it was beautiful, but a little dark."

"Was I?" Leonora sat up straighter, her sketchbook falling into the tall grasses.

"Yes, do you know what it was?"

"No . . . no, I don't . . . unless . . . did it sound like Rachmaninoff?"

"Rock who?"

Leonora smiled. "Rachmaninoff. He was a Russian pianist and composer, and I was dreaming. . . ." How much of her dream should she divulge to Annabelle? She didn't know the girl, though there was a kind sympathy to her that was inviting. Yet, Leonora was wary. She knew that her dreams were strange and sacred. She'd wait to get to know Annabelle better before she told her more about her dreams, her work.

"Yeah?" Annabelle gazed out toward the goats, chomping noisily on their grasses. "That sounds cool. Was the dream about the composer?"

"You might say that . . . but I can't remember much right now."

"Yeah, dreams are like that." Annabelle nodded, pulling a slender piece of grass out of the earth. Raising it to her lips, she bit down, chewing meditatively.

"I wonder what time it is." Leonora stood and brushed off her navy slacks.

"I'm not sure. Time isn't one of my things, but from the sun's angle, I'd say it's about five-ish." Annabelle shaded her eyes with her delicate hand, gazing up into the golden haze.

"Oh, dear!" Leonora exclaimed. "I honestly don't know what's come over me! I need to meet François back at the house. We're giving a soirée for a local artist and I promised I'd help set up the venue."

"Cool. Can I help?" Annabelle asked.

"You aren't busy?"

"Nah, I've got all the time in the world."

Leonora nodded. Yes, she thinks this now, but soon she'd learn otherwise. Time was fleeting, as the saying goes. Yet, for now, why not take advantage of Annabelle's offer?

"Okay, if you'd like. I'm sure we could use the help."

"Great. I just have to make a phone call. To my mom. Would it be okay if I borrowed your phone?"

"Sure, of course. Where does she live?"

"Santa Barbara. I know that's long distance, but I promise, I won't talk long."

"It's not a problem." Leonora gathered up her sketchbook and pencil, wondering what Annabelle's mother was like and what she did in Santa Barbara. Deciding to not ask for the moment, Leonora began to walk down the path. "Do you mind walking to our place?"

"I love to walk!" Annabelle proclaimed, falling into stride next to Leonora with a rhythm that matched hers perfectly. What is it about this girl? Leonora wondered, that makes her so easy? So alluring?

Maybe she'd discover more with this phone call.

Leonora didn't let on, but she was an obsessive eavesdropper. The phone call to Santa Barbara would be an opportunity to practice her art.

If only François weren't on the premises yet!

"Yeah, Mom, everyone is so awesome here . . . yeah . . . he's super cool . . . I really like him . . . uh, uh . . . yes . . . well, we did some painting together in his studio. It was totally awesome! And I met this other artist, her name is Leonora, you'd like her . . . yeah, not only is she an artist, but I dunno, she does other stuff too . . . like science and dreams, and it's just totally cool, you know? She's super nice. In fact, she's letting me use her phone to call you. . . ." Annabelle paused, beaming over at Leonora, who quickly turned back to her tasks in the kitchen preparing fare for the party. "Mom says thank you!" Leonora smiled, nodded as Annabelle turned her attention back to the call. "Yeah . . . okay, yeah . . . really? Wow! Super rad, Mom! Way to go! Yeah . . . okay, well I'll talk to you later. Say hi to everybody for me in Santa Barbara! Bye-bye . . . love you."

Annabelle beamed at Leonora. "Mom wants to meet you. Maybe she'll come visit."

"That would be nice," Leonora said, noncommittally.

"Yeah, but it's hard for her to get away. And well . . . I dunno . . . she has this other thing that she's committed to there and. . . ."

Annabelle's voice trailed off, uncertain.

"Well, it'd be wonderful to meet her if she does come to visit. What does she do in Santa Barbara?"

"She's an artist."

"Really? What kind of art does she do?"

"Oh, like sculpture and painting and found art and whatever, you know?"

Leonora nodded. So. Annabelle's mother was an artist in Santa Barbara. Interesting. No wonder Annabelle was artistically inclined. Though sometimes the artistic gene skips a generation, as in her own case. Her parents were both academics and, as such, interested in the arts, but didn't practice them.

"So, what do you want me to do to help with the party?" Annabelle asked.

"Are you here to help, ma belle?" François appeared in the doorway, a rakish grin on his handsome mug.

"Yeah, if you need me?" Annabelle asked, all hope and enthusiasm.

"I bet we can find something for you to do, right Leo?" François quipped.

"Yes." Leonora sighed inwardly. After all, she had invited Annabelle to help, and she knew that François would revel in this. Very well, she thought. Let the party begin.

"Why don't you help with the vegetables, Annabelle. Can you cut them up for hors d'oeuvres?" Leonora asked.

"Sure! That sounds fun!"

François chuckled as he opened the refrigerator and pulled out a bottle of wine. "Anyone for some refreshment?"

"I'd love a glass of wine!" Annabelle sang.

Popping the cork, François reached for the wineglasses and poured hearty glassfuls for Annabelle, Leonora, and himself.

Taking the glass, Annabelle sipped. "This is delicious! Now where are those vegetables?"

Grinning, François turned and opened the fridge again, grabbing the plastic bags of veggies. "Here you go," he proclaimed, winking at Leonora.

Sipping her wine, Leonora leaned against the counter for a moment, a swoon of sound enveloping her, a sudden loud cacophonous scale circling in her brain. The chords rang heavy, powerful. She sank for a moment into their sublime embrace. Rachmaninoff. He was, as always, very, very, very seductive.

Camilla

SANTA BARBARA, CALIF., 1992

Camilla hung up the phone, a vague uneasiness oozing out of the line and into her fingertips. Why? Her daughter seemed happy and engaged. Santa Cruz appeared to be a perfect place for her to land at this point in her life. Yet, Camilla knew that the secret would come out because of Annabelle's proximity to Adam. It had to. How could it not? One way or another, Annabelle would discover that her connection to Adam was more than just mentor and student. That he was related to her on a much deeper level. Or not.

Who was it that said blood was thicker than water?

Camilla shook her head, who the hell knows? All she did know was that Adam might figure out the connection. Or Annabelle might figure it out.

Or this Leonora? Who was she? And what was her connection to her father? Was Adam in love with her? Did he mean to replace Pauline with this Leonora?

Camilla gazed out the windows at the distant sea below, its gray-blue lines falling from the island on the horizon. The water's blues becoming darker and more alluring.

She must finish that painting that she'd started. When was that? Six months ago? A year? Why was it so hard for her to finish anything lately? Granted, she'd just sold a sculpture to Mrs. Rembrandt (Camilla smiled ruefully), patron saint of the Santa Barbara Arts Commission. But that piece she'd done years ago. She'd not been able to finish anything . . . Not since. . . .

Camilla sighed. Maybe she needed a change of scene? Maybe she should get out of town? But where?

"Camilla? Ma petite chérie? Is everything okay?"

She turned to behold her dear father, Édouard, who'd appeared at the threshold of the living room, his entry quiet as a cat stalking its prey.

"Oh, Papa!" she murmured, turning away from the window to face him. "Yes, everything is fine. I just got off the phone with Annabelle and. . . ."

"Yes?"

"Well, I'm not sure. She seems fine, but I have this feeling that I've sent her into a hornet's nest. That she'll discover who Adam is and. . . ."

"But wasn't that your intention? Didn't you want her to know him?"

"Well, yes . . . maybe . . . I thought so, but now I'm not so sure. There seems to be other people in the mix, you know? There's another woman, an artist or scientist or dreamer or writer? Annabelle was vague, but there's something about her, this woman—her name is Leonora—that I don't quite trust. I can't say why but—"

"Then why don't you go for a visit? Santa Cruz is beautiful. You would enjoy the nature, and you could paint the vistas."

"How do you know just exactly what I am thinking before I even think it?" Camilla cried, hugging him.

She felt his warm and sympathetic energy, yet also his fragility. He was no longer the young man who had brought her here to the ranch all those years ago. Camilla felt a surge of sorrow well up in her chest as she pulled away.

"I know you very well, my child," Édouard replied. "How could I not?"

Camilla nodded, knowing how much this meant. Was she ready to see her "real" father again? Would Adam welcome her? Or would he resent her for losing touch for so many years? And what of Édouard? Would she hurt his feelings by going to Santa Cruz? Ostensibly to check on Annabelle, but they both knew that the trip would be more than this. That she wanted to reconnect with her father and also see who this woman was. This Leonora.

"Of course, you know me better than anyone, Papa," she replied, smiling tenderly. "I will pack my bags tonight. Maybe I'll just hop in the car and drive up 101 as the sun sets! Surprise Annabelle!"

"Are you certain that is such a good idea?" Édouard asked.

Camilla shrugged. "Why not?"

"I leave it to you, my child."

Camilla kissed him on the cheek, excited now with the prospect of her trip. Annabelle would be so pleased!

And Adam?

She felt again that vague uneasiness creeping into her fingertips. But shook it away. Of course, he'd be delighted to see her!

And with this thought, Camilla skipped up the stairs to begin packing for her impromptu surprise trip to Santa Cruz. She'd check on Annabelle. Reconnect with Adam. And this Leonora? She'd find out just who this woman was and what her relationship was with her father.

Even if it meant telling everyone her Secret.

Leonora

"This one. . . ." Leonora took a few steps back, her perspective changing with the subtle shift in distance, "is exquisite, Monarch. Your perspective around Natural Bridges, the light and dark of the sea, the overall mood of the piece. . . ." She paused for a moment, trying to find the right words. But could words describe a work of art, truly? Part of her believed so. That, yes, language was important to the critic and thus preservation of the arts; yet on the other hand, the work spoke for itself. It was sublime. It was divine.

"When I first came to Santa Cruz, I was struck with its natural beauty." Monarch stroked his well-kept goatee. "My work tries to capture the divinity of nature. I am in awe of Mother Earth and all of her glories. I am her humble servant, documenting her canvas. My camera is only a lens that she allows me to use."

"Yes." Leonora nodded. Part of her had little patience with the woo-woo aspect of his art-babble, but another part of her embraced what Monarch was saying. Wasn't nature the ultimate artist? And weren't they all simply her servants, doing her bidding, using her canvas to create the works that they claimed as their own, when in fact, the artist was Nature herself?

"Having fun, my sweet?" François sidled up next to her, champagne bottle in hand. "More bubbly?"

Monarch held out his empty flute. "I normally do not imbibe, but as this is my first opening and you have so graciously hosted this small sample of my work, I have allowed myself the ecstatic experience of alcohol-induced gratitude."

François chuckled. "Whatever you say, Monarch. The champagne is here for the drinking." He filled Monarch's empty flute. "And how about you, Leo? A bit more of the bubbly?"

Leonora hesitated. More champagne might be just what she needed to endure the rest of the evening. Parties were not her thing. While she understood the value of promoting new artists, especially in their small hamlet, she generally shunned such events. Tonight, though, was Monarch's night. And she believed in him. Even if he had renamed himself after a butterfly.

"Sure, thank you." She held out her glass, eyeing François's manly forearm as he poured, a slight tingle running up and down her core.

She watched him saunter away, bottle in hand, stopping at the next group to ask if they wanted refills. She could hear Annabelle's sweet giggle, ringing out and into the room. And then the faint notes of Martha Argerich's piano: Chopin's *Raindrop Prelude*. The notes high and then deep, the repetitions haunting and ethereal.

"Hey, Leonora!" Annabelle was at her side now, beaming. "Wow! This photo is so cool!"

"Why, thank you." Monarch stepped forward.

"Are you the photographer?"

"Yes, I am. But I can't really take credit for Mother Nature's work."

"Wow. Like, yeah, that's true, I guess? But you took the photo and so you saw what she had to offer, right?"

It was Monarch's turn to beam. "I suppose that's one way to look at it. And are you a photographer, too?"

"Me? No way." Annabelle giggled. "I like to paint but I'm still learning, you know? Leonora here and her friend Adam are helping me."

"Ah. Where is this Adam?" Monarch glanced around the crowded room.

"He should be here soon," Leonora said, wondering where the hell he was. He had said he'd make an appearance when she'd told him about the party. About Monarch and his work, thinking that Adam would appreciate Monarch's focus on Nature. He should have been here by now. Yet he was probably down in his studio, working on that piece that he'd been obsessing over for weeks now. "I see it, Leonora. In my mind's eye. The cosmos is showing me an image. It is full of energy, light, and beams. Yet . . ." He'd stopped, frustrated in the telling of his process to her. She'd nodded, understanding completely. What was it about the creative process that was so elusive sometimes? She, too, had visions, yet when it came time to commit these images to the canvas, they slipped away.

"I bet he's still working in his studio," Annabelle offered, seemingly reading Leonora's mind. "That painting he's working on now. . . ." Annabelle paused, thinking. "I dunno . . . it's pretty awesome, don't you think, Leonora?"

"Indeed." Leonora smiled, glancing over at François as he opened the door to let in Adam and a woman. Who was this? She was a stranger, obviously just into town. Leonora didn't know how she knew this, but she felt it. Here was a traveler. An interloper?

She watched as François took her coat, shook her hand, offered her champagne. The woman was petite, pretty, with dark curly hair and porcelain skin. Adam stood at her side, his arm around her, possessive? Familiar? Why was it that Adam always had some woman on his arm? Leonora wondered.

"Mom?" Annabelle cried softly, giving Leonora a quick look of helplessness, before weaving through the crowd to greet the woman.

Leonora continued to stare as Annabelle embraced the stranger. Adam stood behind the two of them, catching Leonora's stare, before leaving the two women and striding across the room to stand before her.

"I see that the party is quite a success," he murmured.

"Who is that woman?" Leonora couldn't help herself.

"An old acquaintance," Adam said.

"Really?" Leonora tried to keep her tone even and disinterested, but her heart pounded.

"Yes, now is this the work of the young photographer you

were telling me about?" Adam leaned in to look at the photo of Natural Bridges.

"Yes, it's mine. Allow me to introduce myself. I am Monarch, chronicler of Gaia."

"Indeed?" Adam grinned, winking at Leonora as he shook Monarch's hand, and grabbed a flute of champagne from François's passing tray.

Leonora stood for a moment, next to the two of them, chatting softly.

Breathing deeply, she gazed across the room to where Annabelle stood with her mother. Leonora downed the last drop of her champagne, set the glass down, and then marched across the room toward the two women.

Pauline

She is sitting on a bed, in a hotel room by the sea. Where? She isn't sure. It could be France. It could be Mexico. It could be New Jersey . . .

Pauline is not alone. There are others visiting in the hotel room, sitting on the balcony, chatting and drinking at the room's little table. Is Adam there? Maybe Breton? And Remedios? She can't be sure. Perhaps.

She lies back on the bed, resting her head on her hands, and stares up at the ceiling, her eyes moving toward the horizontal surface of the wall. What is that she sees? It is almost camouflaged, a pale yellow barely standing out on the faded white of the wall. At first, she thinks it is a spider, but then it grows in size, until it is as large as a tarantula. It clings to the side of the wall, not moving for a moment. Then, to her astonishment, bright flowers begin to grow at the ends of its legs: blue, red, yellow, orange, purple. Each leg dons a brightly colored opening bud at its end.

The flowered tarantula begins to climb down the wall toward her. She shifts away from it. Does she scream? Does she alert the others?

She thinks perhaps she does, but no one else seems to notice the creature, and so she watches in fascination as it moves down the wall and toward the sliding-glass door. To escape out onto the balcony and into the sea?

She rises to open the door for it; by now it is enormous. It has become a giant pale-yellow octopus with the beautiful bright flowers at the ends of each of its legs.

She opens the sliding-glass door. The creature pauses for a moment on the threshold, as if looking at her, but of course, since it is a dream, it has no eyes.

Fascinated, Pauline stands away from the door, watching in wonderment as the creature slinks out and into the sea. The pale-yellow head disappearing under the water. The bright flowers floating for a moment on the sea's surface before being sucked under by the powerful current.

A clock *tick-tocked, tick-tocked* loudly next to her bed. Pauline struggled to consciousness as the image of the flowered creature lingered in her mind.

"Pauline? Darling? What are you doing sleeping in the middle of the day?"

She opened her eyes. Adam stood over her. She saw the worry in his bright blue eyes.

"You're back," she murmured, the fog heavy through a throbbing headache.

"Yes," he said, sitting down on the bed next to her. "Are you quite all right?"

Pauline rubbed her eyes, trying to catch the image of the flowered octopus before it swam away. "I'm fine. Just tired. How was your trip?" Pauline felt the pounding ache intensify, making her vision slightly fuzzy. Was she fine? Yes, she told herself. She often had such headaches, though they'd become more frequent of late . . . and more fierce.

Adam shook his head, a sadness emanating from him. "I will tell you later. But now, let us go to my studio. I have something I want to show you."

"A new work? But you must have arrived home late? How could you be painting already? How long have I been asleep?"

Her questions floated into the air, unanswered, the octopus still tugging at her consciousness. The pain at the back of her eyes fighting for prominence. Rising, she glanced at herself in the mirror. The dark circles under her eyes gave her away—the days of crying and worry, the late nights with Remedios and Breton drinking and talking, the sessions with Wolfgang writing and writing and now this pain. She tried not to wince as another shooting stab struck her from behind her ears to the very soul of her eyes.

Pauline glanced over at her husband. Wouldn't Adam see all of this? She would have thought so. But when he was in this mood, in the throes of the creative process, Adam saw only what was on the canvas, even if the canvas was not before him.

"Shall I fetch you a cup of tea?" he asked, suddenly solicitous. Maybe he did notice her weariness? Or maybe it was simply his English politeness, that manner that always cared for her but also kept her at a distance.

Nodding, she reached for her sweater, the afternoon breeze suddenly chilly. "Sure, tea. That would be nice," she answered, following him out of their room into the too-bright white sun. The pain subsided, for now, as she brushed a stray curl behind her ear.

"And you must tell me of the dream you were having when I woke you," he called back to her.

"Dream?" Pauline ran her fingers through her hair. "Did I say I was dreaming?"

Adam turned and waited for her, a playful smile on his lips. "No, darling, but I can tell. Don't you know that about me? How in tune I am with you and your every fantasy? Wasn't the dream about me?" he joked, holding the door to the studio open for her.

Pauline laughed softly, "Yes, dear, as a matter of fact it was. . . ." But she knew that the dream wasn't about Adam at all. Something else was going on . . . something flowered and watery. Something alien and surprising. Of course, Adam could be these things, but she felt as though a part of her were floating away . . . this pain, these aches. . . .

Oh, bother, she thought. Just get up, get dressed, drink a cup of tea and then . . . then . . . after she was awake, she could think more about the meaning of the dream. Or not.

Pauline rubbed her eyes, straightened her shoulders, and followed her husband into the blinding golden afternoon.

"I call it *Beings Being in the Cosmos!*" Adam proclaimed, standing back from the enormous canvas, filled with shooting comets, pink islands, emerald tubes.

"It is breathtaking," Pauline murmured, taking a step toward it.

"It isn't finished yet, or at least I don't think so," Adam said.

"Yes, I understand. Sometimes it is difficult to tell, is it not?"

"Indeed." Adam stood close to her, the heat of him creating a tingly warmth in the cool studio.

Pauline bent close to examine the painting, its enormous canvas covering a huge corner of the studio. The forest greens, the golden stars, the fuchsia spirals . . . it was dizzying. She took a step back, trying to hide the swoon that threatened to overtake her.

"Darling?" Adam caught her, holding her steady. "You are not well. Here, come sit down." Pauline allowed him to lead her over to the cozy couch, setting her down tenderly.

"Thank you, dear, I'm fine. Just a little flushed from the heat and not quite awake yet." Pauline leaned back into the sofa, closing her eyes, the swirls of Adam's painting swimming before her, taking her back to another time, another man. "I call this one *Space Unbound*, Wolfgang had announced, echoing her husband's proclamation just moments before. What was it about these men and their art? They treated the work like famous people, or even their own children, complete with names and personalities. She'd studied Wolfgang's art in the same way on that day. "What do you think?" he had asked. "You know how I value your opinion." He had gazed at her with a mixture of respect and lust. Pauline tried to ignore the latter, but found herself succumbing in spite of her best intentions. After all, Adam had left her for this "Mimi" woman, a woman he claimed he didn't love, yet . . . he was with Mimi and not with her. Wolfgang was here, now, in the flesh, and a very attractive flesh at that . . . But then, again, the headache. It had made its ugly appearance on the scene as she gazed into Wolfgang's world of swirling golds, aquas, and lilacs. It was as if the painting had swallowed her up and then spit her out again in a tremendous swirl of energy, the headache a direct result of this journey. Of course, she knew that this wasn't the case, but it had felt like this and. . . .

"Is she quite all right?" a familiar man's voice entered her consciousness.

"She says that she is, but I am concerned, Wolfgang. Has she been like this while I was away?"

Pauline struggled back to consciousness, opening her eyes to behold the two men, towering over her.

"I am fine now," she said, sitting up straighter.

"You certainly don't seem yourself," Adam said, sitting down next to her and taking her hand in his. "I think we'd better get you back to bed."

"No, honestly. I'm fine. I just need another cup of tea."

"I'll fetch one for you," Wolfgang said, turning to head back out of the studio.

Pauline watched him retreat, his back straight, his walk sure. Adam stroked her hand, tender.

"I think you need to tell me what is really going on," he commanded softly.

Pauline nodded, taking her hand from his. Should she tell him about Wolfgang? Is that what he wanted to know? Or no, she knew that this wasn't his intention. He knew she was ill. He could sense it. She could, too. But until this moment, she could not admit it. She didn't want to worry him. And there was a part of her that didn't believe she was sick.

Maybe she wasn't. Maybe the headaches were simply a temporary response to her situation. Yet there was a part of her that knew better. And she knew that Adam had a right to know, even if it pained her to tell him.

"Here is your tea," Wolfgang breezed back into the studio, holding the cup of revitalizing liquid in his strong hands. "Be careful, it's hot."

Gratefully, Pauline welcomed the tea, taking a soothing sip. The warmth of it filled her with a sudden burst of energy. Smiling, she gazed up at the two men. "Thank you, Wolfgang. That is delicious. Now, weren't the two of you showing me your latest work?"

"I think we should get you back to the house," Adam said.

"Nonsense," she said, taking another sip of tea, feeling a heady warmth that was surprising and welcome. "Tell me more about *Beings*, darling."

She could tell Adam was torn between concern for her and for his "baby." Which would win out? For now, she hoped it would be the art. She didn't feel up to talking about anything serious now, whether it be her health or what had happened with him and Mimi in L.A. And now with Wolfgang here, well, she knew any real discussion was impossible. For the moment.

"*Beings?*" Wolfgang prompted. "Is that what you've called it?"

"Actually, I call it *Beings Being in the Cosmos*," Adam said, striding away from Pauline and circling over toward the painting. "What do you think?"

Wolfgang turned toward Pauline for a moment, raising one dark eyebrow, before following Adam to the corner of the studio where *Beings* lay in wild cosmic undulation.

Pauline sat for a moment, breathing deeply, trying to steady herself, before rising slowly and joining the two men to examine Adam's "baby."

———

At the study's threshold, the large white cat sat grooming, his whiskers glinting magically in the late-afternoon sunlight. He wasn't listening, exactly, but he made his presence known with a gnashing of fur and teeth interrupting Wolfgang's musings.

Pauline sat at her desk, its surface covered with papers, a typewriter front and center. A flutter of a breeze gently rustled the pages as she closed her eyes. For a moment, she felt at peace, but then the sensation of words cascading from another plane caught her in their spiraling embrace.

"But the function of the pictorial image is not merely the prolongation of the remembrance"—What was he saying? Something about a picture? Of what? How could a picture be long? It could, of course, but . . . Pauline rubbed her temples, the fogginess heavy—*"of a perceived entity or the organization of visual debris scattered in memory."*

"Pauline?" Wolfgang's voice echoed in her brain. "Are you quite well?"

"Yes, yes. . . ." She struggled to smile. "I'm fine. What were you saying?"

"I wondered if you agreed with this idea of memory and the visual? That the true value of the image, through which artistic activity is connected with human development. . . ."

Pauline heard his voice drone on; she tried to grasp his words, but her head . . . it throbbed so. She felt a heaviness that weighed her down, down, down. She fought it, but the pain turned black and then purple, thick clouds of fuzziness. She closed her eyes, letting the images of dark roots and earth cascade down upon her. She was sinking. She was powerless. She was falling. . . .

". . . lies in its capacity to project a new realization which does not have to be referred for its meaning to an object already existing."
[28]

"Pauline!" Wolfgang cried, jumping up from his desk to catch her before she fell, her chair tumbling back.

The cat, startled, turned tail, bolting out into the courtyard.

Pauline felt strong arms catch her, enfold her. She was safe now. Wolfgang would take care of her. And Adam . . . he would come. Wolfgang would take her to him. Adam would know what to do. How to make the pain go away.

"Oh, no, señor!" Remedios stood now at the threshold of their study. "What has happened? My Pauline! Are you ill?"

Wolfgang carried Pauline over to the mauve divan, laid her gently down. "I don't know what happened, Remedios. One moment we were discussing my latest idea for the magazine, and then the next moment, I looked over and she had collapsed." Wolfgang shook his head, anxiety painting his pale face.

Remedios knelt down on the floor next to the little couch, pushed a stray curl behind Pauline's ear. "She is quite ill. . . ."

"Do you know what is wrong with her?"

"I have an idea. But I can't be sure. I know who can help, though."

"A doctor?"

"No, not exactly. I know of a curandera, a healer, who can look to her."

Wolfgang sighed, shaking his head. "A healer? But will Adam approve of that?"

Remedios held Pauline's hand in hers, stroking it tenderly. "I do not know about Adam. All I do know is that my friend, she needs help, and she needs it urgently. I will take her to Serena. She will perform the ritual. She will discover what is the illness that is the plague in our dear Pauline. I will take her now. Today."

"Where is this Serena?" Wolfgang asked.

"She is not too far. In the mountains. Up Rio Santiago."

"Oh . . . where am I?" Pauline whispered, trying to sit up.

"You are in your study, Pauline. Please do not strain yourself. Rest. I will take care of you," Remedios answered.

"Did I faint?"

"Sí, sí, I think that you did, but only for a moment. Where does it hurt? The pain?" Remedios asked.

Pauline felt the heavy black fog again. "My head. . . ." she whispered, falling back down on the thick square pillows.

Closing her eyes, she sank back into her mind, the sounds of Remedios and Wolfgang's voices soothing.

"Can you carry her?" Remedios asked.

"Yes, of course, but shouldn't we tell Adam?"

Remedios frowned, shaking her head. "I do not think so. Pauline is frail. She is in crisis. We must get her to the curandera immediately. Before the illness is too far on its path."

Wolfgang nodded, gathering Pauline up in his arms, following Remedios out into the golden light.

"Where are you going?" Adam demanded, striding down the path toward them.

"Pauline is ill," Remedios answered. "I am taking her to a curandera. She will heal her."

"What do you mean she's ill?" Adam stood before them, gazing down at his limp wife in the arms of his friend.

"I don't know," Wolfgang answered. "She seemed fine earlier and then when we were talking about the next issue of *DYT*, suddenly, she just collapsed."

"Collapsed!" Adam cried. "Here, give her to me. I will take care of her."

Remedios blocked Adam. "No, señor. You have done enough. It is because of you. Because of your behavior, that Pauline is ill. I will take care of her. I will take her to Serena and she will be healed."

"You bloody well are not taking her to any bloody healer! I won't have some witch doctor treating my wife. I will take her to a reputable physician. In town."

"No." Pauline roused herself, the fog lifting for a moment. "I won't go with you. I want to go with Remedios."

"How do you know what you want? Have you heard what she's been saying?" Adam demanded. "She wants to take you to some quack. Some spiritualist. Some healer."

"But Adam, you believe in such things, don't you?" Pauline whispered. "How could you not. The art you create. It is the healing of creativity. It is. . . ." Her voice trailed off, as Adam took her from Wolfgang into his arms.

He stood for a moment, gazing down at her. Then nodding toward Remedios, he turned toward his car. "Where is this healer?"

Remedios nodded. "She is not too far. In the mountains. I can drive your car. I do not think it is a good idea for you to come, too."

"But she is my wife. . . ."

"Sí, sí, this is true. But for Pauline to heal, she must do this by herself. You must not interfere if you want her to recover."

"I cannot let you take her from me like this," Adam protested.

"Adam, darling," Pauline murmured. "Let me go. Remedios will take good care of me. Do not worry. . . ."

"What is going on here?" Breton approached, puffing loudly.

"It seems my wife is ill," Adam sighed. "And Remedios insists upon taking her to some Mexican healer."

"Why that is a splendid idea!" Breton proclaimed. "The Indigenous peoples know of rituals that can heal all. You will let them go, will you not?"

Adam glared at his friend. "It seems that I haven't much choice."

"Please, put her in the car," Remedios commanded. "We haven't much time before the sun sets. It is best if we arrive before dark."

Reluctantly, Adam circled to the other side of the old Ford, placing Pauline gently into the passenger seat. Pauline felt his strength, his protection, but also his resistance. Yet she knew that she must go. That the pain was taking over. And he could not help her.

"You see?" Breton slung an arm over Adam's shoulders. "Pauline is in good hands. She will be given a magical elixir that will cure her malady. It will all be most illuminating. We shall follow her tomorrow. For tonight, mon ami, we will stay here at the hacienda. We will drink and eat. We will tell tall tales. We will send strong empathic messages up the mountain to heal Pauline. All will be most excellent!"

Remedios held out her hand for the keys. "Listen to your friend, Adam. You have done enough. Pauline must do this alone. Without your interference."

Adam searched in his pocket for the keys, digging them out, slowly handing them over to Remedios. "You will take good care of her?"

"Sí, sí. She will be in the best care. Do not worry, señor."

Remedios thrust the key into the ignition, starting the car. Pauline woke to the rumble of the engine, her head throbbing, mirroring its grumble.

"Will we be there soon?"

"Sí, sí, sí, Pauline. Soon."

Turning to glance out the back window, Pauline saw the silhouettes of the three men. Two turned away, sauntering back toward the house. But the third, he stood there, watching. Pauline felt his stare, penetrating the dusk, till the car rounded the corner, and he disappeared.

Mimi

"And . . . cut! That was perfect, sweetheart! You captured the true ennui of Simone. I knew you could do it, kiddo."

Mimi gave the director her sweetest smile. Of course she captured Simone's despair. She'd lived it, hadn't she? It was a piece of cake, as they say here in America, playing this spoiled heiress down on her luck after her husband had been killed in the war, leaving her alone and penniless. *Simone Walks Away.* The film's title was apt, was it not? she thought ruefully.

Oui. This was her life now, too.

Mimi stalked off the set, holding her head high. She would not let anyone know this though. She would live her life. She would make motion pictures. She would be a Hollywood star. Just like Greta Garbo. Or Marlene Dietrich.

Mimi Ravel? No. Not anymore. She was her own woman. With her own identity. Now she was Valentina. She would be a great film star. She would live her dream. Even if she were alone.

"Hey, toots, you up for a drink?" The handsome actor was suddenly at her side, grinning rakishly at her as Mimi hurried from the set.

"I'm a little tired, monsieur. Not tonight. Maybe another time. . . ."

"Promise?"

"Of course," Mimi lied, quickening her pace.

"Tomorrow?" he called out after her.

She gave him a dismissive wave, sighing her purple cloud. Men. She'd had enough of them. And women, too, for that matter.

Genevieve. Damn that woman. Mimi knew that she'd be at home, waiting for her. Or she'd be off at some party, after her race. It didn't matter. Genevieve was trouble. And Mimi wasn't in the mood.

Maybe she should go out for that drink after all. Stopping, Mimi turned and gazed down the long hallway she'd just stalked up.

"Oh, Phillip!" she called out, sweetly. "Maybe I will have that drink after all."

Phillip broke away from the little group he'd been chatting with, rushing up to her. "Sure, baby. Let's do it." He grinned, swinging his arm around her possessively and leading her out into the balmy California night.

Adam

"Man proposes and disposes. He and he alone can determine whether he is completely master of himself, that is, whether he maintains the body of his desires, daily more formidable, in a state of anarchy." [29]

Adam sipped his drink, fingering the stem of the wineglass absently. He was listening to Breton, of course, but there was a part of him that was tired. Being here in L.A. again brought back memories, and not all of them pleasant.

"You must concur, mon ami?" Breton demanded, glaring at his friend.

"Indeed, yes. . . ." Adam stared over toward the door as a striking couple entered the Kit Kat Club. The man was tall, sandy blond hair wavy and thick, a chiseled face and grin that bespoke a confident, manly aura. The woman was petite, with dark curly hair surrounding a pale chiseled visage. He would paint her if he were inclined to portraiture, but. . . .

"Someone you know?" Breton followed his gaze.

"No, no, I don't think so."

Standing, Breton stared at the couple. "Ah, but mon ami, I think you do. Is that not Mimi? And the man? He is a stranger, but a mighty lion is he!"

Adam frowned. Could it be? That in all the bars in L.A., Mimi would show up here? He watched them weave through the tables, her crimson gown showing off her shapely form.

Yes, it was she. Mimi.

Adam felt his heart beat faster, his breath coming faster. After all this time, did he confront her? Would she tell him anything? He needed to know. She had eluded him all these years. Yet he still hungered for the answer: What the bloody hell had happened to Camilla?

Rising, Adam downed the last of his drink.

"Adam, you go to her now? To do what? You will make a scene?" Breton chuckled. "How delightful. Let me accompany you. I would witness the confrontation for you. It will be an exercise in the surreal, non?"

"Yes, perhaps," Adam muttered testily as he strode across the crowded room toward Mimi and the man's table in a dark, smoky corner.

"Mimi," he spoke quietly, yet with force. Did Mimi just shiver? The movement was imperceptible, except to him, attuned as he was to her even after all these years.

"Yes?"

"It is you," Adam said.

"I—"

"Mimi? Who is Mimi?" the man asked, staring at his companion.

"I do not know," Mimi said. "This gentleman is mistaking me for another perhaps?" She stared at Adam, daring him to pursue.

"No, I don't think so." Adam glared down at her.

"But this is Valentina!" The man proclaimed, chuckling. "Don't you recognize her? Her films are all the rage!"

"Is that so?" Adam said. "I'm afraid I've not seen her films. But I have watched her act in another life."

The man frowned, turning toward Mimi. "I had no idea that you had made motion pictures before. In France, perhaps?"

"Yes, yes. . . ." Mimi stood, taking Adam by the elbow. "Not here," she hissed.

Adam shook his arm from her grasp. "I'm not going anywhere until I get some answers from you!"

"I don't know what you think I know," she cried.

"Camilla! Where is she? Where has she been all these years? You've been hiding her from me, her father, her own flesh and blood. I have a right to know where you've been stashing her!"

"Bravo!" Breton clapped loudly. "C'est magnifique! The Lion is here in the Artist and not in the facsimile of her companion."

Adam ignored Breton, now taking Mimi by the arm. "If you won't tell me here, then let's take a walk, shall we?"

Mimi's eyes flooded with black. "No, I will not go with you," she cried, trying to pull away.

"Listen, buddy, I don't know what's going on here, but you heard the lady, she doesn't want to go with you. Now, why don't you be a good boy and let us get back to our drinks?" The man took a swig of his drink, rising.

Adam did nothing to contain the rage pulsing through his being. He gripped her tightly. For an instant, he stared down at Mimi as she struggled to free herself. Enough, he thought, letting her go. Taking a step toward the man, Adam swung hard, hitting him square in the jaw, knocking him over onto the table, crashing the glasses onto the floor. Dark red liquid spread, floating bits of shattered glass sparkled.

The man stood for a moment, then teetered, falling to the floor. Adam watched as Mimi rushed to him, lifting his head, cradling him gently. "Oh! Phillip! Are you okay?" Then turning on Adam, she hissed, "You animal! Look what you've done!"

Adam stared at them for a moment, his hand stinging from the blow, before turning and walking away, Breton's clapping ringing out into the warm dark night.

Camilla

SANTA BARBARA, CALIF., 1958

"Oh, it's yours . . . believe me. . . ." Camilla sighed, staring out the sweet window that showed a stunning view of the waves breaking on the shore. Surfers dotted the water, black bugs floating, waiting for the next set to come in.

Camilla wished she were one of those black bugs. But instead, here she was, in Duke's shack, trying to make him understand.

"I'm just sayin', baby. It could be someone else's, you know? Like what about that cat that you went to Ojai with last month? What was his name?"

"Jake."

"Jake, right. Couldn't it be his?

"No. Jake and I are just friends. He's a business acquaintance of the family."

"Yeah, right. . . ." Duke sauntered over to the tiny kitchen, opening the fridge, pulling out another beer. "You want one?"

"No, thank you. All I'm asking, Duke, is that. . . ." What was she asking? It wasn't like she wanted to marry him. He was fun for a fling, but husband material? Nope. She had other plans for her life besides having a child at the tender age of twenty-one. Finishing art school. That was her dream. And now? With a baby on the way?

What was she going to do?

"Like I said, baby, I'm not really in like . . . you know . . . any position to support a child. I have a lot going on."

"Oh, sure, like what? Your surfing?"

"As a matter of fact, yeah, surfing is where it's at for me. I want to surf the world. The big contests. Hawaii. Australia. Costa Rica."

"And how will you pay for all that?"

"I'll win big, baby. That contest money can add up. And you know, a kid isn't in the game plan, if you catch my drift."

"I hate to interfere with your life's dreams, Duke, but you have to step up. Take responsibility. This child is half yours and the least you can do is—"

"Hey, I ain't marrying you, if that's what you want."

"No, that isn't what I was going to say."

"Why don't you get your rich family to help out? Why do you need to involve me at all?"

"I thought you needed to know . . . I thought you'd want to know . . . I. . . ." Camilla felt a shudder of familiarity. The echo of all those fights between her parents. Her mother refusing to give her up. Her father, not really her father . . . and her real father? Where was he? Why didn't he want her? Was she that broken? Didn't he love her? Would she have the same challenge with this child she was carrying? That Duke would just cast her and his child aside, well . . . it hurt. . . .

Camilla felt the tears begin to puddle. In vain, she tried to control them.

"Hey, baby, don't cry. . . ." Suddenly solicitous, Duke came up behind her, circling her waist with his strong brown arms.

"Can't you just. . . ." He paused, taking a sip of beer, nuzzling her ear. She felt his beery breath and recoiled as he muttered, "you know . . . get rid of it?"

Camilla gasped, turning around to face him, "Do you mean get an abortion?"

Duke shrugged, a sheepish grin making her skin prick. "Well, I mean, girls do that sort of thing nowadays, right? It's not like it'd be the end of the world. And you're not ready for a kid right now, right? What about art school? Aren't you going back to L.A. in the fall?"

Pulling away from him, she felt a sudden wave of grayness envelop her. That had been the plan. But now? Well, she would just have to postpone school. She'd have this child. Her father would support her and his family—they would understand.

Or would they?

She felt a rush of shame and confusion. What the hell was she going to do? Why, oh why, had this happened?

Was history repeating itself? Was she just proving that she really was her mother's daughter?

One thing she did know. She would not get an abortion. She couldn't. She already was in love with this baby. Somehow, she knew it'd be a girl. She'd name her Clara. She'd dance and sing. She'd be musical and artistic. She'd grow up in a home with love and warmth.

Who needs Duke?

Camilla wiped the tears from her eyes, "I've got to go."

"Where to, baby? Hey, don't get frosted! Listen, how 'bout we go for a swim? The water's like wow, crazy, man! Surf's up!" He chuckled, downing the last of his beer.

"No, I don't feel like swimming," she said, grabbing her purse off the worn divan and opening the front door, the fresh ocean breeze lifting her spirits.

"Okay, well . . . I. . . ." Duke shrugged, standing behind her, shading his eyes to gaze out at the sea. "You sure you don't wanna join me in the water? Or . . . maybe later?"

"No, Duke. I don't think so."

"Okay, well, I'll see you 'round."

Camilla nodded, thinking how she wasn't going to waste another moment with Duke Lambert.

Heading down the path, she felt the soft sand crunch under her feet. The sun's warmth on her face. The sea breeze caressing her skin. The surf's crashing filling her soul with its music.

Yes, maybe a swim was just what she needed.

She just didn't need Duke, or any man, to join her in the water.

Leonora

The redwoods whispered to her, *He has a secret . . . he has a secret . . .* Leonora listened, wondering. What secret could Adam have? She had a feeling that it involved Camilla. But what could it be?

And was it any of her business?

Leonora strolled behind Adam and Camilla on the grassy path, the sun-dappled pebbles skittering under her feet. Snippets of the conversation ahead floated over to her: "Annabelle charms . . . her nature . . . cosmic urgencies abide to . . . Édouard, he plays. . . ."

She heard the words, vapors of sifting clouds, evoking colorful wisps of blue and fuchsia and emerald. Part of her wanted to catch up to them, join in their dialogue. But another part, the stronger part, kept her back, listening to the redwoods' whispering, *He has a secret, he has a secret . . .*

Maybe the whispering wasn't about Adam at all, she mused. Maybe the redwoods were whispering about another man . . . François?

Frowning, Leonora decided she didn't want to think about François's secrets. Not today. It was too lovely here, strolling down the woodsy path, the scent of the pines strong on the breeze, the comfort of having Adam close. And Camilla?

Leonora stared at the back of the slender woman, her dark

head leaning in toward Adam. Listening. Not to the redwoods, but to him.

"Leonora," Adam stopped, calling back to her. "I was just telling Camilla about your latest project."

Leonora nodded as she caught up to the pair. "Indeed?" she murmured.

"Yes," Camilla smiled shyly. "I, too, am fascinated by dreams and what they can tell us about ourselves, of course, but also how they can be a source of inspiration and. . . ." Her voice trailed off, unsure.

Leonora nodded, wondering how much Adam had divulged. Had he told Camilla about her latest dream? She'd been in an outdoor café. It had been crowded and warm, with masses of people vying to order coffees up at the bar. She'd tried, repeatedly, to order a coffee for Annabelle, but every time she thought the order was ready, something happened. The coffee spilled. Or the barista, who she thought was Adam, had forgotten her. Or someone else snagged the coffee away from her before she could pick it up. This went on and on and on, and she became more and more frustrated with her inability to procure a simple drink for Annabelle. Finally, she reached the bar for the umpteenth time, and Adam had smiled down at her. "I made a special pizza." He slid onto the counter a beautiful perfect pizza, with red sauce and yellow cheeses arranged in little circular ball designs. Over the top of the pizza was a translucent blue film, thin and exotic. "Do you know what that is?" he asked, pointing to the blue covering. "It is a blue gardenia. I sliced it very thin, and then layered it over the top of the pizza. Next, I baked the pizza, quickly, at a very high heat so as not to destroy it. Do you think that Annabelle would like a slice?" Leonora had nodded, transfixed by the pizza's blue beauty. "Yes, I'm sure she would." And then Adam had cut her a slice, handed it to her, and Leonora weaved back through the crowd to present the blue gardenia pizza slice to Annabelle, who had taken it with delight.

Leonora had the idea to paint the blue gardenia, its energy, its life-giving force and nourishment. She'd told Adam about this idea, but she had thought that it was a private conversation between the two of them. She wasn't sure what she thought about his sharing this intimacy with Camilla.

"It sounds like a marvelous dream, full of inspiration and energy," Camilla said now, her violet eyes gazing sincerely into Leonora's chocolate ones.

"Yes . . . well . . . it is just an idea at this point," she said, shading herself from the sun suddenly bursting through the redwoods.

"I look forward to seeing its manifestation," Adam said, taking Leonora gently by the elbow. "Do you think you'll have time to work on it soon?"

"That depends," Leonora said, still vaguely miffed at his . . . what? Betrayal? Did she believe that his sharing of her idea with Camilla was really so dramatic?

Part of her did. She wanted to keep her ideas to herself, or if she did share them with Adam, then she wanted him to keep them between the two of them. At least until she'd started the project.

Now, it seemed as if it were no longer hers. That Camilla had somehow absconded with it. This was nonsense, of course. Camilla, as an artist herself, was only interested in her art, too. Yet, it nagged at Leonora. This intimacy between herself and Adam seemed somehow shattered, or at least intruded upon by Camilla.

"Hey, hi, guys!" a bright, familiar voice rang out into the woods.

"Annabelle, Monarch!" Adam called back, releasing Leonora and striding into the open meadow. "What are the two of you doing out here?"

"Well, sir," Monarch cleared his throat, serious. "I was just showing Annabelle how the light, when it filters through the trees at this time of day, can create the perfect photographer's paradise."

"Indeed," Adam chuckled.

"Yeah, it's so cool!" Annabelle exclaimed.

"What are you photographing?" Camilla asked.

"If you come this way," Monarch nodded toward a sunny flowered grove several yards away. "I'll be more than happy to show you."

Leonora glanced over at Adam, who winked at her, his blue eyes crinkling in charming amusement as the group of them followed Monarch over to the grove. Leonora followed him, thinking how Monarch probably had more than photography on his mind as she caught a knowing glance from Camilla.

Camilla

Watching her daughter with Monarch, her sweet enthusiasm spilling into the meadow, Camilla couldn't help but think of another child. The one who never had a chance. The one she'd lost.

Duke's child.

She had been so scared, only a girl, and Duke? Well, he had predictably been no help at all. Yet, she'd wanted that child, which had taken them both by surprise, but then. . . .

Camilla felt the old feelings of loss and darkness knocking at her even in the golden warmth of this glorious day.

She'd lost the baby. It hadn't been more than a few months into the pregnancy, but she had been devastated. Her depression and sadness had overtaken her with such power that she couldn't function. Her family hadn't known what to do with her. In those days, there was little that could be done. The types of pharmaceuticals of today weren't in existence back then. So, they had had her committed. To a sanatorium in Santa Barbara. The Casa Tranquila. It had been anything but. Camilla shook her head ruefully as she gazed at Annabelle's sunny form bending down to examine some arrangement of pine needles.

"So, you see, sir," Monarch was saying, his voice grave and pompous, "if you examine nature closely, it presents a wealth of content to manipulate into one's artistic vision."

Adam chuckled, "Yes, I can see that. . . ."

Camilla tried to follow their gazes, tried to pull herself back out of the past. Yet, sometimes, when she looked at Annabelle, even with all the love she had for her daughter, she couldn't help but be reminded of the other daughter. The one she'd lost. The time she'd lost. The part of herself that would never recover.

Clara.

"Camilla?" Leonora interrupted her.

"Oh, yes?" she smiled, disoriented for a moment.

"What do you think of Monarch's idea?"

"I. . . ." Camilla felt a faint rush of blood to her head. "I think . . . I. . . ."

"Mom?" Annabelle rushed to her side. "Are you okay?"

"Yes, yes. . . ." Camilla murmured. "I just think I need to sit down. The heat . . . and I didn't eat much for lunch, I'm afraid."

Camilla felt a strong arm encircle her waist, easing her down into the grassy meadow, before a purple blackness swept over her consciousness, leading her down, down, down into the familiar abyss.

Leonora

"Papa?" Camilla murmured, trying to lift her head.

"No, please . . . rest, Camilla," Adam commanded tenderly.

Leonora's mind raced. Questions spilling out into the blue matter of her brain . . . if Camilla was Adam's daughter, then who was her mother? Pauline? But Leonora thought that Pauline hadn't had any children. Could she be misinformed? Was she remembering incorrectly? Or when she thought about it, maybe Adam hadn't said much to her about Pauline and their life together. So, perhaps it was possible that Camilla was Pauline's daughter.

Yet, Leonora thought not. She couldn't quite think why. It just seemed wrong. In any case, if Camilla were Adam's daughter, this made Annabelle his granddaughter. So, Annabelle would know who Camilla's mother was, right?

Could she possibly broach the subject with Annabelle?

Again a nagging feeling of intrusion filled Leonora. What business was it of hers? Did she need to know all of Adam's past?

Part of her longed to. Another part feared it.

Why?

Leonora felt the blue cells of her brain begin to strain. She had to let them rest for a moment. She knew that if she continued to question, she'd just overwhelm herself. Besides, there was the drama unfolding before her that demanded her attention.

"I'm okay," Camilla murmured. "I'm so sorry."

"Don't apologize," Adam said, stroking the top of her hand softly.

"But I. . . ."

Leonora felt Camilla's confusion, but also something stronger. It was as if Camilla weren't really present with them, here in the woods. It seemed as if she were far away. Someplace familiar, yet also a place that distressed her.

Leonora knew of this place. She tried to stuff it down, but it flooded her at times. Especially when with François. But also sometimes when she painted. Or more precisely, when she didn't or couldn't paint. She'd sit in her studio, the light filtering in perfectly. The blank canvas would be in front of her. She may have set up a still life to work from, but more often, she relied on her imagination. She'd set her paints out. She'd close her eyes. She'd see an image. Of the sea. The sky. The clouds. A figure. With a parasol. A triad of birds circling overhead.

But then when she took her brush in her hand, even after loading it with blues and grays, she'd pause. Hesitant. Confused. Afraid even? Of what?

She couldn't say. All she knew is that some days, she'd sit with this feeling for a time and then force herself to paint. But other days, she'd throw her brush down in frustration, tears puddling, spilling onto the canvas. She'd storm out of the studio. Angry at herself for her lack of productivity.

On the other hand, there was that euphoria of a painting begun. The first layer fills her with an excitement of anticipation and color: Prussian blues, lemon yellows, Payne's grays . . . The next layer astounds and delights. She leaves it, in process. Goes for a walk, the euphoria enveloping her in sweet ecstasy.

Leonora glanced up at the sky. A puffy cotton cloud dancing overhead before she was pulled back into this reality. A voice, flooded with worry, interrupting.

"Hey, Mom, you okay?" Annabelle was kneeling down next to her mother, holding her other hand.

"Yes, dear, I'm fine. Honestly, I just didn't eat much today and the sun and the. . . ."

"I think we need to get you back to the house," Adam said. "Can you sit up?"

"Yes, I think so. . . ." Camilla slowly sat up, shading her eyes from the sun with the back of her hand. "Oh, but I do feel a little woozy." She laughed softly.

"Here, let me. . . ." Monarch came forward, stretching out his young tanned hand.

"Thank you," Camilla said, placing her hand in his.

"No worries. I got you," Monarch said, as he gently but firmly helped Camilla to her feet, Adam on the other side of her, steadying Camilla with tender care.

"Can I be of some assistance?" Leonora finally asked.

"No, no, I think we've got her," Adam said. Leonora caught his eye; he was warning her. Of what? Didn't he want her here? Was she in the way of this family scene? Not a part of it? But Monarch wasn't part of their family. And here he was, leading Camilla slowly back down the path toward the house.

Annabelle hovered close to her mother, "It's okay, Mom. We'll get you home and then I'll make you a nice cup of tea and a snack, okay?"

"Yes, dear. That would be lovely," Camilla said.

Leonora followed behind the group, frowning slightly. Their conversation becoming further and further from her hearing, her sky-blue consciousness.

Camilla and Adam. Adam and Camilla. Father and daughter. Of course. . . .

"Hallo, Leo. Hungry?" François greeted her with a lazy grin, glass of Merlot in one hand, wooden spoon in the other, the smell of garlic, basil, and onion filling the air.

Leonora shook her head. "No, thank you. Not right now. I just need to sit for a moment."

Lifting an eyebrow, François grinned. "Glass of vino?"

"Yes, please, that would be nice."

Pouring her a glass, he handed it to her, then turned back to the kitchen, humming the theme to Beethoven's Sixth Symphony.

Leonora frowned slightly, taking a sip of wine, letting the rich red liquid rest in her mouth for a moment before swallowing.

"I had a day today," François called out over the sautéing.

Leonora took another sip of wine, letting his line hang in the air. She wasn't in the mood to chitchat, but then again, what was she in the mood for? It'd been a strange afternoon and it would take time for her to process its events.

"I was in the gallery, and guess who showed up?" François asked, sauntering into the living room to join her.

"I have no idea," Leonora responded halfheartedly.

"A woman who says she knows you."

"Indeed?"

"Yes, she says that you were childhood friends and that you are very wicked for losing touch with her."

"I can't imagine who it could be," Leonora murmured. Was he making up a story? Trying to engage her with fancy? He did sometimes partake of this strategy when she was distant. She glanced over at him. He seemed sincere, excited even.

"She said her name is Maxine and that you grew up together. Shared the same grand artistic ambitions."

"Maxine?" Leonora frowned. Maxine? Max? Could it be? But how? After all these years? "I'm afraid she must be mistaken. I don't know anyone named Maxine."

François's grin broadened, his eyes glinting golden in the late afternoon light. "That's funny. I wonder who she is if you don't know her. She certainly seemed to know you."

"Well, I hope you didn't tell her anything about me. I mean, she could just be some crazy off the street. You know how this town is."

François nodded. "Yes, perhaps. Could be. . . ." He ambled back over to the kitchen, lifting the lid off the vegetables, opening the oven to check on the salmon. "I think we're ready, Leo. How about some food? Maybe that will jog your memory."

Leonora rose, finishing the last of her wine. Maxine Morgen. Max. Maxi . . . Of course she remembered her. But damned if she was going to tell François about her. At least not tonight. What could Max be doing here in town? What could she possibly want?

Leonora remembered that Max had a sister, Samantha. Sam. Sammy. She smiled to herself at the memory. Yes, maybe this was the reason she was in town? To visit Samantha? Maybe Sam lived in Santa Cruz? And Leonora was just an afterthought?

Leonora sat down at the table as François served the food, poured her another glass of wine. She took a bite of the fish, tasting its lemony goodness. Food would help. And more wine, she thought, as visions of Max, dancing on top of her childhood bed, tossing pillows and stuffed animals to the ceiling, flitted inside her mind. Cascades of feathers floating down in a rain of chaos. Or the time they climbed over the next-door neighbor's heavy cement fence, sneaking into the yard one golden afternoon. Chickens in their pens clucked nervously. Winking at Leonora, Maxine had nodded toward the cages as Leonora followed. Max quickly danced around the cages, releasing the pent-up fowl. Then Mrs. Pullman hollering at them from inside the house, the screen door slamming as she strode out onto the porch. "What the hell you girls doin'? You git out of here right now! I'm gonna call your mothers." And Maxine had hooted and waved Leonora back over the fence. The two of them collapsing on the sticky green lawn in conspiratorial hilarity. Or the time they—

"Leo? Hallo? You in there?" François was waving his fork, a bite of salmon at its end, in front of her face.

Leonora shook herself, a small smile playing at the corner of her lips. "Yes? Of course . . . I. . . ."

"I think I caught you," he grinned.

"Caught me?"

"Ummmm . . . yup." François popped the salmon bite into his mouth.

"At what precisely?" Leonora asked, ruffled.

"You tell me." He reached for the wine, poured her another glass before helping himself.

"Honestly, I don't know what you're talking about."

"Okay. . . ." he nodded, taking a sip of wine. "Have it your way."

Leonora smiled, "I usually do."

He chuckled, scraping his plate with a crust of bread. "That you do, sweetheart, that you do."

Camilla

Camilla shifts in her sleep, the image of the canvas, white and clean, lying on the floor in front of her. She has two buckets of paint: one blue, one yellow. She begins to pour the yellow paint onto the canvas; it is thick and mustardy. Then she pours the blue on top of the yellow. The yellow must be dry now since the colors are separate, not blending into a grassy green. The blue lands as a thick blob in the corner of the yellow canvas. She stands back to survey her work. Then suddenly, a set of six legs begins to slowly grow out of the canvas. They look like the muscular, fit legs of athletes, toes pointed, each toenail donning blue polish, a complementary aqua to the blue blob on the canvas. The legs grow up and out and then stop after the knees, creating a strange leggy circle, like water ballerina legs popping out of the water, but instead they are poking out of the canvas.

She shifts in her sleep, sighing. "What do you think?" she asks Jarod. He walks around the canvas, stroking his goatee. "I like it. I think you should call it *Dance of the Princesses*."

"You do?" Camilla frowns, walks around the canvas. "I don't really see any princesses."

"For an artist, and an absurdist one at that, you certainly can be literal at times."

"I. . . ." Camilla felt herself begin to rise to consciousness, but not before the feeling of inadequacy envelops her. Why must Jarod always criticize her so? She should never show him her work. It only leads to heartache.

"Mama? Mama . . . ? Are you okay?"

Camilla felt herself being gently shaken.

Opening her eyes, she beheld her daughter, worry lining her pale face. "Clara?"

"Clara?" Annabelle frowned. "Who's Clara?"

Camilla tried to sit up, but her strength was still tied to the dream. "Oh, darling, no . . . I'm sorry, I was dreaming. Of course, Annabelle."

"Yeah. . . ." Annabelle sat on the bed, stroking her hand.

"Who is Clara?" Adam asked, looming over her.

"Oh . . . no one . . . I was dreaming. You know how dreams are."

Adam nodded, slowly. "Of course." He gazed down at her for a moment. "I think you are still feeling the effects of the afternoon's collapse. Lie back down. Do you fancy anything? Maybe something to eat?"

"No . . . no . . . not now." Camilla sank back into the softness of the pillows. "I think I just need to rest some more. If that is okay with you?" She glanced at her two cherished ones. How had she gotten to this place? What would happen next? Why had she called out Clara's name?

"I think we should let your mother rest," Adam said gently, taking Annabelle by the elbow and guiding her toward the door.

"Sure, sure. Just let us know if we can get you anything," Annabelle said, giving her mother one last worried glance.

Camilla watched as the two of them left the bedroom, closing the door behind them. A feeling of exhaustion overtook her as she closed her eyes, a vision of Jarod shaking his head at her, a glimmer of crimson encircling his face. And a child, running toward her, laughing joyously, tossing butterflies in the air. They flew up and out, oranges and yellows, filling her consciousness, before she drifted off to sleep.

Pauline

Pauline felt at peace. Floating in the soothing bath of lavender, sweet basil, and lemon that Serena had concocted for her, she closed her eyes. The hot rock that Serena had placed next to her warmed the water, embracing Pauline in a safe cocoon.

Last night had been strange. The ritual around the egg and its magic. Serena had told Pauline how the egg had healing powers—how it collects the bad vibrations. If Pauline would lie very still, she would feel the power of the egg. Pauline had done so. And Serena had held the egg above her, chanting a song, softly, in Spanish, as she gently waved the egg over Pauline's prone form. The headaches began to fade, their intensity diminishing as she lay there under Serena's ministrations.

Later, when Serena had put her to bed, placing the egg in a glass underneath the mattress, Pauline had drifted off into a deep, healing sleep. She dreamed of swimming in a blue-green sea, surrounded by violet dolphins and yellow fishes. Her swim was free and easy, like flying. There were no impediments to her stroke. She could swim like this forever.

When she woke this morning, Serena had drawn this bath for her, telling her how when she had cracked the egg into the glass that morning, the yolk had told the story. The healing had begun. Now,

Pauline must rest. She must submit to Serena's magic powers.

And today, floating in this heavenly bath, Pauline heard Remedios's voice: "You must follow the directions of Serena. You must not question. You will feel your body and your mind and your spirit heal and grow. But you cannot question. And if you do as Serena bids, you will feel a feeling that you have not felt before."

Remedios had paused, smiling at Pauline, slyly: "Peace. It is better than tequila!"

They had both laughed.

Now, Pauline knew that Remedios was right. Serena's magic was better than tequila.

But at the same time, she could feel that her stay here on Cerro San Miguel was limited. That this chance she had would be fleeting. She didn't know if this feeling was because of her illness or Serena's magic, but she knew that she had little time in this place.

She would write her novel. It would be filled with artists and writers and dreams and cats. Maybe she'd throw in a couple of elephants!

Pauline smiled to herself as she sank into the tub.

Yes, a novel. The time was now. She would write her story. . . .

Before it was too late . . .

Pauline rested under the shade of Serena's jacaranda tree, breathing in the crisp dazzle of the mountain air. It was dizzying. It was delicious. It was healing.

Where to begin? she thought. Staring at the notebook lying open in her lap, the blank page glared at her. Where did her story start? Adam, of course. It all started with Adam. The moment she first laid eyes on him at his lecture in New York City. The chills she felt up and down her spine, the butterflies fluttering in her soul. She had never heard anyone speak like he did. She had never seen anyone with such passion and presence.

She knew it was corny, but it had been love at first sight.

Yes, this is where her story would begin. That afternoon at the lecture. He was speaking of the surrealists. Today, looking back, she even remembered the exact line that captivated her from Breton's *Manifesto of Surrealism*: "*Put your trust in the inexhaustible nature of the murmur.*" [30] At the time, she had puzzled over its meaning. Adam had quoted Breton at length, speaking of the dream and the unconscious, the process of allowing the automatic thoughts to flow out of oneself and onto the page when writing. To not think. To not censor. To just write.

Didn't one have to think hard and long about what to put on the page? she had wondered at the time, just beginning to think of herself as a "writer." Yet, today, after Serena's treatment, Pauline felt refreshed, open, unresisting.

She glanced down at the blank page again, lifted her pen, and began to write:

"Put your trust in the inexhaustible nature of the murmur," Adam quoted, his voice strong, serious, lofty. Pauline listened, rapt as he continued. Yet . . . She couldn't focus on his words. She was stuck. On that line. What did it mean? How could a "murmur" be inexhaustible? Didn't it, by its very nature, fade away into the ether?

She shivered in the vast lecture hall, cold and intimidating. The room filled with intellectuals and artists. She sat in row three, clutching the worn wooden armrests, mesmerized by the man at the podium.

Adam. Adam Sinclair. Who was this man? Why had he singled her out? It was as if he were talking only to her, a lowly waitress, who knew nothing of such lofty philosophies as surrealism or psychology or the interpretation of dreams and the unconscious. . . .

And then what? Pauline paused; the thread lost. What's next? What was she going to write? Oh, damn it all! she cursed to herself. Writing was so hard! She had the idea and now . . . it was gone . . . floating off into some intangible space. . . .

She sighed under the jacaranda's lavender umbrella, a heavy fog enveloping her. Trying to fight it, she stared out into the golden light. Why couldn't she write today? Was it her illness? Or Serena's treatments? Or just the goddamn elusiveness of any act of creation?

A leaf crackled from behind her, light footsteps approaching: "Hola!" Remedios softly greeted her. "How do you feel today?"

Pauline glanced down at her half page of scrawl, frowning, "Oh, Remedios. I don't know. I am so frustrated! I have this idea. For my book. I have a beginning. I was writing. It was flowing and then *poof!* I stopped. It was as if an invisible wall rose up between my pen and the page. Do you know what I mean?"

Remedios nodded, thoughtful. "Of course, my friend. It is a common problem. It happens to me, too."

"It does?" Pauline leaned forward in her wicker chair.

"Sí. I am painting. The image is there on the canvas. I feel the power of the muse. She is guiding my hand, my shapes, my colors. I am in the moment of a great creation. And then. . . ." Remedios laughed softly. "I stop. I cannot put another mark on the canvas. I am paralyzed."

"Yes!" Pauline cried. "That is it exactly. One moment you are writing, you are painting, and the next moment, you cannot. The words do not come. They are in your brain, buried somewhere in that gray mass, but when you try to squeeze them out, the gray mass refuses to cooperate."

Remedios nodded, thoughtful.

"And it happens so suddenly. This block. This void," Pauline continued. "And it sounds like it does happen to you, too. But . . . why, Remedios? And then how to get the words back onto the page? To get that flow of language to move out of your gray matter, articulated into language and then a structure? Breton, in his *Manifesto*, describes 'automatic writing' as not letting the brain have too much power. To just write and not worry about what comes out. But I find this completely impossible!" Pauline exclaimed. "At least today."

Remedios laughed softly. "Oh, my friend, you are too serious. I think that Breton is right. If you can let go and write, then the words will come."

"But I can't!" Pauline cried, tears threatening. Why was she so frustrated? Why was everything so hard?

Feeling a tender touch on her shoulder, Pauline turned toward Remedios, trying to force a smile. "I'm sorry. I'm just tired."

"Yes, of course you are. Perhaps today is not the best day to work on this project more than you have."

Pauline saw her glance down at the half page she'd written. Remedios continued. "I see that you have done some writing, sí? This is a good thing. Perhaps just let it rest for now. We can take a short walk."

Closing her notebook, Pauline nodded. Yes, a walk might help. At least it would get her up and out of this chair.

Rising, Pauline stood for a moment and stretched. Reaching for the lavender, she breathed in the jacaranda's life.

"I have some news," Remedios began as they started to walk.

"News?" Pauline fell into step with her friend.

"Yes, it's about Adam."

"I'm not sure that I'm in the mood today," Pauline said, shivering slightly in spite of the heat.

"Yes, I understand," Remedios continued. "But I think that this is something you will want to know."

"Very well," Pauline sighed, thinking again of her thwarted writing. And how Adam seemed to be a part of her frustration. Yet, oh how she missed him, too. Why was she so conflicted about him? Was this push and pull going to haunt her always? Were these polarities surrounding Adam always going to be part of her existence here at Cerro San Miguel?

"He wants very much to come to visit you," Remedios began, looping her arm through Pauline's.

"I don't think I can see him now. . . ." Pauline murmured, feeling a sudden exhaustion overtake her. "I think I need to return to my room," she said. "I'm feeling a bit lightheaded."

"But of course," Remedios said, worry lacing her voice.

Pauline leaned on her friend, feeling her strength and compassion as she slowly made her way back to Serena's magical sanctuary, thinking of Adam, thinking of her writing, thinking, thinking, thinking. Perhaps Breton and Remedios were right. She thought too much!

Feeling the fog descend upon her, Pauline clutched Remedios's arm for support. Yet even as she began to fall, she thought of her writing. She would describe this fog. This illness. This place.

Yes, that's what she would write. When the fog lifted. That's what she would write.

25

Mimi

HOLLYWOOD, CALIF., 1944

"He must be stopped! I cannot have him intruding upon my life in such a violent fashion! You must do something, Édouard!" Mimi took a long drag from her cigarette, tapping her little foot in frustration as she held the phone to her ear. "Yes, I understand that, but can't your family watch her for a few days? No? Why not? What else are they doing? Don't they just play tennis and sip martinis by the pool? . . . Please don't call me that anymore. I am Valentina! Mimi. She is dead. Gone. Buried. She is no more. I am a star. I will grant you that the paparazzi and the papers, they do love a good story. But my art! I cannot have Adam intruding upon my work. You should have seen him, Édouard! He was an animal! A beast! Who knew that he had such. . . ." Mimi paused, taking another drag of her cigarette, gazing out her sliding-glass door at the shimmering pool for a moment. A little smile crept over her face. Of course, she knew that Adam was a passionate man. Hadn't she been the seductive recipient of his advances? And, yes, it had been long ago, yet Mimi felt a shiver of pleasure rise up through her at the memory.

But now! This relentless quest to get Camilla back. It had to stop. And since Édouard had her, well, then, couldn't he help? Didn't he have any ideas? She crushed her cigarette out in the heavy aqua glass ashtray.

The man was useless!

She nodded into the phone. "I understand, Édouard. Yes . . . very well . . . I just thought, mistakenly it seems, that you might have an idea of how to stop him. I cannot go on like this . . . very well, put her on . . . Hello, ma chérie. How is my pet today?" Mimi glowed for a moment at the sound of her daughter's bright voice on the other end of the line. Telling her about an art project she had just finished in school. Something to do with sand and shells and paint and music. "That sounds divine, my pet . . . yes, save it for me. I do want to see it so. . . ."

Mimi lit another cigarette, inhaling deeply. The purple cloud of resignation drifted up into the high-beamed ceiling, floating ominously as she held the phone to her ear. "Listen, my pet, can you put your father back on the phone, please? Yes . . . yes . . . Mama will visit soon. I promise . . . bye-bye, my pet. . . ." Mimi shivered under the purple cloud, a sudden chill overtaking her. "Are you positive that you can do nothing? Or is it that you refuse? . . . Very well. I only thought that perhaps . . . yes . . . okay . . . you enjoy your day . . . I must go to work now. . . ."

Mimi hung up the phone, sighing deeply, a vision of sand castles and golden paint dancing before her for a moment. Camilla . . . she did miss her so. But what could she do? She had her career to focus on. She had no time for her daughter. Or her ex-lover, passionate as he was. He must be stopped. But how?

"I couldn't help but overhear. . . ." a familiar voice rang out behind her.

Turning, Mimi felt a mixture of fire and fog rise in her. "How did you get in here?"

"It was easy," Genevieve replied. "You left the front door open. You shouldn't be so careless, Mimi. You never know who might wander in."

"I told you that I never wanted to see you again. And please, do not call me that. I am. . . ."

"Valentina?" Genevieve laughed, a sparkling catlike growl.

"Yes, I know. I read about your little incident in the papers. Is that what you were on the phone to your 'husband' about?"

"Not that it is any of your business, but yes. . . ."

"I have an idea." Genevieve sauntered into the sunny living room, reaching for a cigarette from the pack of Camels lying on the glass table.

Mimi glared at her.

"Do you have a light?" Genevieve purred. She leaned toward Mimi, the cigarette dangling seductively from her full lips.

Sighing, Mimi reached for her purse, fumbling for a moment in its cavernous contents for the lighter before finding it. Flicking it for Genevieve, she lit the cigarette.

"Ah . . . merci. . . ." Genevieve took a long drag, then sat down on the divan, crossing her long, lean legs. "Do you want to hear my plan?" she grinned.

"Very well," Mimi answered, knowing that if nothing else, Genevieve was resourceful. Sitting down on the chair across from her, Mimi lit another cigarette for herself. Took a quick puff, and then gazed at Genevieve serenely. "But I haven't much time. I'm due at the studio in forty-five minutes."

Genevieve's feline eyes sparkled, "Oh, it won't take that long to explain. I know you are a very busy woman. A 'star,' as you say."

"Yes." Mimi felt the purple cloud above her begin to turn a menacing crimson.

"First," Genevieve began, uncrossing and crossing her legs, "we need to. . . ."

Mimi leaned forward in her chair, riveted, as Genevieve began to detail her plan to purge Adam from her life. It was preposterous. It was dangerous.

Yet . . . Mimi thought, it might just work. It might just work. . . .

"Hello?" Mimi paused, dramatically, allowing a soft sniffle to echo into the receiver. "This is Valentina. I need"—she paused again, wiping an imaginary tear from her cheek—"to please speak with Adam immediately." She glanced over at Genevieve, who stood behind the kitchen bar, exhaling cigarette smoke that floated above her in lazy circles. "What do you mean he is not there? Who is this? Ah, Monsieur Breton, of course, yes . . . Mimi . . . yes, Valentina is my stage name. You understand, oui?" Another not-so-subtle sniffle rang out into the air. Mimi glanced over at Genevieve, who winked wickedly, giving her a thumb's up before taking another drag from her cigarette.

"No, no . . . no message. I must speak to Adam . . . no, I do not understand. What elephant in the room, monsieur? I am sure you are mistaken. This is not the case . . . Do you know when Adam will return? . . . I see . . . Can you not go to his studio to retrieve him? Oui, I understand that he is working, but it is imperative that I speak with him as soon as possible. . . ." Mimi let out a gasping breathy sob. "No, no . . . I am fine, monsieur. Well, no, in fact I am not. This is why I need to speak with Adam . . . What is it about? Oh. . . ." Here, Mimi allowed a true sob to overtake her. "It is about my daughter. Our daughter, Camilla . . . no . . . no, I cannot tell you, monsieur, just do please tell Adam to call me immediately . . . Oh, could you? That would be divine, monsieur. Oui, the sooner you can get him to call me, the better it will be. . . ." Mimi took out a handkerchief, blew her nose into it with sobbing drama. "Merci, monsieur. I am so sorry . . . I cannot speak any longer . . . I . . . I must go now . . . Au revoir. . . ."

A loud clapping began from across the room as Genevieve stepped from behind the kitchen bar. "Brava! That was a fine warm-up, my love. An Academy Award is in your future."

"I wish that I had spoken to Adam and not Breton." Mimi frowned, rising from the emerald divan and stomping over to the sliding-glass door. A pale moon rose in the hazy sky. A hummingbird buzzed around frantically in the pink hibiscus, hovering for a moment in mid-flight, before zooming across the pool.

"It is a good practice," Genevieve said, sauntering over to join her. "I think you had just the right touch of tragedy and restraint, especially for a relative stranger. Now, you must dive more deeply into your acting skills. You must bring out all of your grief and anguish when you speak with Adam. Did Breton say when Adam would call you back?"

"No, he did not. He only said that Adam was in his studio. That he had asked not to be disturbed. That his work was not to be interrupted. His work!" Mimi scoffed, turning to face Genevieve. "Can you believe that he forgets us so easily? That he can simply go back to his work?"

Tossing back her pretty curls, Genevieve laughed with abandon. "Oh, ma chérie! You told him that he had no chance of reclaiming his daughter. That you had no idea where she was. That he may as well forget her. What did you expect?"

Pouting, Mimi reached for the pack of cigarettes, shaking one out. Holding it in her lush lips, she leaned toward Genevieve, who lit it for her, gleefully. "I expected that we would matter more to him. That he would be so bereft that his 'work' would no longer be possible. That he would mourn his daughter and search for her till the end of his days."

"Oh, Mimi!" Genevieve reached over to push a stray curl from Mimi's eyes. "You are just too romantic for your own good. You must harden yourself for the next phone call. Or. . . ." Genevieve paused for a moment, gazing into Mimi's distraught eyes. "Perhaps this is a good thing. This feeling of anger and frustration at what you perceive to be Adam's abandonment of you and your daughter. This could be emotion to channel into your next performance, n'est-ce pas?"

"I suppose." Mimi sighed her purple cloud, plopping back down on the divan as she took a long drag of her cigarette.

She stared at the phone. "Why does it not ring!" she cried.

"Why does he not call me back! I will not stand for this treatment! I will call him again. Now!"

Mimi picked up the phone, beginning to dial. Lunging toward
her, Genevieve grabbed the receiver out of her hand. Pushing her
back into the soft cushions, she placed the receiver back on its
stand.

Leaning over Mimi for a moment longer than necessary,
Genevieve began to laugh. "Oh, Mimi. You are so funny. You must
wait. He will call. Trust me. Breton was convinced, I am sure, by your
performance. It is only a matter of time. Have patience, my darling."

Mimi glared at her, took a long drag off her cigarette, crossed
her slender legs. "I am hungry."

"But of course, a snack. Let me see what we have."

"I want smoked salmon sliced on sourdough, white wine, it
must be Château de Puisserguier, Saint-Chinian blanc, and. . . ."

Genevieve rose and headed into the kitchen, her laughter
filling the room. Mimi turned back toward the phone and gently
lifted the receiver. Starting to dial Adam's number, her hands
trembled slightly. Would he believe her? Could she convince
him?

Mimi finished dialing, listened to the faint ringing on the
other side of the line. His voice floated across the line, strong,
impatient?

"Adam . . . ? Is that you? . . . Yes, it is"—she started to say Mimi,
but then changed her mind—"Valentina . . . Yes, I know you think
me frivolous for this name but it is who I am now. But that is not
why I called . . . to argue about such things . . . I have some
news. . . ." And here she sniffled loudly, wiping a real tear from her
eyes. "Terrible news . . . tragic news . . . I . . . oh, Adam . . . it is
Camilla . . . she. . . ." Mimi began to cry in earnest, pulling up from
the depths of her being the grief that puddled inside her. She cried
into the receiver for a moment, letting the tears fall into the ear
piece. "There has been an accident. A horrible accident . . . and
our Camilla . . . oh, Adam. . . ." Mimi broke down now, crying as

she handed the phone over to Genevieve, who had placed the tray of salmon snacks on the coffee table before her.

"Adam? Yes, Genevieve here . . . no, Mimi can't talk now. She is too upset . . . yes, I know . . . but she is completely incapacitated . . . No, she can't come back to the phone . . . I am so sorry, but there has been a terrible accident. . . ."

Mimi wiped her eyes, reached for a snack, bit into it, chewing thoughtfully, while she listened to Geneveive say, "I hate to tell you this, but Camilla is dead . . . no, I don't know the details . . . yes, of course. . . ."

Mimi let out an ear-piercing mournful wail, filling the room with its reverberations. "Yes, that is Mimi. I must go to her now . . . she is in shock. You can understand . . . yes . . . of course, I will call you with the details . . . but I don't think that they plan to hold any kind of service . . . the body. . . ."

Mimi raised her face to the ceiling, inhaled deeply, then opened her mouth wide and screamed, her grief and rage rising to fill the room.

"I must go, Adam. I am so sorry . . . goodbye. . . ."

Genevieve hung up the phone, glancing over at Mimi, who handed her a glass of wine, raising her own toward her.

"To our performance." Mimi giggled, sipping the wine.

"Oui, our performance. C'est magnifique!" Genevieve drank, her green eyes glimmering.

"Do you think he bought it?" Mimi asked, taking another salmon snack.

Genevieve grabbed a snack for herself, taking a hearty bite. "Oui, how could he not, ma chérie? You were truly an artist. You are a great actress. He will trouble us no more. . . ."

Laughing gaily, Mimi flopped back on the couch, her eyes sparkling. "Come here, my love. Let me thank you."

Genevieve sat down beside her, playing coy, but not very well. Mimi knew she would accept her gratitude.

Mimi began to kiss Genevieve passionately, hungrily, feeling a sudden surge of power. She pictured herself on the stage, the lights flashing, the crowd applauding. Her gown would be resplendent, low-cut, black, and sparkling. She would smile, magnificently, but demurely, accepting the golden statue in her hands for a moment, feeling the weight of it. Taking a deep breath, she would gaze out at the audience for moment, drinking in its adoration. "First, ladies and gentlemen, I would like to thank the Academy for. . . ."

Adam

HACIENDA DEL ARTISTA, MEXICO, 1944

Grabbing the can of midnight black, Adam stood for a moment gazing down at the blank canvas, holding the paint aloft. It felt surprisingly light, as if the can contained no liquid at all. He took a deep breath. Inhale . . . Exhale . . . Slowly . . . And then, swinging the can back behind himself, he tossed the paint up and into the air. It swirled away from him, black globs and dots and lines. He watched, detached, as the paint landed on the canvas, spreading into a cosmos of midnight luster, the white of the canvas creating an eerie luminosity in contrast.

"Damn her to bloody hell," he seethed aloud, letting the paint journey up and down, back and forth across the canvas. He saw a comet, black as the devil. He saw a tree, struck by lightning. He saw a sliver of a moon appear over a tree, bending and twisting in the night.

Adam glanced at the paints lining the studio floor: crimson, lemon, tangerine, avocado. Turning back toward the moving black of the canvas, he stood still for a moment, watching, then backed up and away, squinting.

Did it need the crimson? Mimi's color? "Damn her," he muttered again. "Does she think I am a bloody fool? That I would believe such a tale?" he cried out into the studio, his voice echoing up and into the cool cement walls.

Adam glared at the can of crimson paint, willing it to do what? Lift itself up? Heave itself onto the canvas? Take Mimi's inane spirit and hurl it into the cosmic midnight?

Leaning back against his worktable, Adam sighed, frowning as he turned on the radio. Schubert's Fourth Symphony in C minor, the *Tragic Symphony*. Grinning ruefully, he turned up the music, sinking into the strident sawing of the violins tugging at his heart.

Camilla could not be dead. He would feel it. Mimi, along with that vixen, Genevieve, had concocted the entire charade. Granted, it had been quite a performance. Yet Mimi had always been a third-rate actress, not that that didn't have its appeal. But he knew that the story was full of holes. When he had asked about the details around the accident, none could be given. When he asked about the funeral service, Genevieve had given some nonsense about the viability of the body.

As if he would believe anything that Mimi or Genevieve told him! He had his men out looking for Camilla, and they had traced her to some ranch in Santa Barbara. He would find out the exact location. He would go to Camilla. He would not allow Mimi to keep his daughter from him. . . .

"Bonjour, mon ami!" Breton hailed him from the entryway of the studio.

Adam waved him in, turning down Schubert.

Sauntering into the room, Breton paused in front of the black and white canvas. "Oh, mon ami, whatever is the matter? This"—Breton clucked his tongue—"it does look to be a tragedy of the grandest kind, n'est-ce pas?"

"You might say that." Adam shook his head, began to circle slowly around the canvas. "Do you think it needs something else?" he asked.

"I would say so, mon ami," Breton answered. "A work in progress, oui?"

"I suppose," Adam said, stopping to gaze at a thread of black dripping like a fine web on the corner of the canvas.

Adam glanced over at his friend, who was walking around the canvas in the opposite direction from him. "I see here a symptom of the anguish. A cosmic unfolding of the cloud. A tsunami of inquisition. A simmering of despair. Tell me, mon ami, what has inspired such a passion?"

"Mimi."

"Ah." Breton continued to walk slowly around the canvas. "I did speak with her earlier. She did sound most distraught. What is the problem?"

"The problem," Adam sighed, "is that she's a bloody idiot!"

Breton threw back his head, chuckling joyously into the cavernous chamber. "Ah, Adam, you simplify. She is clever. In her way. And if I am not mistaken, she is plotting a scheme against you?"

"How did you know that?"

Breton shrugged, "I had a vision as I spoke to her. The vision was one of an immense purple cloud, its vapor oozing out of a kangaroo's pouch. And as Mimi spoke to me, asking me to please find you, to bring you to the phone, I saw this kangaroo leap up and into the cloud, its hind legs enormous, thumping up into the azure sky. It disappeared from my view for a moment, until it came tumbling down from the sky and landed directly in my view. It stared at me with its animal eyes, and then it spoke, 'She lies. She lies. She lies . . .' Naturally, I thought nothing of this vision at the time other than a figment of the surreal that is always with me, but now that I hear that Mimi has upset you, well, I can only say, mon ami, the kangaroo knows. The kangaroo knows."

Adam stared at Breton for a moment, letting the story of the vision sink in, before letting out a tremendous laugh. "She does lie! She told me that Camilla was dead. That there had been some sort of accident, but I would know if my daughter had died."

"But of course, you would! Mimi is fantastical! To think that she could tell you such a fabrication. Why, it is the height of the absurd!"

"Exactly. I can feel where Camilla is. I see the turquoise sea, steep mountains, golden sky. My men have almost located her. She's somewhere in Santa Barbara, California."

"Ah! C'est magnifique! You must go to her!" Breton cried,

shaking his mop of hair in wild animation. "Now! Today! I will drive you in my automobile! We shall have a journey. It will be most fruitful. We will find Camilla and we will bring her here to safety! And Mimi? What do you propose to do with her, mon ami?"

Adam sighed, gazing down at the crimson can of paint. "I haven't decided yet," he answered, heaving the can up and holding it for a moment, before tossing it up into the air and watching it fall in bloody fragments onto the midnight scene that lay before him.

Breton clapped his hands, loudly, joyfully. "Ah! That is what it needed! The blood of the duplicitous woman lies in our path. Come, mon ami, let us leave this place for now. Leave this art for now. I hear the kangaroo, thumping its tangerine tail, calling us to 'hit the road' to find your sweet, sweet daughter."

Taking one last look at the canvas, Adam watched as the red intertwined with the black, shocking against the white, creating a fiendish web.

He would find Camilla. He would bring her back. And he would take care of Mimi.

He only wished that he had his wife, Pauline, by his side. To share his frustration, anger, and turmoil. She would know what to do with Mimi. Though if he thought about it, Mimi was a sensitive subject for Pauline. He wondered sometimes if this is why she had left him. That her "illness," though manifesting in real symptoms, was not somehow a byproduct of his distant lover. And their child. Oh, Pauline . . . where have you gone? Why have you left me? I need you . . . I miss you. Will you ever come back to me? he cried to himself, a vision of turquoise stars rising before him.

"We are off!" Breton cried.

Taking one last look at his canvas, Adam saw a glimmer of gold peeking out from under the black and crimson web.

Camilla. She was alive. She was waiting for him. He would

find her. And then, he wasn't sure, but he trusted something larger. A force that would guide him.

Adam turned, closing the studio door behind himself, breathing in the crisp violet air as he fell into step next to Breton.

Leonora

She is outside, in the bright sunshine, by a blue, blue bay, on a green grassy knoll, watching as dozens of powerboats with loads of tourists take off across the water. Leonora unfurls a large red banner, another friend, a woman, holds the other end. The woman is familiar, but she can't quite grab on to her identity. Yet, Leonora knows that this woman is someone she can rely on. Someone she knows. Someone from her past?

On the banner is a huge fierce lion, his mane circling his majestic head in feline glory. Leonora and her friend are protesting this intrusion upon the bay by these powerboats, these loads of tourists. The huge lion banner will scare them away. He is fierce. He is ferocious. He will prevail!

Leonora glances up into the sky. She sees vibrant-colored flying circles: yellow, blue, green, purple, red. The flying circles are the size of paper plates and they twirl and swirl up in the aqua sky and then float down toward her, spinning and buzzing. They land on the top of a worn wooden fence, balancing on its top, spreading their paper plate wings. When they face her, she sees that each paper plate contains a tiny person who stands in the center of the plate, holding it open. The tiny person is attached to the paper plate and is the same color as the plate. The red plate contains a miniature red person encircled by the paper plate wings; the yellow plate contains a tiny yellow person encircled by the paper plate wings, and so on.

Leonora is delighted and amazed by the colorful paper plate-flying people. She wonders if they are reinforcements to help protest the tourists. If the lion has somehow summoned them from the heavens with some sort of magical powerful pull. . . .

"Leo? Oh, Leooooonooora?" François's voice rang into her consciousness. She struggled to stay in the dream. To try to reach the flying plate people, but a sudden hearty shaking took her away.

"Leo, wake up." François was sitting on the bed, his weight shifting her toward him.

"Who are you?" she muttered.

François chuckled. "Oh, that's a good one, luv. You want to play that game, do you?"

Leonora opened her eyes, trying to focus on what was going on around her. Fluorescent outlines of the plate people danced before her as she slowly sat up.

"What is it?" she asked now, pushing the plate people from her too-present reality.

"Oh, are we a little grumpy?" he teased.

"No, no, I'm fine. You just woke me up in the middle of a dream and. . . ." She paused. Should she tell François about the flying plate people and the protesting lion? And the friend? Who was she? Leonora frowned as she swung her long legs over the side of the bed.

"A dream, eh?" François grinned at her. "You know, luv, your dreams scare me sometimes. But they thrill me, too. It's a fine line with you and your subconscious."

He laughed. Heartily.

"I'm glad you find my dreams so"—Leonora struggled for a suitably insulting adjective—"illuminating."

He laughed again, this time slapping his thigh in mock appreciation. "Yes, Leo. That's it, 'illuminating.' But we can speak about all this later. The reason I woke you out of your always-fascinating dream life is because you have a phone call."

"I didn't hear the phone ring," she murmured.

"No, of course not. You were . . . well . . . wherever you were. But you're here now, right, aren't you, luv? Your friend Maxine is on the line."

"Maxine?" Leonora shook her head. Maxine? What was he talking about? She didn't know anyone named Maxine. Unless . . . yes, that's right. He had mentioned that her childhood friend was in town and had wanted to see her. Yet, how had Max gotten her number? And what did she want?

"I hope you don't mind that I gave her our number, sweetheart." François rose, arching his back.

"Actually, I do. I wish you had asked me first."

François shrugged. "Sorry. Too late now. She's waiting. Or maybe she's hung up by now."

Leonora felt like snarling at him, like channeling the fierce lion of her dream. Standing, she stalked past him into the other room, her bare feet softly padding on the hardwood floor. Picking up the receiver, she felt a tingling nervousness in her hands. "Hello, this is Leonora . . . Maxine? Maxine Morgen? My, it has been a long time. It is good to hear from you . . . no, no . . . I can't right now."

Leonora glanced over at François, who had followed her. He raised a golden eyebrow in her direction, his eyes glinting in unabashed intrusiveness.

"Yes . . . I understand." Leonora tried to wave François away, but he just grinned, sitting down on one of the barstools next to the counter where the phone was.

"Very well . . . yes, I think that will work. I have to check my schedule . . . I will call you back . . . yes . . . yes . . . I will, Maxine . . . I promise . . . yes . . . you, too . . . okay . . . goodbye."

"Now that sounded intriguing!" François swirled mischievously on the barstool. "Care to share?"

"No, I don't." Leonora stared at the phone for a moment, wondering if it would fly away. Maybe the paper plate people would swoop down, scoop it up, and whisk it away into the heavens. The Red Lion would roar, chasing the phone up and out into the ether. And her friend, the one who . . . Damn . . . Leonora felt herself sway, a slight dizziness overtaking her. The friend. In her dream. Maxine. That's who she was.

Why was she dreaming about Maxine? What was Maxine trying to tell her? Or show her? Obviously, at least in the dream, Maxine was an ally. Someone to help her. Yet, Leonora felt a fluttering in her belly, then shuddered slightly. "I think I'll go for a walk," she announced.

"I can't make you a cup of tea?" François asked. "Or maybe you need something a little stronger?" He glanced at his watch. "It is almost cocktail time."

"No . . . no, I just need some air."

"I can come with you?"

"No, I need to be by myself," she said. Slipping on her boots, she grabbed a sweater off a hook and opened the door, breathing in the sumptuous afternoon of pine and sunlight. Already she felt better. Yes, a walk in nature always helped clear her head. Bring her back to reality. Keep her grounded. She closed the door behind her, shutting out the echo of François's laughter.

Leonora began to walk briskly, the pine needles crunching under her feet, the sunlight warming the back of her head.

"Leonora?"

She turned, startled for a moment. "Oh, Adam . . . I. . . ."

"I apologize for the intrusion," he said.

"No, no . . . it's fine. I just didn't hear you. I—"

"Do you mind if I walk with you?"

"No, no, of course not," she murmured. Adam was always welcome to join her. No matter what her state.

"Are you certain?" he asked. "You seem a bit—"

"Oh, I'm fine, just fine." She tried to smile, but felt a grimace rise instead. "I just was rudely woken up from a nap in the middle of a dream and. . . ." Her voice trailed off.

"Ah, indeed," he nodded. "I understand perfectly. Do you want to tell me about your dream?"

Leonora grinned, slowly. "Yes . . . yes, I do," she began as a blue jay screeched in the boughs above them. Glancing up toward the sound of the squawking, Leonora caught a glimpse of bright color: bright saucers of red, yellow, blue, and green spun and swizzled in the pale sky.

Her voice quiet, she began, "I was on a green grassy knoll and. . . ."

"That François of yours," Maxine sipped her chardonnay, pausing dramatically for a moment, "is quite a dashing cad, isn't he?"

Leonora bristled. How dare she! Maxine better keep her claws out of her husband! It was for precisely this reason, well, not François specifically, but Sergei . . . Leonora felt an overwhelming longing drape over her at just the thought of him . . . his eyes, his hair, his arms. . . .

Maxine had "stolen" him from her all those years ago. This is precisely why they'd been estranged all this time. They'd both been students at the Sorbonne, becoming best friends and bonding over art, music, and dreams. Maxine had been a childhood friend, a naughty one at that, she mused ruefully, but they had lost touch. Then one day, walking in the autumn light, Leonora had heard a familiar voice. "Hey, Leo! Wait up!" Turning, she'd found Max skipping toward her. It had been surreal to say the least. But they had reconnected, sharing everything, until, one night. . . .

Leonora shivered. She couldn't go there right now. The "incident" was still too traumatizing.

And so . . . now, here she was, sitting across the table from Maxine, sipping wine in the golden light on the patio of the Crêpe Place.

What the hell did Maxine want from her now?

"François? A cad?" Leonora now murmured. "I suppose so."

"Yet, I would imagine that's part of his appeal, n'est-ce pas?"

"What did you want to see me about?" Leonora ignored the bait. She wasn't going to dredge up their mutual attractions to the same "type" of men.

"I. . . ." Maxine began, suddenly shy? Leonora had never known her to express any sort of timidity. And there was a part of her that liked this. Maybe she had the upper hand in this scenario. Yet, again, why had Maxine contacted her?

Leonora sipped her own wine, not helping Maxine in the least. Let her explain herself for once, she thought.

"Well . . . I'm not sure if I'm being too presumptuous, or. . . ." Maxine's voice trailed off.

Leonora resisted laughing sardonically, but nodded imperceptibly instead. "I can't say unless you tell me why you're here," she said.

"Yes, well . . . I know, I mean, I've read some of your articles about dreams and—"

"Really?" Leonora took a sip of her wine. She had never pegged Max for a reader, especially one of academic journals or papers.

"Yes, well, it's a long story."

"I'm listening."

"No, really, it's boring how I came to know about your work, Leo, but the reason that I needed to talk to you is of the utmost urgency."

Leonora raised a dark brow. "Indeed?"

"Yes . . . well, maybe I should just tell you about the dream. . . ."

"You had a dream that I should know about?" Leonora asked, wondering if it had to do with stealing boyfriends.

"Yes, well, it's not about you, if that's what you're thinking."

"I'm not thinking anything yet," Leonora lied. "Go on, tell me about your dream."

"Well," Maxine sighed deeply, taking another hearty sip of her wine, "the dream seemed to be some kind of warning. Some sort of prophecy. And I know from your work that this is something that interests you, am I right?"

"Yes." Leonora's heart quickened in spite of her reticence around the source.

"Anyway, I had this dream. It was one of those—oh, how do you describe it? One of those apocalyptic dreams?"

"The world was ending?"

"Yes, yes, that's it exactly!" Maxine cried, glancing around the patio to see if anyone had noticed her excitement. The hippie clientele was deep into their crêpes and chai, not paying her a bit of mind.

"Okay, and so what happened to end the world?" Leonora asked.

"Well . . . maybe this is all quite common, but it was distressing to me. I was at some seaside house or resort or place with my family and this enormous tsunami rose up from the sea out of nowhere, entirely covering the beach and the house in water and sweeping away my whole family! Even my cat!"

Leonora smiled, nodding. She felt almost glad that Maxine had lost her cat. "That sounds terrible," she murmured.

"Yes! Yes, Leo, it was! It was terrible! For some reason, I was spared, but I had to run very quickly away from the rising waters or I would have been swept away, too. So, I ran up a hill to try to get to safety and did take shelter in a structure, some sort of bombed-out house with the roof open to the sky, and when I looked up, I saw this menacing orange cloud of poisonous gas filling the heavens and descending onto the earth. People were suffocating under this cloud. That's how I knew it was poisonous, and I knew that if I didn't get away from it, I'd suffocate too. Oh, Leo, it was just terrible. . . ."

Maxine paused for a moment, wiping a tear from the corner of her eye. "Anyway, I thought, what if this dream portends the end of the world? Shouldn't I tell someone? And then I thought of you and your work with dreams and. . . ."

"I'm no psychologist," Leonora said, "but it sounds to me like maybe you're going through some sort of crisis in your own life. That this 'apocalypse' you're describing is simply a symptom of your subconscious manifesting the turmoil in your life. Are you having any issues presently?"

Maxine nodded. "Yes . . . yes, I am, Leonora. I don't know if you remember that I married Sergei?"

Leonora felt her fingers tighten around the stem of her wineglass. "Yes, of course."

"Yes, well. . . ." Maxine sniffled. "We divorced . . . he left me for a younger model." Maxine smiled bitterly, running her fingers through her dark tresses.

Leonora couldn't help but feel a spasm of glee. Served her right! But did this mean that she would go after François? Damn!

"I'm sorry to hear that," Leonora said now, trying to keep the smug you-deserved-this-and-more thoughts out of her tone.

"Yeah, well, I will always regret losing our friendship over him," Max sighed. "Especially since well . . . you know. . . ."

"No, I don't."

"He always loved you more. I could tell. Even after we were married, when we made love. . . ."

Leonora gave her an icy stare. But Maxine continued, oblivious. "I could tell, he was thinking of you. He wasn't really into me. And so . . . I suppose it was inevitable that we would break up, you know?"

Nodding, Leonora restrained herself. It wasn't her style to gloat, but today, it was hard to keep it inside. She took the higher ground though, going back to the dream. "Yes, well, I suppose this may be why you had the dream. Why the poisonous orange cloud was trying to destroy not only the world, but you, too."

"Oh, Leo!" Maxine gushed, tears now streaming down her cheeks. "I miss you so! Can you ever forgive me?"

Leonora softened. Why not? It had been a long time. And Sergei was in her past. It wasn't just Maxine who had betrayed her. He had, too. Maybe more so. "Of course," she said.

"Really?" Maxine cried, wiping her cheeks. "You don't know how much that means to me! I've been living with this guilt for all these years and. . . ."

"Hello, ladies!" François hailed them as he strode across the courtyard.

"Oh, dear!" Maxine retrieved a tissue hurriedly from her purse. "I can't let him see me like this!"

Leonora frowned, an uncontrollable seething filling her. Maxine better not try anything, she thought. Otherwise, that poisonous orange cloud may portend more than the end of the world.

"Oh, Maxine, you look so lovely," François cooed.

"I do?" Maxine tittered, cocking her head to one side in flirtatious abandon.

Leonora bristled. Goddamn her. Goddamn him. Why the hell can't François just leave other women alone? Yet, Leonora had to smile inwardly. If he did that, she thought, he wouldn't be François. But honestly? Why now? And why with Maxine, of all people? Granted, Maxine was looking rather breathtaking in a late-afternoon-sun sort of way. But couldn't François rein it in just a little bit? And Maxine? Couldn't she control herself around handsome men? Especially, *her* handsome men!

"We were just talking about dreams, François," Leonora said. "Something I know you have no interest in—"

"Au contraire!" he replied, pulling out a chair with a flourish and settling in. "Dreams are one of my favorite topics!"

"Really?" Maxine gushed.

"Really?" Leonora asked.

"Yes, really, ladies. Now, tell me all about your dreams. Which one of you is the dreamer today?"

Checking her rage, Leonora watched her husband wink at Maxine. Oh! The nerve of the man!

"Actually, I was telling Leonora about a dream I had," Maxine said, faux shy. "But I hardly know you, sir! I'm not sure I'm ready to tell you of my innermost secrets."

"I adore secrets." François winked at Leonora this time, hailing the hippie waitress as she ambled by. "Excuse me, miss? I'd love a glass of Bordeaux when you've a chance."

"Bore what?" Hippie waitress asked, puzzlement covering her round moon face.

"Ah. . . ." François leaned back in his chair. "Just bring me a glass of the house red wine. And for you ladies?" He nodded at their nearly empty glasses. "Refills?"

"Oh, yes, please!" Maxine enthused. "I shall need some liquid courage if I'm going to be telling you about my dream."

"Excellent!" François exclaimed as Leonora ordered two more glasses of chardonnay.

"Cool." Hippie waitress nodded as she slowly wrote out their order. "I'll be right back."

"Take your time, sweet pea," François called after her.

"I don't think she'll have a problem with that," Leonora observed as the waitress stopped to pet a customer's golden retriever hiding under one of the tables. "Oh, pretty pup! What's his name? Ocean? Cool. He's so soft. . . ."

"Now, back to your dream?" François leaned toward Maxine, his eyes glinting copper in the sunlight.

"Well," Maxine giggled softly, glancing over at Leonora, who tried not to roll her eyes, "I was telling Leo—"

"You call her Leo, too?" François exclaimed.

"Yeah, since we were kids. She has a lioness in her, you know?" Maxine took a gulp of her wine, glanced nervously over at Leonora, who felt like growling.

"That is remarkable!" François said. "I've always called her Leo, and I agree. There is the feline soul lurking inside her."

"Exactly!" Maxine exclaimed.

"Now, sorry to interrupt, but what dream were you telling Leo?"

"It was a horrible dream." Maxine shuddered dramatically. "I'm not sure I can tell it again."

"Oh, poor baby." François patted her arm, smarmy sympathy oozing from his fingertips.

"Yes. It was just awful!" Maxine began to sniffle again, wiping a stray tear from her eye.

"There, there . . . it's okay, luv. It's just a dream, right, Leo?" François soothed.

"Actually," Leonora began, "the reason Maxine contacted me in the first place is because this dream seemed larger than just a personal issue-based manifestation. The apocalyptic quality of the dream, while often hinting of personal upheavals, was, in this case, too devastating for Maxine to ignore. She thought, perhaps, it was a prophecy of some sort. And while, you know, François, how my work doesn't exactly deal with prophetic aspects of dream life, Maxine thought that I might be able to help. Is that right, Max?"

Maxine nodded, sniffling in dainty helplessness.

"Here you go," Hippie waitress returned, announcing each wine's name as she lifted the glass from her tray and placed it in front of them. "A chardonnay for you. And another chardonnay for you. And for you, sir . . . a house red and . . . I hope I got it right?" she asked, her tone reflecting her unique ability to care a little but not a lot.

"Looks great, sweet pea." François beamed up at her. "We'll let you know if we need anything else, okay?"

"Sure, got it," she said, backing away in a wavy hippie stupor.

Leonora took a large sip of her wine, letting the soothing buttery silk sit on her tongue for a moment before swallowing. "In any case, François, I hardly think that Max's dream will be of any interest to you. Don't you have someplace else you need to be?"

Leaning back in his chair, crossing his lanky legs, François chuckled. "Nope. No place at all, Leo. I'm all ears." He turned toward Maxine.

"I . . . where was I?" she glanced over at Leonora helplessly.

"You were telling me about the enormous orange cloud that was poisoning the populace."

"Oh, yes! That's right." Maxine took a sip of her wine, batted her lashes at François, then began. "The orange cloud covered the entire sky. I remember looking up and all I could see was orange vapor. It was moving, and it was menacing. I remember trying to get away from it. Someone had a yellow bike. I asked if I could borrow it. For some reason, I thought I could ride this yellow bike faster and away from the orange cloud. That I could escape it if I pedaled fast enough."

"Sounds frightening!" François exclaimed. "What does the yellow bike mean, Leo?"

"I have no idea," Leonora answered, turning her attention toward Maxine.

"But isn't everything in the dream important?" François grinned. "I thought that's what your work was all about. Dreams. Symbols. Archetypes. That sort of thing." He waved his hand in the air, dismissively. "Are you hungry, dear?" he asked Maxine. "I would imagine all this dream narration works up an appetite, n'est-ce pas?"

"Ooooh. . . ." Maxine cooed. "I love it when a man speaks French to me."

"Leonora! Oh Leonora!" a soft voice called out from across the café's patio. Turning, Leonora saw Camilla weaving between the tables in rapid panic. Her face was pale and flushed at the same time. Her hair windswept and wild. What could be wrong? Leonora wondered.

Out of breath, Camilla now stood in front of their table. "Oh, Leonora, I'm so glad I found you." Her voice trembled.

"Camilla, what is it? This is my friend Maxine. . . ."

"Pleased to—" Maxine began.

Ignoring her, Camilla gasped. "It's Adam! Oh, Leonora! You must come quickly! I don't know what to do! He's—" Camilla broke down in sobs, grabbing the side of their table to steady herself.

Rising, Leonora hurried over to her side. "Camilla, please . . . it's okay. Tell us what happened. What is wrong with Adam?"

Leonora tried to contain her rising anxiety, but the feeling of tiny birds beating in her breast nearly felled her, their quivering wings creating a dizzying effect.

"He was working in his studio . . . and oh!" Camilla began, wiping her eyes. "Leonora! Please, you must come with me."

"Yes, of course, Camilla. Right away. François, you'll take care of Maxine, won't you?"

He grinned at her. "Sure thing, luv. She's in good hands with me."

"Is there anything I can do?" Maxine asked Camilla, half-heartedly.

Camilla stared at her for a moment before shaking her head. "Leonora, please, come quickly. He is asking for you!" She yanked Leonora by the elbow, clutching her in desperation.

The tiny birds fluttered more violently against her ribcage as Leonora grabbed her purse, allowing Camilla to lead her out of the restaurant away from her husband, her friend, and the prophecy of dreams . . . What could have happened to Adam that has put Camilla in such a state? He was fine when she saw him last, after their walk, sharing their dreams.

"Here, here's the car," Camilla pointed to the dilapidated vehicle parked in front of the Crêpe Place.

"Why, that's Adam's truck," Leonora exclaimed softly.

Camilla nodded, "Yes . . . yes . . . it is . . . Oh, Leonora, I don't think I can drive? Can you?"

"Of course." Taking the keys from her, Leonora helped her into the passenger seat before hurrying around to the driver's side, climbing in, slamming the door, and starting the engine.

As she pulled onto Soquel Avenue and headed up the hill, she glanced in the rearview mirror. The sun was setting. The clouds were gathering.

They were a rich, luminous, foreboding orange. . . .

Leonora is driving an unfamiliar car, a tan sedan. She is speeding. Careening. She glances over at Camilla, who smiles back at her from the passenger seat. Nervous. Small. Scared?

Leonora nearly misses hitting a steep cement wall of one of the buildings in the narrow gray alley, high warehouse walls creating an industrial tunnel that she zips through. The buildings rise up, endlessly, into the cool gray sky. She is reckless. Steps on the gas. Harder. Hears a malicious cackle now from the passenger seat. Turns to see not Camilla, but Maxine. She has a gun. In her lap. She caresses its smooth silver barrel. Winks at Leonora. Wicked.

Leonora turns her attention back to the road, marveling at the gun's seeming innocuousness. Its silver silence.

The target?

Sergei.

"You're sure he'll be there?" Leonora asks, nervous, excited, the fear heavy in her blood. The anticipation racing through her mind.

"Yes, he's always there. Taking a break. Parked in his car. Sitting there. Smoking." Maxine harrumphs, then glances over at Leonora. Her next words are cold, calculating: "You know what to do."

Leonora nods as she speeds through the narrow gray alley.

She sees his car. Parked at the curb, his cigarette smoke drifting lazily out the driver's side of the car.

"Okay . . . now . . . slow down," Maxine commands, raising the gun and taking aim.

She fires.

Sergei slumps over the steering wheel. Gone.

Did he even see who shot him? Leonora wonders. Did he know who the killer was? Who wanted him dead?

Maxine let out a long, silent scream-sigh. In the dream, there is no sound now. After the murder. No sound of the gunshot. No sound of the car's engine. No sound from Sergei as he takes his last breath.

Leonora steps on the gas, speeds out of the alleyway. Fear and exhilaration envelop her.

Sergei is dead. Maxine killed him. Leonora soothes herself . . . it wasn't me. She didn't pull the trigger . . .

Yet, she was culpable, wasn't she? She had driven the car. She knew what Maxine was going to do.

Leonora, in the dream, experiences intense feelings of regret and misgivings. What had they done? It was irrevocable. This taking of another's life. And why? Did he really deserve to die?

She turned out of the alley, out onto a wider boulevard. But there were no other cars around. No people on the streets. All was empty and gray.

Leonora glances in the rearview mirror. An enormous orange cloud is covering the sky. If she drives fast, maybe it won't overtake them.

Leonora shudders as she steps on the gas. . . .

"Pauline . . . ? Pauline. . . ."

Leonora roused herself, rubbing her eyes, trying to wake from the dream.

"No . . . Adam, it's Leonora . . . Pauline is—"

"Leonora?" Adam tried to sit up in the bed.

"Please, don't get up." Leonora rose from the chair where she'd fallen asleep. The dream still too vivid to forget. Why had she and Maxine killed Sergei after all these years? What did the dream mean? What did the orange cloud signify?

"I beg your pardon," Adam murmured softly, "I thought you were Pauline . . . the resemblance. . . ."

Leonora nodded as she passed the dresser with the photo of Adam and Pauline in Mexico, posed in front of their hacienda, a large white cat lounging at their feet. Glancing at her own reflection in the mirror, she felt a surge of energy. The resemblance was uncanny. The same high cheekbones and pale skin. The same dark, curly hair. The same deep brown eyes.

Could she be Pauline?

Even for her, the notion was absurd. That one could die and then come back to life as another. And the timing? Perhaps it was possible. Pauline had died before she had been born. Or had she? Leonora gazed steadily at her reflection, then back at Pauline's image. A sudden chill shook her core.

Adam was vague about Pauline's death. When? Where? How? Or had she even died? Pauline was such a mystery.

Leonora continued to stare at the photo. There was something so familiar about Pauline. Of course, she'd heard Adam speak of her, but not at length. But it seemed as if she knew her, intimately. Her hopes and dreams about writing and relationship. Her first meeting with Adam and the excitement around this man.

She had felt the same way. The first time she met him. Hadn't she? Did Adam inspire this sort of reaction in all the women he met? she wondered.

She turned toward the bed where he lay now, tired and old and . . . dying? Leonora refused to believe this. He still had so much work to do. And she had so much to learn from him. He couldn't leave her. Not now.

Approaching the bed, she sat down on the chair next to it, pulling up close to him. "How are you feeling?"

"How the bloody hell do you think?" he muttered, chuckling softly before a thick cough took over.

"Oh, Adam!" she exclaimed softly. "Please don't tax yourself. It will take time to recover. The doctor said you needed to rest."

"To hell with rest. I have work to do!" he proclaimed, trying to raise himself from the mountain of pillows.

Gently, Leonora touched him on the shoulder, shy but forceful. "I know, I know. But the work will be there when you are recovered. For now, rest." She pushed him tenderly back; he was too weak to protest. Her heart cried.

"Papa?" Camilla's soft worried tone floated across the room. "Oh, Papa, you're awake. How are you feeling?"

Leonora exchanged a look with him, knowing his reaction to this question would be tempered for his daughter. She watched as he took Camilla's hand in his. "I'm fine, sweetheart. Just weak."

"Yes, of course, Papa. We were so worried. When I found you. Collapsed in your studio like that—oh . . . !" Camilla wiped a tear from her eye.

"There, there," he comforted her. "None of that now. I will be right as rain before you know it."

"Promise?" she asked.

"I promise."

Leonora rose and moved away from the bed to leave the two of them alone. But she couldn't help gazing at the photo one last time. Pauline gazed back at her, her spirit and passion filling Leonora.

Yes, Pauline was here. Leonora could feel her.

She knew Adam felt her, too.

How could he not? Her spirit was palpable and her love was strong. Leonora listened for a moment to Adam and Camilla's hushed voices, before a feeling of foreboding descended. It was the dream, she told herself. But she knew it was more than this as she left the room, softly closing the door behind her, a scent of lemons, honey, and lavender circling the air above her.

Pauline

SANTA CRUZ, CALIF., 1992

Floating above Adam, who lay sleeping, alone for now, Pauline absently stroked the large white cat purring next to her. "Yes, Pablo, you're right. Adam needs us. Of course, he has his daughter from that tramp Mimi!" Pauline sighed, emitting a puff of green gauziness. It floated up to the ceiling of Adam's bedroom, trapped for a moment, before dissipating into the air. "And, I do understand that he loves Camilla. And she loves him. And then there's this woman, Leonora, holding something back. Do you know what I mean, Pab?"

Mrrrrooooooowwww!

Laughing softly, Pauline stroked him. "I knew you would! But even with these women who love him and care for him, I know that there was never any woman for him but me. We were married, for heaven's sake! And granted, I had to leave. But that wasn't my fault. I was sick. I didn't want to burden him. He had so much work to do. Such fine work. Such a genius! And, as it turned out, the time away from him was good for my work, too. I wrote my book."

Pauline paused for a moment, petting the cat absently. "I wonder what happened to that book?" she mused.

Mrrrrooowwww!

"You don't say?" she joked, tossing her head back, the thick curls dancing.

"I remember," Pauline continued, staring down at Adam who shifted in his sleep, "that Remedios took it. She said that she was going to take care of it. I never found out what she meant by that. Did she keep it for herself? Did she find a publisher? Did she give it to Adam?"

Frowning, Pauline floated up for a moment, then sank back down, hovering a few feet above her husband. "Adam, darling? Can you hear me?"

"Who's there?" Adam struggled to open his eyes, yet this was not Pauline's intention.

"Damn!" she cried softly. "*No*, don't wake up. I will come to you in your dreams, darling. Be still. Back to sleep. I'm coming."

Pauline watched as Adam turned over, settling on his other side, then let out a deep sigh. "Pauline?" he said softly. "Is that you . . . ?"

She floated down toward him, leaving the large white cat for a moment. "Stay there, Pablo."

Mrrrrooowwww.

"I'll only be gone a moment. Just wait for me."

The cat blinked his golden eyes at her, then began to groom.

"That's a good boy. Now to my love," she murmured as she felt herself grow smaller and smaller, till she was the size of a small kitten, then a mouse, and finally a cricket.

"Pauline. . . ." Adam repeated, as Pauline became paler and paler, till there was only a whisper of her left. She floated to the side of his head, hovered for a moment above his ear, before disappearing into its tunnel that led the way into his psyche.

Adam

"What do you mean I can't see her?" Adam paced the length of the waiting room as Serena and Remedios stared.

"She says that she is too tired, Adam," Remedios began. "That she needs to rest. That your visit, while this would be a wonderful thing, would so tire her. You understand, sí?"

"No! I do not understand! I bloody hell do NOT understand. I demand to see her immediately. You will take me to her!"

"Por favor, señor," Serena began. "Calm yourself. Your energy will only hurt yourself and your dear wife and. . . ."

"My energy!" he fumed. "I'll show you some bloody energy!"

"Adam, please." Remedios walked over to him, gently took him by the elbow, led him to a chocolate love seat in the corner of the dusky room. "Sit, please. . . ." she commanded. "I have something for you. From Pauline."

Adam fell into the sofa, grateful for its support. He suddenly was overcome with an enormous fatigue. The strain of his wife's illness. These two women's refusal to let him see Pauline. He could not—no, he would not—believe that Pauline didn't want to see him. Why would this be? Was she really dying? If this were true, then he must see her. They mustn't keep her from him. He would not allow it.

"Here, she wanted me to give you this." Remedios stood before him, a thick manuscript in her hands, the pages bulging from a cobalt blue felt cover.

"What is this?" Adam took the manuscript from her, marveling at its weight. Its beauty.

"Pauline's novel. She has been so hard at work on it," Remedios said, sitting down next to him. Adam noted her nod at Serena across the room, who took her leave. "She wanted you to have it."

Adam stared down at the book, then back up at Remedios. "Why doesn't she give it to me herself?"

"Adam." Remedios stifled a tear, then wiped her eye. "Pauline . . . she. . . ."

"NO!" he roared, standing up and shaking. "NO, I won't believe it. Take me to her! She would not leave me. It is unfathomable!"

"No, no . . . señor, she has not passed over. The transition, it is not complete. But she is so weak . . . and . . . I am afraid that her time here in our world is nearly over." Remedios shook her head, the tears falling silently onto her lap.

"But if she's still here. . . ." Adam pleaded, "then I must see her. I don't want this bloody book!" He hurled the manuscript across the room, hitting the wall with a tremendous thunk. The pages spilled out and flew in yellow-and-white slices of life. "I want Pauline! I must see Pauline!"

"Adam, darling. . . ." Her voice floated into his consciousness, into his dream.

"Pauline? Pauline, is that you?" Adam glanced up at the ceiling of the room, to the sound of her voice. Its musical lilt raising his hopes.

"Yes, darling, I'm here. I'm so happy to see you. You don't need to get so excited. I'm fine. I just need to rest. Now please, pick up those pages!" She laughed, her mirth circling him. "I worked hard on that book and I am most incensed that you'd treat it with such disrespect!"

"Pauline, where are you? I can hear you, but I can't see you." Adam stood and twirled slowly around, still gazing up at the sound of her voice.

"I'm here, I am always here, my love. Now! Pick up those pages, put them back in order. Thank goodness I numbered them!" She laughed. "And read it. It is my story, but it is also your story. For you are my story. You must know this, my love. Now, I must go."

"Pauline, no. Don't go. Please don't go. I must see you!"

"Remember to read the book with the notion of its fictitious nature. Keep that paradigm of reality you insist upon with literature at bay. Yes, it is about you. It is about me. It is about us. But it is also about something bigger. You will understand, darling. I must go now. Toot-a-loo!"

"Pauline, no! NO!!"

Adam felt a heavy weight on his mind, a foggy unforgiving clamp. And then a lightness. A freeing. A feeling of joy and wonder took over. Waking now, he glanced around his room. All was still. Quiet. He gazed up at the ceiling, and for a moment, he thought he saw a large white cat grinning down at him, blinking golden eyes laughing at him, before disappearing into the ether.

The book. Where had he put the book? He knew it was someplace safe. But where the bloody hell could it be?

"Adam?" Leonora appeared beside him. Adam noted the worry cascading from her handsome face.

"Leonora?"

"Yes, are you quite all right?"

Adam sighed, damn these women. They're always asking him if he's all right. Of course, he's not all right! He must get out of this bed. He must find Pauline's book.

And he must get back to work. The painting. It is unfinished. And Pauline's book. Yes, this will be the key. . . .

Mimi

Mimi stretched lazily on the chaise lounge, wriggling her toes in the bright sun, the nails painted a seductive ruby red. Her hair wrapped in a golden turban, her eyes shaded by enormous sunglasses, she reached for her drink. Frowning, she lifted the empty glass, then called out, "DALE! DALE! I am thirsty!"

She sighed purple and violet, then watched as a young couple, a boy and girl, skated down the boardwalk, playfully knocking into each other. She was clad in cut-offs and a lemon bikini top. He was scruffy with swim trunks hanging low and no shirt.

Watching them skate away, Mimi wondered where her life had gone as Dale scurried in with her cocktail.

"Your wish is my command," he joked, setting the martini down on the glass table next to her.

A withering glance stifled his playful banter. "I wish that Antonio would arrive!" she complained. "Can you arrange that? I don't know why that man is always late!"

Dale shrugged. "He's Italian?"

"I'm French!" she exclaimed. "And my time is valuable."

She took a sip of her drink, letting the alcohol meld into the sun-swept consciousness of her brain. Her operetta was taking shape. It was full of passion, drama, and murder. The protagonist, a beautiful French siren, was married to a wealthy German industrialist. Yet, the wife was understandably bored by her husband and so had taken on a secret lover, a young artist, a painter. . . .

"Ah! Valentina!" a rich baritone floated out onto the patio.

Mimi turned slightly, extending her pale hand. Antonio took it in his sturdy tanned one, bent to kiss it. "You are ravishing as always."

"Yes, I am," she agreed. "You're late! Where have you been?"

He waved his hand in nonchalant negation. "Oh, I am very busy, mademoiselle. But for you, I am here!"

Antonio took a seat in the chaise lounge next to hers, eyed her martini. "That looks like a fantastica idea!" he exclaimed.

"It is," Mimi said, "but before you start in on the cocktails, show me what you've got."

"Very well," Antonio pouted, reaching for his portfolio containing piles of scores in process. Shuffling through them for a moment, he began his placation: "Now, you must understand, mademoiselle, that while you have a most fabulous narrative and the themes in your lovely head are enchanting, dramatic, and romantic, it does take time for me to transcribe, sí?"

Mimi sat up and gazed out at the sea. A pair of seagulls circled over the shore. "I want Alessandria to do something!" she proclaimed. "I have an idea. . . ."

She smiled slyly, leaning over the pages of the score that Antonio had laid before her. "Here!" she pointed to a phrase. "This is where she will do the deed."

"Deed?" Antonio grinned. "That does sound dastardly. Do tell Antonio."

"Mimi! MIMI!"

"Oh, damn," Mimi muttered to herself. "Genevieve! I explicitly told you that Antonio was coming over today. That we'd be working on my operetta and should not be disturbed."

"So sorry, darling." Genevieve strode out onto the patio, kissing Mimi on top of her turban and nodding at Antonio, who gave her a little wave. "I completely forgot that you were working today."

"Well, I am," Mimi said. "And while I realize that you think little of my work, I would appreciate it if you would not—"

"Any more of those cocktails around?" Genevieve interrupted. "Dale? Oh, Dale!"

"Yes, mademoiselle?"

"Could you whip up some more of your divine martinis?"

"Oui, of course."

"And it looks like Antonio needs one, too, don't you darling?"

"Well . . . I. . . ." Antonio began, sheepishly glancing over at Mimi, who rolled her eyes.

Rising in dramatic abandon, Mimi threw her arms up in the air, relinquishing all pretense of productivity. "I am going for a walk!" she announced.

"What do you mean?" Genevieve teased. "You never go for a walk."

"Well, I am now. I need to think! I have an idea in my head and I need to work it out. Antonio, do not drink too many martinis. I shall return. And I expect you to be ready to work when I do."

"But of course, signorina. Your wish is my command."

"Where have I heard that before?" Mimi muttered as she grabbed her oversized polka-dot sun hat and adjusted her round white shades. Grabbing her notebook, she gave Genevieve and Antonio a withering gaze before turning her back on them, slamming the patio gate.

For a moment she stood at the edge of the boardwalk, watching the gulls circle over the sea. Oh, she thought, why can't I just fly away from it all? Why must Genevieve always be so annoyingly intrusive? Why must Antonio always be late? Why, why, why!

"Mama!" a familiar soft voice rang out behind her.

"Grandmamma!" a younger, energetic one behind it.

Camilla? Annabelle?

Mimi sighed her purple cloud, but it was tinged with a bit of gold sparkle now. She'd just visit with her daughter and granddaughter for a bit. Catch up. It had been too long since she'd seen them.

"Grandmamma." Annabelle was outside the gate now. Standing next to her was a stranger, handsome in his hippie way, towering at her side. "This is Monarch."

Mimi turned around and gave Monarch her pale hand. "Enchantée," she murmured as she followed them back through the gate into the patio. She'd go for a walk later. To hell with the creative process.

Linking arms with her granddaughter, a feeling of warmth tingled through her as Annabelle began to prattle on about this and that: "Monarch is an awesome photographer, Grandmamma. He wants to interview you and do a photographing session and what do you think? Could you do that? It'd be so cool. . . ."

Leonora and Adam

SANTA CRUZ, CALIF., 1992

Leonora cradled the book in her lap. Reverently, she ran her fingers over the deep blue cover. Lightly.

Pauline's book.

"You want me to read it?" she asked Adam.

"Yes, of course. It was meant for you."

"What do you mean? How could it be meant for me?"

Adam glanced over at the enormous series of canvases laid out flat on his studio's great gray floor. The first layer of golds and tangerines drying before he could apply the next layer of gray-greens and ethereal silvers. He had an idea for this painting. It would chronicle all of his inner quest that had previously eluded him. He felt its power. Its calling. Yet, he also knew it would be his last. And his time, here in this sphere, he also knew, was short. . . .

But first, Pauline's book. For Leonora.

Sitting down next to Leonora, he gazed down at the book. "Open it."

Leonora fingered the front cover, a chill running down her spine. She felt a warmth, too, at her core. A kind of bubbling up of magic. Anticipation. A sweet wisp of air grazed her cheek, a soft laughter echoed in her mind, a distant rumbling, a cat's purr? filled her soul.

Lifting the thick cobalt cover, she turned to the pale blue title page:

Palette of Blue by Pauline Sinclair.

"Palette of Blue?" she murmured. "Why is it called that?"

Adam chuckled softly. "You'll have to read it to find out. However," he paused, stroking his chin for a meditative moment, "if you think about it, I think you already know. Why the book possesses this title. What its meaning is. And what is inside the book."

"But how could I?" she asked, frowning slightly, thinking of the palette of blue and what it could mean. The ocean. The sky. The cosmos. The soul. All are blue, are they not?

Again, a soft laughter echoed from above. Glancing overhead, Leonora caught a glimpse . . . of what? A pale blue wisp of smoke. A dark blue wink of a cat's golden eye?

"Go ahead, turn the page, Leonora," Adam commanded gently.

She did. Read the quote on the first page: "'A pox on all captivity.' —André Breton." [31]

"Breton? You knew him, right?" she asked.

"Oh, yes!" Adam chuckled. "He was my constant compadre and my eternal humorist, besides supporting me in all that was surreal. Pauline adored him. As did everyone. Well, except for maybe his wife!"

"Indeed?" Leonora frowned.

"Oh, to be honest, I don't know. Remedios always claimed this."

"Remedios Varo? The artist?"

"Yes, she was a wonder to behold. Though. . . ." Adam paused, remembering how Remedios had taken Pauline away from him when she'd become ill. How he had begged her to let him visit Pauline. He would always resent Remedios for this. Though he understood, now, looking back, that she was just trying to protect Pauline. To do what Pauline had asked. Yet, there was a part of him that didn't believe Remedios when she had told him that Pauline didn't want to see him. The book, though, back to Pauline's book.

"Please," he implored, gently intense now. "Turn the page. . . ."

Leonora's heart was aflutter. What was this feeling of trepidation? Why did she have this fluttering in her breast? "Leonora, don't be afraid. . . ." she heard from above. "The book is for you. The book is about you. The book is about Adam and me and art and life. It is your book now. . . ."

"Did you hear that?" Leonora stared at Adam.

"Yes," he murmured.

"Who is it? Could it be . . . ?" Leonora let her voice trail off. She had heard the voice. It was clear and confident, yet tender, too.

"Pauline knows that the book is in good hands," Adam said. "She knows that you will steward it to its rightful place in the world."

"Me?" Leonora asked. "But why me? What can I do?"

"I think you know," Adam said. "Or if you don't yet, you will. Read the book. Absorb its stories, its themes, its fantasies. And then, you will hone your own palette of blue."

"But I don't understand," Leonora frowned again. "What is the significance of the palette of blue? I know in your art, Adam, that blue is part of your palette, but it is not the only hue of your canvases. You create your worlds with golds and greens and tangerines. You circle the canvas with spheres of silver and crimsons. A palette of blue? It seems so limiting," she finished.

Adam laughed, his mirth filling the cool empty studio. "Oh, Leonora, you can be so literal sometimes. Think again. Close your eyes. Imagine the palette of blue. What do you see?"

Leonora felt the heft of the book, its thickness weighing on her lap. She felt so tired all of a sudden. She closed her eyes. Leaning back into the sofa, a lightness enveloping her. And then she saw it: the palette of blue.

It was a sea of blue. A sky of blue. It was cats of blue. And children of blue. It was trees of blue and shoes of blue. François

was blue. And Maxine, too. Leonora's writing was blue. Her
dreams were blue. Her science was blue. Blue was all she needed.
It encompassed all of life. It homed in on what was real and what
was imagination. It created a world of depth and beauty. It surrounded her with a cool soothing sanctuary.

She was swimming in it.

The palette of blue.

She opened her eyes, a sensation of lightness and serenity
filling her. Adam had gone back to his canvases, was circling
them, palette in hand.

And she saw it now. What he did. Who he was. How he was all
of her and she was all of him. They were one.

She would hone her palette to blue. It would take time. It
would take practice. It would take patience.

But Pauline's book, it would be her teacher. She would read
the book. She would live the book. She would be the book.

The *Palette of Blue.*

Epilogue

Leonora watches as the students file into Adam's studio. Tentative. Awestruck. She senses their reverence: they can feel him. His presence still emanates from the walls, the paintings hung there, yes, but also his worn shoes, covered in red, yellow, green dots; his dozens of brushes, laid out on the table, just as he left them the day he died; the Post-its on the wall, sample titles for paintings scrawled on each: *Cosmostopia*, *Nature Dreams a Star*, *Pauline Posits*.

"He used to stand up there," Leonora points to the high inside balcony that overlooks the gray cold studio floor and walls, "and contemplate his work. See what he had done. Observe. Notice. A different perspective from above . . . I used to come in to talk. We'd look at the work together, then tire, need a break and so go out for a walk, in the warmth of the sun, the scent of the pines. Nature spoke to him. As I think it does to all of us."

Leonora pauses, her reverie echoing in the vastness of his studio.

"I know this may sound odd," one of the students ventures to speak, "but I can feel him. . . ."

Leonora nods. "Yes."

"I don't know if it's because of the way you've preserved his studio in all the loving detail that you have, or if somehow, he is still here . . . or. . . ."

"He is still here." Leonora waves at the massive paintings of luminescent stars, cosmologies, the bright dots of tangerine, lime, and cobalt leaping off the canvas, creating energy in the cold still room. "I remember him at the end. He didn't want to stop painting. The day I tried to take him to the hospital, he said, 'No! I need to paint. I need to complete this work that I've begun. I can feel it. It's almost there . . . if only . . .'"

Leonora shakes her head, holding back the tears. She would not cry in front of strangers, even sympathetic ones. "But he never did finish that work." She points to a large canvas, the white splashes spinning like windmills, the blue dots dancing over them, "He collapsed . . . here on the floor. . . ." And now she does stifle a sniffle, but then sighs, deeply, before her cool smile prevails again.

"Please, do take a look around." She motions to the students. "But be so kind as to not touch anything. I don't believe Adam would mind, but. . . ."

Leonora can't finish her thought. The students nod, thoughtful, silent, as they separate into individuals to take a closer look at the artist's last works. . . .

Leonora allows herself a moment of joy. Remembering that first day she'd ventured into his sphere. "How do you do?" he'd asked.

How did she? And now? How does she?

"Hey, hi. . . ." Annabelle pokes her head in, tentatively. "Wow, hello, everyone. . . ."

The students nod, murmur a few hellos back.

Leonora smiles, beckons Annabelle to come in.

"Sorry to interrupt, but I got those paints you asked for, Leonora. You ready to work on our project? Maybe later this afternoon?"

Leonora nods, a glow of gratitude filling her. "Yes, Annabelle. That would be fine. You can just leave the paints over there in the corner."

"Cool. . . ." Annabelle sets the supplies down in the corner of the studio, behind Adam's workbench, then glances around the room at the serious group of students.

"You guys here to see my granddad's work, yah?"

"Yes, they are," Leonora answers.

"Cool. Let me tell you about this one. . . ."

Leonora watches as Annabelle leads the group over to the largest work on the wall, a massive green ocean sprouting cosmic tangerine dots and golden spirals.

"He was working on this one when. . . ."

A student asks another question, and Leonora moves away to survey the pile of supplies Annabelle has left. Peeking in the bag, she sees the tubes of paint: Prussian blue . . . cerulean blue . . . ultramarine blue . . . Her eyes linger for a moment, then shift to the lemon yellow, permanent rose, phthalo green, and tangerine. She reaches for the rose, fingering it for a moment as she leans gently against Adam's worktable: she feels his energy, his strength, his passion, and yes, his love. . . .

It will be good to get back to work with Annabelle, Leonora muses. And Adam? The student was right. He was still here. Observing. Prodding. Chuckling.

"How do you do?" She remembers the first day she met him, his greeting echoing so clearly still after all these years.

Very well, thank you. Leonora smiles to herself as the answer leapt into her mind, Annabelle's voice, musical and alive, echoing in the coolness of the studio, the prospect of their project filling her with joy, purpose, and yes, Adam.

References

Bogzaran, F. (1996). *The Quest of the Inner Worlds: Paintings by Gordon Onslow Ford*. Dream Creations.

Breton, A. (1924). *Manifesto of Surrealism*. https://www2.hawaii.edu/~freeman/courses/phil330/MANIFESTO%20OF%20SURREALISM.pdf

Breton, A. (1929). "The Second Manifesto" in Patrick Waldberg's (1965) *Surrealism*. Oxford University Press.

Breton, A. (1935). *Mad Love*. University of Nebraska Press.

Green, C. (2022). For Curanderos, Cures Come from the Ground Up. *Whetstone Journal*. https://www.whetstonemagazine.com/journal/for-curanderos-cures-come-from-the-ground-up

Johnson, J. (1998). *Surreal Women* by Penelope Rosemont. University of Texas.

Jung, C. G. (1974). *Dreams*. Princeton University Press.

Onslow Ford, G. (1999). *Once Upon a Time, The O World*. Lucid Art Foundation.

Paalen, W. (2000). "The New Image" in Christian Kloyber's (Ed) *Wolfgang Paalen's DYN: The Complete Reprint Hardcover* (p. 9). Austria: Springer-Verlang/Wien. Paalen, Wolfgang. "The New Image." *DYN Magazine*, (1942).

Sawain, M. (1995). *Surrealism in Exile and the Beginning of the New York School*. The MIT Press.

Endnotes

1. Breton, A. (1924) *Manifesto of Surrealism*. https://www2.hawaii.edu/~freeman/courses/phil330/MANIFESTO%20OF%20SURREALISM.pdf

2. Ibid., p. 7

3. Bogzaran, F. (1996) *The Quest of the Inner-Worlds: Paintings by Gordon Onslow Ford*. Published in conjunction with the inaugural exhibition of the Arts and Consciousness Gallery.

4. Breton (1924) *Manifesto of Surrealism*, p. 14.

5. Sawin, M. (1997) *Surrealism in Exile and the Beginning of the New York School*. MIT Press.

6. Ibid., p. 161.

7. Ford, Onslow. *Quest of Inner-Worlds*, p. 46.

8. Breton (1924) *Manifesto of Surrealism*, p. 11.

9. Breton (1924) *Manifesto of Surrealism*, p. 13.

10. Breton as cited in Waldberg (1965) p. 76.

11. Sawain (1995) p. 167.

12. Breton as cited in Ades (1997) p. 193.

13. Paalen as cited in Kloyber (2000), p. 9.

14. Johnson, Jacqueline. *Surrealist Women*, p. 240.

15. Breton as cited in Waldberg, p. 68.

16. Ibid., p. 70.

17. Breton (1924) *Manifesto of Surrealism*, p. 15.

18. Ibid., p. 4.

19. Breton (1924) *Manifesto of Surrealism*, p. 10.

20. Ibid.

21. Ibid., p. 42.

22. Ibid., p. 7.

23. Jung, C. G. (1961/1974) *Dreams*.

24. Breton (1924) *Manifesto of Surrealism*, p. 42.

25. Ibid.

26. Ibid.

27. "Je Suis Seule Ce Soir," Cancioneros, accessed October 7, 2023, https://www.cancioneros.com/lyrics/song/1929143/je-suis-seule-ce-soir-andre-claveau

28. Ibid.

29. Breton (1924), *Manifesto of Surrealism*, p. 14.

30. Ibid., p. 30.

31. Breton (1935), *Mad Love*, p. 25.

Acknowledgments

This novel began with a tiny spark of an idea after a visit to the Lucid Art Foundation and the studio of the surrealist painter, Gordon Onslow Ford. Without this visit, led by artist and Dean of Arts and Consciousness at John F. Kennedy University, Karen Sjoholm, the novel would never have materialized. Thanks, too, to Fariba Bogzaran, for sharing her love of Onslow Ford and her reverential tour of his studio.

There were so many people who helped with the creation and revisions of the novel. Thanks to my sister, the writer Laura Lohnes, for her kind but insightful critical eye during the first drafts of the novel. If she hadn't sat with me over Zoom every Saturday afternoon for three years, I doubt this book would have ever been finished! Thanks, too, to the poet and writer Owen Hill, for his help with those big revisions. And to my marvelous copyeditor, Mikayla Butchart, editor extraordinaire, for her granular miracle working with line edits. Serge Morel, Frenchman and swimmer, helped tremendously to translate the various songs, phrases and dialogue from the French. Also, thanks to Melissa Kirk, for her feedback on the initial contract for the book. Without her translations of the legalese, I might have stopped the process before it began!

Much gratitude to Dr. Ruth Saxton, author of *The Book of Old Ladies*, and former writing professor of mine from Mills College. She helped pave the way for me to pursue the publication of this project with her encouragement and wisdom. Her own experience with She Writes Press (SWP) and "getting her book out into the world" helped spur me to contact this publisher and answer questions about the process of "publication"!

Because of Dr. Saxton, I did submit the manuscript to SWP,

and what a wonderful, intelligent, and efficient team they've been! I'd like to thank them for all of their help and support: Publisher, Brooke Warner; Samantha Strom, Senior Editorial Project Manager and Senior Acquisitions Editor; Managing Editor, Krissa Lagos, my patient and smart Project Manager, Lauren Wise; and my fabulous, multilingual proofreader, Jennifer Caven. Without their unflagging assistance and encouragement, I never would have been able to get through this process. Thanks to Rebecca Lown for the beautiful cover. It captures the drama and the color that is such a big part of the novel. I also would like to thank the community of other authors I met through SWP, especially those in my spring 2024 cohort. What a fabulous group of women writers to answer my questions, commiserate with my confusion, and ultimately, buoy me up with their own work and enthusiasm.

A special thanks to authors Jonathan Lethem, Summer Brenner, Owen Hill, and Victoria Lilienthal for their endorsements of the novel. Their belief in the novel was a real boost for me. I am truly grateful for their careful readings and inspiring blurbs.

I'd like to thank my mother, the artist Ruth J. Jameson, for her inspiration and support. I grew up in a house full of art and music because of her. I think without this, my love of art and my pursuit of writing might not have taken the path that it did. Also, to my sister, Paula Jameson Whitney, who has the talent for bringing silliness, intelligence, and heart to any situation. Horses are everywhere, Paula, just ask Leonora. And, many heartfelt hugs of gratitude to my partner, actor and playwright Ian Lambton, who put up with all my nervous breakdowns as the process of this novel unfolded. I adore you, darling, I do!

Questions and Topics
for Discussion

1. Leonora is inexplicably drawn to the painter Adam Sinclair. Why do you think this is? Have you ever been drawn to a "stranger"? If so, who and why?

2. Consider the dreams in the novel. Were these dreams meaningful? Did any resonate with you? Why or why not?

3. The novel is told through multiple points of view: Leonora, Pauline, Mimi, Adam, and others. Is there one point of view that you found most compelling? If so, why?

4. Who is your favorite character in the novel? Why?

5. Who is your least favorite character in the novel? Why?

6. What is surrealism? How does Adam's surrealist friends impact the novel? Why do you think so?

7. Adam makes the following declaration about his artistic process and the meaning of art and the universe: "*I myself am using divisions on a two-dimensional surface—my canvas—so as to reflect the life pattern that exists in the universe, its tension, oppositions, actions and counteractions, and to explore the cosmic pattern by the way I move the planes back and forth in all directions to form the complete living unit*" (p. 57). What do you think he means? How is this important to the novel's themes?

8. If you are an artist, how would you describe your creative process? Is there anything in the novel that resonates with you? That inspires you?

9. Did the novel contribute to your understanding of surrealism and the artistic process? Why or why not?

10. The novel begins and ends with a visit to Adam's studio by a group of art students. How is their experience important to the telling of the story? Why?

About the Author

Photo credit: Karen White Schneider

CAROL JAMESON is an educator, swimmer, and pianist. She created and coedited the online zine *Hello Goodbye Apocalpyse*, a journal of pandemic writings and artwork, and is the author of *The Kaiser Stories* and *It Builds in the Brain*. Currently, she writes two blogs: *Pool Purrs*, a collection of swimming stories, and *Walk with CJ*, a collection of walking stories that began during the pandemic. She has an MFA in creative writing and literature from Mills College and teaches writing in San Francisco Bay Area colleges. She lives in Richmond, California, with her naughty orange tabby cat, Clara.

caroljameson.com

SELECTED TITLES FROM SHE WRITES PRESS

She Writes Press is an independent publishing company founded to serve women writers everywhere. Visit us at www.shewritespress.com.

Estelle by Linda Stewart Henley. $16.95, 978-1-63152-791-3. From 1872 to '73, renowned artist Edgar Degas called New Orleans home. Here, the narratives of two women—Estelle, his Creole cousin and sister-in-law, and Anne Gautier, who in 1970 finds a journal written by a relative who knew Degas—intersect . . . and a painting Degas made of Estelle spells trouble.

Attribution by Linda Moore. $17.95, 978-1-64742-253-0. In this fast-paced novel full of imaginative art world revelations, betrayals, and twists, an art historian desperate to succeed leaves her troubled parents to study in New York, where she struggles to impress her misogynist advisor—until she discovers a Baroque masterpiece and flees with it to Spain.

The Color of Ice by Barbara Linn Probst. $17.95, 978-1-64742-259-2. Cathryn McAllister's carefully curated life is upended when she travels to Iceland to interview a charismatic glass artist who ignites in her a hunger for everything she's told herself she doesn't need anymore: Passion. Vulnerability. Risk. But the new journey this awakening sends her on leads to devastating choices she never could have foreseen.

Don't Put the Boats Away by Ames Sheldon. $16.95, 978-1-63152-602-2. In the aftermath of World War II, the members of the Sutton family are reeling from the death of their "golden boy," Eddie. Over the next twenty-five years, they all struggle with loss, grief, and mourning—and pay high prices, including divorce and alcoholism.

When It's Over by Barbara Ridley. $16.95, 978-1-63152-296-3. When World War II envelopes Europe, Lena Kulkova flees Czechoslovakia for the relative safety of England, leaving her Jewish family behind in Prague.

This Is How It Begins by Joan Dempsey. $16.95, 978-1-63152-308-3. When eighty-five-year-old art professor Ludka Zeilonka's gay grandson, Tommy, is fired over concerns that he's silencing Christian kids in the classroom, she is drawn into the political firestorm—and as both sides battle to preserve their respective rights to free speech, the hatred on display raises the specter of her WWII past.